A HOLMES BY ANY OTHER NAME

THE TWISTINGS AND TURNINGS OF "SHERLOCK HOLMES"

A HOLMES BY ANY OTHER NAME

THE TWISTINGS AND TURNINGS OF "SHERLOCK HOLMES"

BILL MASON, BSI

WILDSIDE PRESS

CONTENTS

INTRODUCTION

In June 2016, I was honored to deliver the opening address at "The Misadventures of Sherlock Holmes," a Minneapolis conference sponsored by the Norwegian Explorers of Minnesota, the Friends of the Sherlock Holmes Collections, and the University of Minnesota. The theme of the conference, of course, was derived from Ellery Queen's landmark anthology, *The Misadventures of Sherlock Holmes* (Little, Brown & Co., 1944).

After reviewing the history of that important book, I launched into a discussion of misadventures (or parodies), including a seemingly-endless recitation of several hundred names used to spoof or imitate Sherlock Holmes. The reception of this performance was gratifying (although I would be hard-pressed ever to attempt it again), and I was immediately asked for a copy of my list. However, I realized even then that simply listing the parody names, while interesting and fun, would not do justice to the subject. Some feverish fit inspired me, therefore, not only to reproduce that list, but to expand and annotate it. This volume is the result.

By way of introduction, I submit the following excerpt from my address in Minneapolis.

Pastiche, as defined by Ellery Queen in the introduction to *The Misadventures of Sherlock Holmes*, is "a serious and sincere imitation in the exact manner of the original author," while parody consists of "humorous or satirical take-offs" with "no reverent scruples." Sometimes, the distinctions between parodies, pastiches, burlesques, spoofs and sketches are not very clear. But for me, pastiches do not qualify as "misadventures." Usually they are too serious, too earnest—and too often, too dreadful—to be considered.

No, when I think of extra-canonical "misadventures," I think of parodies, of satire and humor and impossible situations. In its most primitive form, I picture a Holmes-like character making the miraculous deduction that it is raining outside because Watson comes in with a wet umbrella. Richard Lancelyn Green saw Sherlockian parody being an imitation made, as he said, "for comic effect, with Holmes' exceptional abilities heightened or exaggerated to a point at which the sublime merges with the absurd."

The very first parodies of Sherlock Holmes didn't take long at all to make their way into print. On November 28, 1891—only five months after "A Scandal in Bohemia" was first published in *The Strand Magazine*—an anonymous writer in *The Speaker: A Review of Politics, Letters, Science, and the Arts* skewered Sherlock Holmes' methods of deduction in a short sketch called "My Evening with Sherlock Holmes."

On April 9, 1892, "Adventures of Sherwood Hoakes: An Interrupted Honeymoon" by C.C. Rothwell (writing as "A Cone and Oil") appeared in *The Ludgate Weekly*. This story was followed a month later in the same magazine by his "Adventures of Sherwood Hoakes: The Yellow Cockroach." Other authors joined the fun, and more stories and quickly and quite frequently followed—and have never ceased.

Sherlock Holmes is far and away the most mimicked of fictional characters. He is so universal in his appeal that the more serious pastiches overwhelm us, and the humorous parodies seem limitless. And Holmes is easy to make into a comic figure. All it takes is a deerstalker and a magnifying glass to turn Bugs Bunny, Donald Duck, Jerry Lewis, the Three Stooges or Adrian Monk into a Sherlockian knock-off.

For us, devotees and disciples, the parody writer actually walks a dangerous line. He can make us appreciate the wit, the satire, the humor with such a story. But, at the same time, he must make it apparent that it is a tribute and not a mockery, that there is an affection for Sherlock Holmes and underlying respect for the master. Simply sticking a deerstalker on a crude or demeaning or pornographic personality—which has been done, of course—is not truly a parody. That is just a travesty.

One of the great aspects of Sherlock Holmes is the fact that, just as the character himself is subject to endless variation, so is his name. Ellery Queen noted that the name itself "is particularly susceptible to the twistings and mis-shapenings of burlesque minded authors." Surely, Arthur Conan Doyle, who struggled a little with what he was going to call his detective hero, could not have known just how perfect the name he finally selected—Sherlock Holmes—would be for parody, for rhyme, for the transposing of letters and sounds, for the substitution of suggestive words in the name of a comic character.

Remember what Juliet had to say:

> O be some other name!
> What's in a name? That which we call a rose
> By any other word would smell as sweet.

Sherlockians, however, may not agree with Shakespearians on this subject. A Sherlock by any other name is not the same.

What follows is not just a list, but also a catalogue of 561 parody names derived from a true phonetic gold mine: the name Sherlock Holmes. Many are unique, the exclusive product of a single creative mind. Others are found frequently, although they were most likely continually reinvented rather than copied. The best example of repeated creation is "Herlock Sholmes," the most obvious of parody names, which has 30 citations in this book.

These appellations are gleaned from a multitude of sources. The "twistings and mis-shapenings" of the name Sherlock Holmes can be found almost everywhere: novels, short stories, jokes, cartoons, comics, movies, plays, puppet shows, radio and television programs, the internet, newspapers, magazines, video games, jewelry, toys, music, and even supermarket fliers. All are represented in this listing.

While I do claim this is a longer and more inclusive list than any previously published (and I have been diligent in making as exhaustive a search as I know how to conduct), I have no illusions that it is complete. Probably, a complete list can never be achieved. Doubtless, some will disagree with what has been included and what has been deliberately omitted. Not included are the names of Sherlockian-styled parody characters, impostors, imitators or aliases whose monikers have no particular linguistic connection, in either sound or cadence, to the name Sherlock Homes.

Any errors in attribution are entirely unintentional, and I accept full responsibility for them. They will be corrected gladly in the future, should another version ever appear.

This list has been a pleasure to compile and a relief to bring to a conclusion, lest pursuing it becomes an obsession. Even more, it is a tribute both to Arthur Conan Doyle's brilliant choice of a character name and to the inventiveness of the Sherlockian mind.

Bill Mason, BSI
"White Mason"
Greenbrier, Tennessee
June 2018

QUICK LIST

Airlock Holmes
Armlock Holmes
Arson Clews
Artlock Holmes
Badlack Holmes
Badlock Tombs
Barlock Jones
Barock Holmes
Barratt Holmes
Batlock Holmes
Bearlock Bones
Beerlock Foams
Blaylock Jones
Blowback Foams
Brainy Domes
Brihtric Donne
Bumlock Tomes
Burdock Holmes
Burdock Rose
Burstup Homes
Capslock Holmes
Cedric Coombes
Cellblock Holmes
Cerlocio Olmez
Charles Kolmes
Charley Colms
Charlake Hams
Charlock Coombs
Charlock Halms
Charlotte Holmes
Charlotte House
Chelovick Homes
Cher-Lock Sam

Cherlock Holmes
Chubb-Lock Homes
Chubblock Homes
Chublock Bones
Churlhack Halmes
Churlhock Halmes
Clewlow Holmes
Cockroach Bones
Cocksure Jones
Creighton Holmes
Curlilock Ohms
Curllock Halmes
Curlock Bones
Curlock Holmes
Dalock Holmes
Dennis Bones
Doorlock Bones
Doorlock Combs
Doorlock Homes
Dorlock Homes
Dreadlock Holmes
Dudley Jones
Egglock Holmes
Enoch Bone
Fablock Holmes
Fellock Holmes
Fetlock Holmes
Fetlock Jones
Finlock Combes
Flatfoot Burns
Flintlock Holmes
Foreclose Holmes
Forelock Combe

Forelock Domes
Forelock Holmes
Forelock Hums
Forelock Tomes
Froglock Holmes
Geoffrey Holm
Girlock Holmes
Goldilock Holmes
Goldilock Homes
Grimlock Holmes
Hairlock Cholms
Hairlock Combs
Hairlock Holmes
Hairlock Jones
Hairlock Shomes
Hamhock Bones
Hamhock Holmes
Hamlock Shears
Hamrock Shoals
Hancock Homes
Hardas Stone
Harelock Holmes
Haricot Bones
Harlock Holmes
Harlot Holmes
Hawk-Sure
Hawkeye Soammes
Hawkshaw
Headlock Holmes
Heddlock Phones
Hemlock Bjones
Hemlock Bones
Hemlock Booms
Hemlock Coombs
Hemlock Foames
Hemlock Hoax
Hemlock Holmes
Hemlock Jones
Hemlock Shears
Hemlock Shoals
Hemlock Sholmes
Hemlock Shomes

Hemlock Soames
Hemlock Stones
Herblock Stones
Herlock Domes
Herlock Holmes
Herlock Olmes
Herlock Shoames
Herlock Sholem
Herlock Sholmes
Herlock Shomes
Herlock Soames
Herlock Solmes
Hermlock Holmes
Herr Lock Shömes
Hodiah Twist
Holmlock Blake
Holmlock Shears
Homelock Sherles
Homelock Shermes
Homlock Shermes
Horlock Shem
Hoskell Chomers
Hurlock Shoams
Hurlock Sholmes
Kerlock Shomes
Kermlock Holmes
Kreplock Holes
Laugh-a-Lock Holmes
Lockjaw Bones
Lockley Soames
Loufock-Holmès
Lovelock Holmes
Matchlock Holmes
Mereluck Holmes
Mereluck Tombs
Merlock Jones
Molar Vons
Momlock Holmes
Mooch Sheckls
Morecock Bones
Morelock Holmes
Morlock Tomes

Mukluk Gnomes
Mycock Bones
Mylock Bloodstalker
Myron Honize
Naughton Jones
Nerdslock Combs
Neville Boyles
Oilock Combs
Old Cap Jones
Ozone Holmes
Padlock Bones
Padlock Booms
Padlock Domes
Padlock Holmes
Padlock Homes
Padlock Jones
Padlocked Homes
Parrot Holmes
Persnurlock Holmes
Petcock Holmes
Pharaoh Jones
Philo Combs
Philo Gubb
Philo Holmes
Picklock Bones
Picklock Holes
Picklock Holmes
Picklock Homes
Picklock Soles
Pocklock Holmes
Pollack Hmms
Poplock Holmes
Porlock Moans
Potluck Bones
Psylock Holmes
Puglock Holmes
Pureluck Holmes
Pureluck Jones
Purlock Hone
Purrrlock Holmes
Quarrelrock Hums
Radford Shone

Raffles Holmes
Rex Homes
Rockhard Scones
S. Herlock Holmes
Sa Haapu
Saeloc Holmes
Sanford Haus
Saurian Holmes
Scherlock Holmes
Schlock Holmes
Schlock Homes
Sedgewick Hawk-Styles
Sellem Jones
Semloh
Seol-ok
Shadlock Bones
Shadrach Chomes
Shadrach Holmes
Shadrach Voles
Shagbark Jones
Shallock Holmes
Shamlock Bones
Shamrock Bones
Shamrock Cohen
Shamrock Ferret
Shamrock Holes
Shamrock Holmes
Shamrock Homes
Shamrock Houses
Shamrock Jolnes
Shamrock Jones
Shamrock Wolmbs
Shamshock Phones
Shamus Homes
Sharl Homes
Sharlock Holmes
Sharlowe Com's
Shaw La Coombs
Shayluck Hums
Shearlock Combs
Shearlock Hollmes
Shedlock Combs

Shedlock Holmes
Shedlock Homes
Shedlock Jones
Sheer Look Holmes
Sheer Luck Holmes
Sheer-Luck Holmes
Sheer-Luck Hums
Sheerbach Tones
Sheercheek Holmes
Sheercrocked Moans
Sheerflop Soames
Sheerlock Holmes
Sheerlock Omes
Sheerluck Bones
Sheerluck Bonkers
Sheerluck Brown
Sheerluck Coames
Sheerluck Combs
Sheerluck Cones
Sheerluck Coombes
Sheerluck Cracky
Sheerluck Gnomes
Sheerluck Goof
Sheerluck Holds
Sheerluck Holmes
Sheerluck Homes
Sheerluck Houses
Sheerluck Hums
Sheerluck Jones
Sheerluck Ohms
Sheerluck Roams
Sheeur-Loque Holmes
Sheila Holmes
Sheila-Locke Holmes
Shelby Holmes
Shellac Holmsburg
Shellack Homes
Shelley Gomez
Shelley Holmes
Shellshock Sloan
Shelly Holmes
Shelook Holmes

Sher Lok Holmes
Sherbert Cones
Sherbert Foams
Sherbert Scones
Sherbet Foams
Sherbet Jones
Sherbourne Rath
Shercock Bones
Sherdog Bones
Sherdog Holmes
Sheridan Haynes
Sheridan Hume
Sherk Oms
Sherlark Holmes
Sherlark Honed
Sherlaw Combs
Sherlaw Kombs
Sherlhock Holmès
Sherlick Holmes
Sherlie Holmes
Sherlimerick Holmes
Sherloc Holmes
Sherlock Abodes
Sherlock Ambrose
Sherlock Baffles
Sherlock Blake
Sherlock Bonds
Sherlock Bonehead
Sherlock Bones
Sherlock Boob
Sherlock Brown
Sherlock Bug
Sherlock Chick
Sherlock Clones
Sherlock Cohen
Sherlock Combs
Sherlock Cones
Sherlock Dale
Sherlock Dalek
Sherlock Dodo
Sherlock Domes
Sherlock Doyle

Sherlock Drones
Sherlock Droopy
Sherlock Duck
Sherlock False
Sherlock Ferret
Sherlock Fink
Sherlock Foams
Sherlock Fumes
Sherlock Gnomes
Sherlock Goof
Sherlock Groans
Sherlock Guck
Sherlock Haggis
Sherlock Hams
Sherlock Harms
Sherlock Hawkshaw
Sherlock Haymes
Sherlock Helms
Sherlock Hemlock
Sherlock Hoax
Sherlock Hochmes
Sherlock Höek
Sherlock Hoelms
Sherlock Hohms
Sherlock Holmz
Sherlock Homeboy
Sherlock Homeless
Sherlock Homely
Sherlock Homerun
Sherlock Homes
Sherlock Homes and Gardens
Sherlock Homie
Sherlock Homey
Sherlock Homo
Sherlock Hones
Sherlock Hong
Sherlock Hoomes
Sherlock Hot Stuff
Sherlock Hound
Sherlock Hounds
Sherlock Hums
Sherlock Jones

Sherlock Key
Sherlock Klotz
Sherlock Kush
Sherlock Mario
Sherlock Moans
Sherlock Monk
Sherlock Moose
Sherlock Mouse
Sherlock Murphy
Sherlock Oan
Sherlock Ohms
Sherlock Ol-mes
Sherlock Oomph
Sherlock Otis
Sherlock Phones
Sherlock Pimple
Sherlock Pinky
Sherlock Q. Jones
Sherlock Roams
Sherlock Romes
Sherlock Rooms
Sherlock Sam
Sherlock Shamrock
Sherlock Shamus
Sherlock Sholem
Sherlock Sholom
Sherlock Sleuth
Sherlock Slick
Sherlock Sloans
Sherlock Snoop
Sherlock Soames
Sherlock Sooty
Sherlock Stones
Sherlock Thrones
Sherlock Tones
Sherlock Troll
Sherlock Watkins
Sherlock Watson
Sherlock Wholmes
Sherlock Woof
Sherlock Yack
Sherlock Zones

Sherlocko
Sherlocko Homo
Sherlocko Smith
Sherlocko the Monk
Sherlocks Combs
Sherlockz Homz
Sherlog Combes
Sherlook Ohms
Sherlopp Homes
Sherluck Bones
Sherly Holmes
Sherman Holmes
Sherman Homes
Sherman Horn
Sherman Sherlock
Shermlock Shomes
Sherrinford Holmes
Sherringham Holmes
Sherslav Glomsky
Sherwood Hoakes
Sherwood Holmes
Sherwood Homes
Sherwood House
Sherwood Lang
Sheryl Locke Holmes
Shih Lok
Shilah Coombes
Shirknot Holmes
Shirley Combs
Shirley Holmes
Shirley Holmquist
Shirley Lock Holmes
Shirley-Lock Holmes
Shirlick Holmes
Shirt-Lock Holmes
Shirtlock Holmes
Shoelock Holmes
Sholomon Hume
Shore Rock Halmes
Shoreflock Hums
Shorelock Gommes
Shorelocked Holmes

Shoreluck Hams
Shorl Rock Hums
Shorlrock Homes
Shortwave Ohms
Showman Hoyle
Shrock Holmes
Shroomlock Holmes
Shrr'lok of Kholmes
Shumlock Holmes
Shurl Holmes
Shurl Rock Gommes
Shurlacombs
Shurlock Guck
Shylar Holmes
Shylock Bones
Shylock Combs
Shylock Hames
Shylock Haynes
Shylock Hoax
Shylock Holmes
Shylock Homes
Shylock Homestead
Shylock Hommes
Shylock Hound
Shylock Hyams
Shylock Jones
Shylock Oames
Shylock 'Olmes
Shylock Plumes
Signor Om-mez
Simon Rolfe
Sir Loch Hoames
Sir Luck Helm
Skilock Holmes
Skylark Bones
Skylark Holmes
Skylock Peyton
Slipshod Helms
Slylock Fox
Smallpox Soles
Smearlock Holmes
Smearlock Homeless

Snoopy Holmes
Snowlock Holmes
Solar Pons
Sonar T. Phoom
Sorelock Holmes
Soreluck Hams
Sortluck Ohms
Speedlock Holmes
Spencer Holmes
Spitlock Phones
Spurlock Holmes
Spylot Bones
Squirrel-Loch-Holmes
Squirrel-Lock Holmes
Squirrelock Holmes
Stamford Holmes
Stanway Holmes
Stately Holmes
Stately Homes
Stevenson Holmes
Suburban Holmes
Suburban Homes
Sure-Lock Home
Sure-Lock Homes
Sure-Locked Homes
Sure-Luck Holes
Sure-They-Lock Homez
Surefoot Jones
Surelacks Holmes
Surelick Bones
Surelick Holmes
Surelick Holms
Surelock Grones
Surelock Holmes
Surelock Homes
Surelock Jones
Surelock Keys
Surelocked Home

Surelocked Homes
Surelout Hole
Sureluck Combs
Sureluck Gommes
Sureluck Holmes
Sureluck Homes
Sureluck Hoomes
Sureluck Hums
Sureluck Jones
Sureschlock Homely
Surly Homes
Syaloch
Thinlock Bones
Tide Pooles
Timelock Foams
Townclock Fumes
Turlock Loams
Unlock Homes
Upchuck Gnomes
Urlach Holmes
Warlock Bones
Warlock Holmes
Warlock Horne
Warlock-Jones
Wassup Holmes
Wedlock Holmes
Werelock Holmes
Whodunit Stomes
Whoreluck Hams
Wormwood Soames
Yale Lock Holmes
Yalelock Holmes
Zedlock Holmes
Zerlock Holmes
Zinsheimer Holmes
Ziplock Holmes
Zoolock Holmes

A HOLMES BY ANY OTHER NAME

Airlock Holmes
Airlock Holmes is a designation for the Star Wars detective character Inspector Thanoth in *Darth Vader*, No. 9 (Marvel Comics, Sept. 2015), as conceived by Dylan Todd in his online review of the issue for Comics Alliance, "All for the Wookiee" (Oct. 2, 2015). The term is not used in the comic itself.

Armlock Holmes
Armlock Holmes, drawn by Koko Gonzales, appeared in *The K-Zone Bulletin*, the on-line publication of *K-Zone: Where Kids Rule*, produced by Summit Media of the Philippines. He was one of the 18 Holmes parody characters to take part in "Crisis of Infinite Holmes" (Aug. 2008), an adventure involving Sherlockian characters working together to save their concurrent universes.

Arson Clews
Gene Fowler wrote a long series of parodies featuring Professor Arson Clews and his assistant Boobson for the Hearst newspapers between 1923 and 1925. Three of them, "The Sylvan Puzzle" (Mar. 6, 1924), "The Plate Mystery" (Apr. 13, 1924), and "The Vault Mystery" (June 22, 1924) as they appeared in the *New York American* are reprinted in *Sherlock Holmes in America* (Bill Blackbeard, ed.; Harry N. Abrams, 1981).

Artlock Holmes
Artlock Holmes was a cartoon figure in "Life Is Better Than Art, No. 1" by the artist known as Taz. An entry for the Art Institutes poster design contest, originally drawn Feb. 3, 2008.

Badlock Holmes
"Badlock Holmes" was a burlesque skit written by Wallace Irwin "in which some unique features of the local burglary system will

be shown." Presented at the Theater Republic of San Francisco on March 15, 1903. Badlock Holmes was portrayed by Joe Kane.

Badlock Tombs

Badlock Tombs is one of seven parody names in "Prize Detective Story." Anonymous (*The Weekly Magazine*, May 8, 1897). Retitled "Holmes and the Startled Banker" in *As It Might Have Been: A Collection of Sherlockian Parodies from Unlikely Sources* (Robert C.S. Adey, ed.; Calabash Press, 1998). Hemlock Coombs repeatedly changes his name as he makes a series of trivial deductions.

Barlock Jones

"The Adventures of Barlock Jones" appeared in *Queue*, a hobbled-together publication produced by captured British servicemen at a World War I prisoner of war camp in Mainz, Germany, in 1918.

Barock Holmes

Detective Barock Holmes and His Hound (1909), a silent short film, now presumably lost. Produced by Gaumont Studios of France. The cast members are unknown.

Barratt Holmes

1) "Barratt Holmes and the Strange Case of the Missing Cobblers" (1988) and "Barratt Holmes and the Case of the Phantom Police Killer" (1990) were episodes of *The Russ Abbot Show*, a British sketch comedy television program. Barratt Holmes was portrayed by Russ Abbot, with Jerry Holland as Dr. Wimpy. Produced by Grenada Television for BBC; directed by John Bishop.
2) Barratt Holmes made two more appearances in *Russ Abbott's Fun Book* (BBC Books, 1990). In "The Armchair Mystery" by Joel Morris and Jason Smith, false teeth lead to the killer of a gardener. In "Barrett Holmes and the Red-Headed Mystery" by Paul Minett and Brian Leveson, victims wear red wigs to forestall a deranged attacker. Barratt Holmes is assisted by Dr. Wimpy.

Batlock Holmes

Batman: Arkham Knight is a 2015 action-adventure video game developed by Rocksteady Studios and published by Warner Brothers Interactive Entertainment. "Batlock Holmes" is story-driven mission #62.

Bearlock Bones

"Bearlock Bones: The Story-Book Detective." Anonymous (*The Hartlepool Northern Daily Mail*, Nov. 16, 1895). Reprinted in *The Hampshire Telegraph* (Nov. 23, 1895). Bearlock Bones locates a missing sweetheart for a cross-eyed client.

Beerlock Foams

"The Stolen G-Strings," featuring Beerlock Foams and Swatson. *Candid Tales* (Kirby Productions, June 1950). An adult comic book appearance. A crime is committed by "Sally, the strip-tease pick pocket."

Blaylock Jones

"The Ghost of Plymouth Castle," featuring Blaylock Jones and Datson. In: *Whatever Happened to Uncle Albert? and Other Puzzling Plays*. Sue Alexander (Clarion Books/Houghton Mifflin, 1980). Lady Plymouth summons Blaylock Jones to uncover the cause of strange happenings that threaten her inheritance. A play for children and teen actors.

Blowback Foams

Blowback Foams is one of the "great made-up detectives," as conceived by James Parker in his review of Sherlockian volumes in *The New York Times Sunday Book Review* (Oct. 26, 2015).

Brainy Domes

Brainy Domes (Buster Bunny) and Flotsam (Babs Bunny) appear in "And All That Rot," a segment of "Brave Tales of Real Rabbits." Season 1, Episode 59, of *Tiny Toon Adventures*, an animated television series. Written by Eddie Fitzgerald; directed by Rich Arons; voiced by Charlie Adler. Produced by Warner Brothers Animation for syndication. Brainy Domes searches for the Queen's missing jewels, with Montiarity as the prime suspect.

Brihtric Donne

Brihtric Donne appears in *Druid's Blood* by Esther M. Friesner (New American Library, 1988), a fantasy novel set in Victorian England. Donne is the assumed name of Sherbourne Rath, a detective thought to be deceased. Assisted by Dr. John H. Weston.

Bumlock Tomes

Bumlock Tomes and Dr. Flotsam appeared in two humorous sketches in *The Chicago Tribune*, written by an anonymous author (as "D-Double-E"): "Mystery of the Closed Portal" (Mar. 19, 1947) and "Case of the Dejected Lady" (May 28, 1947). Tomes lives on Butcher Street.

Burdock Holmes

Burdock Holmes is a one-time corruption of Sherlock Holmes' name in *The Supreme Adventure of Inspector Lestrade* by M.J. Trow (Stein and Day, 1985). Reissued as *The Adventures of Inspector Lestrade* (Regnery Publishing, 1998). Lestrade tells Conan Doyle, "I like your stories of detection—that fellow, what's his name, Burdock Holmes."

Burdock Rose

Burdock Rose appeared in two stories by P.G. Wodehouse in *Public School Magazine*: "The Strange Disappearance of Mr. Buxton-Smythe" (Dec. 1901) and "The Adventure of the Split Infinitive" (Mar. 1902). Both tales involve crimes committed at St. Asterick's School. Assisted by Dr. Wotsing.

Burstup Homes

Burstup Homes was a character appearing in a series of four short silent comedy films, all released within a four-month period in 1913: *Burstup Homes* (Feb. 19), *Burstup Homes' Murder Case* (Mar. 26), *The Mystery of the Lost Cat* (Apr. 16), and *The Case of the Missing Girl* (May 7). The films were produced by the Solax Film Co. and directed by Alice Guy. Starring Fraunie Fraunholz in the role of Detective Burstup Homes.

Capslock Holmes

Capslock Holmes, drawn by Koko Gonzales, appeared in *The K-Zone Bulletin*, the on-line publication of *K-Zone: Where Kids Rule*, produced by Summit Media of the Philippines. He was one of the 18 Holmes parody characters to take part in "Crisis of Infinite Holmes" (Aug. 2008), an adventure involving Sherlockian characters working together to save their concurrent universes.

Cedric Coombes

Cedric Coombes was the alias assumed by Sherlock Holmes in *The Strange Return of Sherlock Holmes* by Barry Grant (Severn House, 2010). Holmes, frozen in a glacier in 1914, is returned to life 90 years later and resumes solving mysteries with the assistance of James Wilson.

Cellblock Holmes

Cellblock Holmes, a detective behind bars, drawn by Koko Gonzales, appeared in *The K-Zone Bulletin*, the on-line publication of *K-Zone: Where Kids Rule*, produced by Summit Media of the Philippines. He is one of the 18 Holmes parody characters to take part in "Crisis of Infinite Holmes" (Aug. 2008), an adventure involving Sherlockian characters working together to save their concurrent universes.

Cerlocio Olmez

"A Case of Identity II; or, Art in the Soup Can Take the Strangest Forms!" featuring Cerlocio Olmez and Átsonez. Katherine Karlson. *The Baker Street Journal*, Vol. 20, No. 3 (Sept. 1970). The director of the Prado Museum in Madrid consults Olmez about missing art by "that famous American artist Andrés Warhol."

Charles Kolmes

Charles Kolmes, along with Doc Ouatson and Morty, are the creations of the artist known only as Wells in France. The cartoons appeared in *La Lettre de Baker Street*, a magazine "dedicated to the master detective," under the title *Le Monde Vermeilleux de Charles Kolmes* ("The Rosy World of Charles Kolmes") in the 1980s and early 1990s.

Charley Colms

Charley Colms was a Sherlockian character in three French films: *Charley Colms* (Apr. 5, 1912), *The Dancer's Necklace* (June 7, 1912), and *The Fashionable Set* (1912). Produced by Pathé Freres; written by Gustave LeRouge; directed by René Leprince. Charley Colms was portrayed by Georges Coquet.

Charlake Hams

Charlake Hams is a corruption of the name Sherlock Holmes in *Wilde About Holmes* by Milo Yelesiyevich (Comic Masque, 2008), one of many names used within a bizarre hallucination that occurs when "a delirious Holmes" suffers from "a cocaine frenzy."

Charlock Coombs
"Charlock Coombs: A London Detective in Clarksburg." John G. Gittings. *The Clarksburg Daily Telegram* (Dec. 5, 1903). Coombs, a friend of Arthur Conan Doyle, stops a pumpkin thief.

Charlock Halms
The Ranger Smokes Too Much: An Adventure of Charlock Halms and *The Crying Cat: An Adventure of Charlock Halms*. Pierre Coran (Child's World, 1992). Two children's books featuring Charlock Halms, a rabbit detective.

Charlotte Holmes
1) *Sherlock & Me*, featuring Charlotte Holmes (1980) is the British version of a Japanese anime television series that first aired in 26 episodes (Dec. 1977-June 1978). Charlotte Holmes is the niece of Sherlock Holmes. Released on VHS by Portland Films. In America, the series was titled *The Casebook of Charlotte Holmes*.
2) *Charlotte Holmes and Dr. Watson*. Written by Kitty Beletic. Presented at the Richardson, Texas, Children's Theatre (Feb. 1988). Charlotte Holmes was portrayed by Laura Carter.
3) *The Strange Adventures of Charlotte Holmes*. Hilary Bailey (Constable & Co., 1994). The independent minded sister of Sherlock Holmes maintains a laboratory in her garden and solves a series of cases with the assistance of Mary, the wife of Dr. John Watson.
4) *The Tale Not Told* by Constance Wilder-Wokun (Xlibris, 2000), a "re-telling" of the Sherlockian Canon, reveals that Sherlock Holmes is really a girl, Charlotte Holmes, who grew up with Mycroft in India and eventually became a consulting detective in London.
5) Charlotte Holmes and Jamie Watson, teenaged descendants of Sherlock Holmes and Dr. Watson, appear in two novels by Brittany Cavallaro, both published by Tegen Books: *A Study in Charlotte* (2016) and *The Last of August* (2017), in which they encounter August Moriarty, part of a family of art thieves. A promotional book trailer on YouTube featured Emma Pfaeffle as Charlotte Holmes.

6) Charlotte Holmes is the true identity of Sherlock Holmes in *A Study in Scarlet Women* (2016) and *A Conspiracy in Belgravia* (2017) by Sherry Thomas, both published by Thorndike Press. "Being shunned by society gives Charlotte Holmes the time and freedom to put her extraordinary powers of deduction to use as Sherlock Holmes, consulting detective." Assisted by Mrs. Watson.

Charlotte House

Charlotte House and Jane Woodsen "solve mysteries of the heart" in England during the time of the Napoleonic Wars in two novels by Jennifer Petkus: *My Particular Friend* (Mallard Classics, 2012) and *Our Mutual Friends* (Mallard Romance, 2017). The characters are modeled on Sherlock Holmes and Jane Austen.

Chelovick Homes

Chelovick Homes is a corruption of the name Sherlock Holmes in *Wilde About Holmes* by Milo Yelesiyevich (Comic Masque, 2008), one of many names used within a bizarre hallucination that occurs when "a delirious Holmes" suffers from "a cocaine frenzy."

Cher-Lock Sam

Sherlock Sam is a series of children's books featuring Samuel Tan Cher-Lock by A.J. Low (Adan Jiminez and Felicia Low-Jimenez), published by Andrews McMeel Publishing (2013): *Sherlock Sam and the Missing Heirloom in Katong*, *Sherlock Sam and the Ghostly Moans in Fort Canning*, and *Sherlock Sam and the Sinister Letters in Bras Basah*. Set in Singapore, Sam solves mysteries with the assistance of his robot, Watson.

Cherlock Holmes

1) Cherlock Holmes peers through a magnifying glass, trying to deduce the identity of Santa Claus in an untitled cartoon by Jeffrey R. Huddleston (*The Baker Street Chronicle*, Dec. 1981).
2) "Cherlock Holmes" is a Tumbler site featuring six images of the singer/actress Cher superimposed onto iconic Sherlockian images including a vintage comic, movie poster and book jacket (Mar. 12, 2012-July 24, 2013). Artur Kim, web designer.

Chubb-Lock Homes

Chubb-Lock Homes is an alternative rendering of the title character in *The Adventures of Chubblock Holmes* by Jack Butler Yeats.

Chubblock Homes

The Adventures of Chubblock Holmes. Jack Butler Yeats. A serial comic strip that originated in *Comic Cuts* (London) on June 16, 1894. Later, the character was transferred to the magazine *Funny Wonder*, where it remained until 1897. Assisted by Dr. Potson. Sometimes written as Chubb-Lock Homes.

Chublock Bones

"The Mystery of 2463, Pte. Chugwater." Anonymous. *Fifth Gloucester Gazette*, October 1915. Reprinted in *As It Might Have Been: A Collection of Sherlockian Parodies from Unlikely Sources* (Robert C.S. Adey, ed.; Calabash Press, 1998). In the trenches of World War I France, a series of deductions helps Chublock Bones find a missing private.

Churlhack Halmes

Churlhack Halmes is a corruption of the name Sherlock Holmes in *Wilde About Holmes* by Milo Yelesiyevich (Comic Masque, 2008), one of many names used within a bizarre hallucination that occurs when "a delirious Holmes" suffers from "a cocaine frenzy."

Churlhock Halmes

Churlhock Halmes is a corruption of the name Sherlock Holmes in *Wilde About Holmes* by Milo Yelesiyevich (Comic Masque, 2008), one of many names used within a bizarre hallucination that occurs when "a delirious Holmes" suffers from "a cocaine frenzy."

Clewlow Holmes

The Unrelated Adventures of Clewlow Holmes. Douglas Moreton (Cadds Printing, 1998). A collection of 11 stories featuring Clewlow Holmes and Boniface (Bon) Motson. The accident-prone brother of Sherlock and Mycroft Holmes solves his own cases and encounters Moriarty along the way.

Cockroach Bones

The Adventures of Cockroach Bones. Kevin Reed (The Tiger's Paw, 1997), a series of three short parodies about a detective in the insect world. Followed by *Cockroach Bones and the Five Orange Peeps* (Privately Printed, 2003). Assisted by Waspon, Cockroach Bones lives at 221 Bee on Baker's Street, where he encounters Arachne Adder.

Cocksure Jones

Cocksure Jones, Detective (1915), a short silent comedy film. Produced by Selig Polyscope Co.; directed by Burton L. King. The cast members are unknown. Released Sept. 18, 1915.

Creighton Holmes

The Adventures of Creighton Holmes. Ned Hubbell (Popular Library, 1979). A collection of seven mysteries solved by the grandson of Sherlock Holmes who uses "pure deduction" in his investigations. Creighton Holmes lives at an "address on Baker Street."

Curlilock Ohms

"Curlilock Ohms—Original Highly Moronic Sleuth." Thomas Martin (as "Tony"). *Wit: Modern Mirth and Mystery* (1947). A female detective living in Quaker Street.

Curllock Halmes

Curllock Halmes is a corruption of the name Sherlock Holmes in *Wilde About Holmes* by Milo Yelesiyevich (Comic Masque, 2008), one of many names used within a bizarre hallucination that occurs when "a delirious Holmes" suffers from "a cocaine frenzy."

Curlock Bones

Curlock Bones was an occasional alternative name for the canine character Curlock Holmes, a creation of T.A. (Tad) Dorgan for his "Indoor Sports" comic strip in *The New York Evening Journal* appearing between 1907 and 1921.

Curlock Holmes

1) Curlock Holmes, "a noted detective who has more clues than a pipe has puffs" was the creation of T.A. (Tad) Dorgan, a sports writer and cartoonist for *The New York Evening Journal*. His daily "Indoor Sports" comic strip featured frankfurter and dog characters, including Curlock Holmes. Several of the strips from 1907 are reprinted in *Sherlock Holmes in America* (Bill Blackbeard, ed.; Harry N. Abrams, 1981).

2) Curlock Holmes makes an appearance in the humorous feature "Dog in Society Hotel at $40 a Week." Anonymous (*The Virginia Enterprise* of Minnesota, Nov. 26, 1909).

Dalock Holmes

Dalock Holmes, "the Sherlock Dalek," was designed by the artist known as Adrienne D. as a combination of Sherlockian and Dr. Who themes. Daleks are an extraterrestrial race of mutants in the *Doctor Who* television series. The image is featured on various products, including prints, a throw pillow, t-shirts, hoody, wall clock, and laptop sleeve. Featured on Society6.com, an on-line marketer.

Dennis Bones

The Dennis Bones Mystery Book. Jim and Mary Razzi (Scholastic Book Services, 1978). Dennis Bones, the world-famous canine detective, and his good friend Scotson solve a series of seven mysteries.

Doorlock Bones

Jayville Junction: An Hour and a Half Comedy in a Railroad Depot, featuring Doorlock Bones, the detective. Harry L. Newton (T.S. Denison & Co., 1906). A comedy play, often staged in the first half of the 20th Century. Doorlock Bones is a minor character.

Doorlock Combs

"The Twisted Hairpin," featuring Doorlock Combs, was written specifically for *The Harrisburg (Pennsylvania) Telegraph* (Feb. 23, 1895) by Howard M. Hoke. Combs and his friend Swatson live on Butcher Street and are consulted by Mr. Gingerly Spicer, who fears that his sister has been abducted and her fiancé murdered by a fiery European count.

Doorlock Homes

1) *The Adventure of the Five Puce Map Tacks: A Doorlock Homes Mystery.* Paul Nizza (Fibonacci Corp., 1976). Assisted by Dr. John H. Whatson. Doorlock Homes lives at 221B Bonker Street; his fat older brother is Hayloft Holmes; and his rival is Professor Artie Morey. Whatson plans to marry Miss Morestains in order "to get out of this madhouse."

2) Doorlock Homes is a character in *LEGO City Undercover* and *LEGO City Undercover: The Chase Begins*, both of which are action-adventure video games released in 2013. Developed by TT Fusion and published by Nintendo.

Dorlock Homes

Deduce, You Say! (1956), featuring Daffy Duck as Dorlock Homes and Porky Pig as Watkins. A Warner Brothers cartoon. Written by Michael Maltese; directed by Chuck Jones. Released Sept. 29, 1956. Included in the *Looney Tunes Golden Collection*, released by Warner Home Video in 2003. The heroes pursue the Shropshire Slasher. Voiced by Mel Blanc.

Dreadlock Holmes

1) "The Case of the Missing Tandoori, or What Ever Happened to My Bombay Duck? Being the Ethnic Adventures of Dreadlock Holmes." Miles Tubb. *Calabash Series*, No. 1 (Dyfed, Wales), 1983.
2) Joke: "Q: What do you call a Jamaican Detective? A: Dreadlock Holmes." Anonymous. Online at heichou-fever.tumblr.com.

Dudley Jones

"Dudley Jones, Bore Hunter." P.G. Wodehouse. *Punch* (April 26 and May 6, 1903). Assisted by his friend, Waddus. Called upon to rid the Pettigrew home of an unwelcome and relentlessly boring uncle, Jones succeeds in beating the man at his own game. He literally bores the uncle to death with "stories of adventures on Swiss mountains. A Switzerland bore is the deadliest type known to scientists."

Egglock Holmes

Egglock Holmes is the creation of the artist Priscilla Bellafronte of Brazil. Her gallery quality print featuring a sunny-side up Sher-lockian egg is featured on Society6.com, an on-line marketer.

Enoch Bone

Everybody's Favorite Duck, featuring Enoch Bone. Gahan Wilson (Mysterious Press, 1988). Assisted by John Weston. The "forces of justice" call on Enoch Bone to battle the combined criminal plans of the Professor (Moriarty), the Mandarin (Fu Manchu) and Spectrobert (Fantomas).

Fablock Holmes

Fablock Holmes is the persona assumed by Marco, the friend of the fashionable detective Maddie Springer in *Deadly in High Heels* by Gemma Halliday (CreateSpace, 2015). Marco "might pull out a deerstalker hat and magnifying glass at any second."

Fellock Holmes
"Caught in the Act," featuring Fellock Holmes and Dr. Watso. Bill Conklin (*The Saturday Evening Post*, Aug. 26, 1967). A gigantic rooster is killed in front of the Hollywood Palladium, providing Fellock Holmes with an "electrifying adventure" involving dresses for go-go dancers.

Fetlock Holmes
"The Adventure of the Porcelain Clock: A Parody," featuring Fetlock Holmes. Roger W. Herzel. *The Haverford News* (Haverford College, Pennsylvania), Oct. 27, 1961. Fetlock is assisted by Walnut.

Fetlock Jones
1) *A Double-Barrelled Detective Story*, featuring Fetlock Jones as a nephew of Sherlock Holmes. Mark Twain (Harper & Bros., 1902). A satire of the mystery genre, and specifically of the Sherlock Holmes stories and themes. Sherlock Holmes finds himself in the American West, and his nephew Fetlock Jones kills a silver miner by blowing up his cabin. The novel was adapted for the stage by Robert St. Clair (Baker's Plays, 1954).
2) "Bibliographic Bones," featuring Fetlock Jones, "the great defective." Frank Place. *The Medical Pickwick*, No. 1 (1915). Fetlock Jones and his friend Swatson discuss errors (which they call "bones") in medical references.

Finlock Combes
"A Case of Identity III," featuring Finlock Combes and Dr. Klutzdam. Andrew Page. *The Devon County Chronicle*, Dec. 1971 and Feb. 1972.

Flatfoot Burns
"Flatfoot Burns." *Candy*, No.1 (Comic Magazines, Autumn 1947). A comic book appearance. Private detective Flatfoot Burns (in Sherlockian costume) searches for Aladdin's magic lamp, stolen from lamp manufacturer Mr. Fatty de Light.

Flintlock Holmes

Flintlock Holmes, drawn by Koko Gonzales, appeared in *The K-Zone Bulletin*, the on-line publication of *K-Zone: Where Kids Rule*, produced by Summit Media of the Philippines. He is one of the 18 Holmes parody characters to take part in "Crisis of Infinite Holmes" (Aug. 2008), an adventure involving Sherlockian characters working together to save their concurrent universes.

Foreclose Holmes

"The Ghost of Snaggle Castle," featuring Foreclose Holmes and his assistant Batsin Belfry. *Jerry Iger's Golden Features*, No. 5 (Blackthorne Publishing, Oct. 1986). Reprinted in *Scream Comics*, No. 1 (A List Comics, Oct. 1998). The story is credited to "Slaba Eyce." The ghost is actually the butler, Mayhem, who has been "making counterfeit slugs in the basement."

Forelock Combe

Babes in the Woods, featuring Forelock Combe and Dr. Dash, was a stage comedy produced in about 1894, presumably an adaptation of the traditional folk tale.

Forelock Domes

"The Case of the Poisoned Finger," featuring Forelock Domes and Potson. Anonymous (as "Exile"). *Alma Mater*, March 5, 1924. Reprinted in *As It Might Have Been: A Collection of Sherlockian Parodies from Unlikely Sources* (Robert C.S. Adey, ed.; Calabash Press, 1998). Domes deduces how the son of a count who always wears gloves managed to suffer from a single poisoned finger.

Forelock Holmes

"Forelock Holmes: A Pony in Pink." Lorem Ipsum. A *My Little Pony* and Sherlock Holmes crossover on fanfiction.net (July 2, 2013).

Forelock Hums

Forelock Hums is a corruption of the name Sherlock Holmes in *Wilde About Holmes* by Milo Yelesiyevich (Comic Masque, 2008), one of many names used within a bizarre hallucination that occurs when "a delirious Holmes" suffers from "a cocaine frenzy."

Forelock Tomes

Forelock Tomes appears in an anonymously-written "The Private Detective" in *The Leighton Buzzard Observer and Linslade Gazette* (July 14, 1896) and in other British newspapers on various dates. Tomes makes a series of deductions from an umbrella left outside his door, but his conclusions turn out to be off the mark. Assisted by Dr. Dotson.

Froglock Holmes

1) "Froglock Holmes: The Case of the Missing Spouse," also featuring Dr. Flopson. Suni V. Perez (Unpublished MS, Feb. 1981). The characters live in Baker Bog.

2) "The Search of Froglock Holmes." *Case of the Missing Number: Solving for Unknown Numbers*. Candace Watkins (Teachers Pay Teachers, PDF Acrobat File, 2012). An educational tale designed to aid mathematics comprehension.

Geoffrey Holm

"No Rhyme or Reason," featuring Geoffrey Holm. Marsha Prouty (*Mycroft's Messenger*, No. 19), Oct. 1980. Assisted by Dr. Dawson.

Girlock Holmes

Girlock Holmes (2014) and *The Angels Tear* (2014) are fan fiction stories featuring Emma Holmes, a descendant of Sherlock Holmes, who travels to Japan and teams with Detective Conan. Anonymous (as "Feathered Fox"). Posted on wattpad.com.

Goldilock Holmes

"Sherlock is a Lady with Perfect Feet: Scotland Yard's New Wrinkle." Arthur Veysey. *Chicago Tribune*, Jan. 24, 1948. A premise of the article: "Sherlock Holmes is out of date. The modern star sleuth is Goldilock Holmes."

Goldilock Homes

"Give Me Lib, or Give Me Death," featuring Goldilock Homes. Rod Reed. *Ellery Queen's Mystery Magazine*, Sept. 1973. A group of female detectives (all characters based on famous fictional detectives) meets to solve the robbery of a toy manufacturer and prove they are not second-class detectives.

Grimlock Holmes

Grimlock Holmes, a bear detective inspired by *Grimm's Fairy Tales*, drawn by Koko Gonzales, appeared in *The K-Zone Bulletin*, the on-line publication of *K-Zone: Where Kids Rule*, produced by Summit Media of the Philippines. He was one of the 18 Holmes parody characters to take part in "Crisis of Infinite Holmes" (Aug. 2008), an adventure involving Sherlockian characters working together to save their concurrent universes.

Hairlock Cholms

Detective Hairlock Cholms, No.1. "The Mystery of the South Pole." J.L. Le Hir (writer and artist). A Dutch comic book, published by Mondria (1981). Hairlock Cholms is a feline Sherlockian detective, assisted by a canine Watson.

Hairlock Combs

1) "His Crowning Sorrow," featuring Hairlock Combs, "the village barber." Anonymous (*Wells Journal*, Feb. 23, 1905). A short joke credited to *London Opinion*.

2) *Babes in the Wood*, featuring Hairlock Combs, a "lady detective." Book by Josh Barry; music by Edmund C. Brierly. A musical pantomime of the folk story in eleven scenes. Opened Dec. 21, 1905, at the Alexandra Theatre in Widnes, England, and ran through Feb. 1906 in Widnes, St. Helens, and Blackpool. Jenny Clare portrayed Hairlock Combs.

3) "The Detective Man," featuring Hairlock Combs, was a comedy sketch presented at a Volunteer Aid Detachment (V.A.D.) Hospital in Reading, England, on Dec. 16, 1915. Hairlock Combs was portrayed by a wounded soldier identified only as Pvt. Steadleman.

4) *The Case of the Screaming Bishop* (1944), featuring Hairlock Combs and Gotsome. A short animated film. Produced by Columbia Pictures; written by John McLeish; directed by Howard Swift. Released Aug. 4, 1944. Hairlock Combs investigates the theft of a dinosaur skeleton.

Hairlock Holmes

1) "Hairlock Holmes, Detective, Solves an Anachronistic Mystery." Floyd Horowitz. *The Baker Street Journal*, Vol. 14, No. 4 (Dec. 1964). A play script for young people.

2) "The Adventures of Hairlock Holmes." Kane Pickerill. An interactive online narrative featuring Hairlock Holmes, a rabbit detective (bombfish.com). Posted Nov. 30, 2009.

Hairlock Jones
Hairlock Jones in the Case of the Pirate Pirate DVD Maker. Assisted by Tom Motson. Produced by the Youth Film School of Brighton, East Sussex, England (Oct. 7, 2014). A short film featuring students.

Hairlock Shomes
Hairlock Shomes is a comic book character by Freddy Milton, appearing in a series of parodies in *Seriemagasinet*, published in Stockholm, Sweden, 1974-75. Magnus Knutsson collaborated with Milton on at least two of the stories.

Hamhock Bones
"Murder at 13 Rue de Ditoot," featuring Hamhock Bones and Whatson. Art Buchwald. *Wampus* (University of Southern California, Feb. 1947). Reprinted in *A Century of College Humor* (Dan Carlinsky, ed.; Random House, 1971). A murder is solved amid frequent references to college courses and campus life.

Hamhock Holmes
The Adventure of the Wild Turkey: From the Continuing Adventures of Hamhock Holmes, By Billy Joe-Bob "Bubba" Watson and *The Red-Necked League: From the Continuing Adventures of Hamhock Holmes, By Billy Joe-Bob "Bubba" Watson*. John Atkins and C. Bryan Gassner (Wilson's Basement Dwellers, 1998). Exploits of redneck mystery solvers from an Alabama trailer park.

Hamlock Shears
Hamlock Shears is a one-time corruption of the name Smallpox Soles, the Holmes parody character featured in "The Marischal Manor Mystery." Anonymous (*Alma Mater*, Oct. 31, 1923). A play, reprinted in *As It Might Have Been: A Collection of Sherlockian Parodies from Unlikely Sources* (Robert C.S. Adey, ed.; Calabash Press, 1998).

Hamrock Shoals

Hamrock Shoals is a one-time corruption of the name Smallpox Soles, the Holmes parody character featured in "The Marischal Manor Mystery." Anonymous (*Alma Mater*, Oct. 31, 1923). A play, reprinted in *As It Might Have Been: A Collection of Sherlockian Parodies from Unlikely Sources* (Robert C.S. Adey, ed.; Calabash Press, 1998).

Hancock Homes

Hancock Homes, "master detective," appeared in *Popeye* daily comic strips, by E.C. Segar and distributed by King Features Syndicate, Feb. 4-22, 1933. They are collected in *E.C. Segar's Popeye, Vol 3: Let's You and Him Fight*. Kim Thompson, ed. (Fantagraphic Books, 2008). Popeye calls in Hancock Homes to investigate a case of election fraud.

Hardas Stone

"Round the Pink Pill-Box: A Study in Pathological Romance," featuring Dr. Hardas Stone. Anonymous (as "Castor Oyle"). *Lika Joko*, Dec. 1, 1894. Reprinted in *As It Might Have Been: A Collection of Sherlockian Parodies from Unlikely Sources* (Robert C.S. Adey, ed.; Calabash Press, 1998). A parody of both the Sherlock Holmes stories and Conan Doyle's medical tales in *Round the Red Lamp: Being Facts and Fancies of Medical Life* (Methuen, 1894).

Harelock Holmes

"Harelock Holmes and His Search for the Golden Carrot." Jadeyn Feuillerat, Hunter Greicar and Carrie Greicar (Fiction Press, April 18, 2014). "A lesson to children about judging someone." Harelock Holmes searches for Moledigger, who has made away with his prized possession.

Haricot Bones

"The Struldbrugg Reaction," featuring Haricot Bones and Dr. Dawson. John Sutherland. *The Magazine of Fantasy and Science Fiction* (July 1964). Reprinted in *The Game Is Afoot: Parodies Pastiches and Ponderings of Sherlock Holmes* (Marvin Kaye, ed.; St. Martin's Press, 1994). Bones, a wheelchair-bound, 95-year-old detective, searches for killers in New York and the secret of eternal youth.

Harlock Holmes

Harlock Holmes, a space detective, drawn by Koko Gonzales, appeared in *The K-Zone Bulletin*, the on-line publication of *K-Zone: Where Kids Rule*, produced by Summit Media of the Philippines. He was one of the 18 Holmes parody characters to take part in "Crisis of Infinite Holmes" (Aug. 2008), an adventure involving Sherlockian characters working together to save their concurrent universes.

Harlot Holmes

Harlot Holmes is the designation for a "slutty Sherlock," as conceived by the artist and photographer known as "MM" on her "Wit or Miss Online" blog (May 22, 2009). "It's not elementary, dear Watson. It's my birthday."

Hawk-Sure

"Hawk-Sure the Detective and Whatsis." *Tick Tock Tales*, No. 1 (Magazine Enterprises, Jan. 1946). Hawk-Sure, in full Sherlockian costume, is robbed in his own office by a thief who "returns to the scene of the crime," just to prove the old saying correct. A one-page comic book appearance.

Hawkeye Soammes

Hawkeye Soammes and Dr. Potson appeared in two episodes of *Count Duckula*, an animated television series on ITV in Britain and Nickelodeon in the USA. "All in a Fog" (Season 1, Episode 9), written by Peter Richard Reeves, first aired Nov. 1, 1988. "The Great Ducktective (Season 3, Episode 7), written by Jimmy Hibbert, first aired Dec. 3, 1990. Both episodes directed by Chris Randall. Series produced by Cosgrove Hall for Thames Television. In both episodes, Count Duckula is falsely accused of murder. Voiced by Jack May.

Hawkshaw

1) "Hawkshaw the Detective" by Gus Mager debuted in *The New York World* on February 13, 1913, and ran until 1922 in various Pulitzer-owned publications. The character was based on Mager's "Sherlocko the Monk," which he was forced to discontinue because of objections from Arthur Conan Doyle. Mager tweaked Conan Doyle by signing his Hawshaw strips as "Watso," the parody name

of Watson in the Sherlocko series. The character was revived and endured from 1931-1952, as a "topper" for *The Captain and the Kids* comic strip. *Tip Top Comics* (United Features Syndicate) included "Hawkshaw the Detective" frequently during the 1940s.

2) "Murder in the Library," featuring Hawkshaw. Harold Gray. *Mirage*, Nov. 1933. Reprinted in *As It Might Have Been: A Collection of Sherlockian Parodies from Unlikely Sources* (Robert C.S. Adey, ed.; Calabash Press, 1998). Assisted by Dr. Watson, Hawkshaw takes part in the investigation of the murder of Sir Jasper, who was killed in a house full of detectives.

3) *Hawkshaw the Detective*. Tim Kelly (Pioneer Drama Service, 1976). A play featuring the "enemy of the criminal element, master of disguise," whose motto is "Hawkshaw's the name, detection's the game."

Headlock Holmes

1) "Headlock Holmes" was a recurring skit on *The Merrymakers*, a music and comedy variety program on KHJ Radio in Los Angeles during the summer of 1932. At that time, KHJ was the west coast affiliate of the CBS Radio Network. Headlock Holmes investigated such mysteries as "why Dracula died of ptomaine after taking a bite out of Watson's left knee."

2) Headlock Holmes appeared in two comic appearances by Don "Duck" Edwing (writer and artist): "The Adventures of Headlock Holmes: From the Diary of Doctor Watsnew" in *Duck Edwing's Madventures of Almost Superheroes* (Warner Books, 1990) and "The Adventures of Shirley Holmes (Headlock Holmes' Ugly Sister)" in *Mad's Creature Presentation* (Warner Books, 1993). Also featuring Mrs. Crudson of 221 Half-Baked Street and Holmes' brother Micrin.

3) Headlock Holmes and Flotsam appeared in a satirical "pastiche" serving as political commentary about straw man tactics in a column by Milwaukee-based syndicated columnist Rick Horowitz in November 2003. The column appeared in several newspapers around the United States under various headlines. Holmes' conclusions are tagged, "Alimentary, my dear Flotsam... It's enough to make you sick to your stomach."

Heddlock Phones
Heddlock Phones appears in "The Return of Donan Coyle" in *The Belshill Speaker* (Mar. 19, 1927). Anonymous as "Suatel." Complaining to Dr. Swotson about "superfluous verbage," Phones proceeds to make completely erroneous deductions based on a single headline.

Hemlock Bjones
"Quite Simple!" featuring Hemlock Bjones, "a great detective." Edward H. Dreschnack. Bjones reveals that a murdered man is a bachelor because he is missing only one button from his shirt. The short item appeared in several American newspapers in February and March of 1925.

Hemlock Bones
1) "Hemlock Bones' Mystery." *Los Angeles Times* (Oct. 7, 1900). Anonymous, but credited to the *Baltimore American*. Bones, who smokes four cigars at once and toys with nitroglycerine bombs, contemplates the identity of an accident victim.
2) Hemlock Bones and Dr. Wopsome were characters in two political columns by Thomas F. Logan, the Washington correspondent of *The Philadelphia Inquirer* (May 24 and Aug. 16, 1909). In Logan's regular "Behind the Scenes at Nation's Capital," Bones and Wopsome consider the woes of Democrats.
3) "The Mishaps of Maggie, or The Ten Dollar Misery," featuring "Hemlock Bones, defective" was a serial in at least 12 parts, summarized daily in *The Tacoma Times* by the columnist known as Selah. Bones assumes various bizarre disguises during the course of the story.
4) "Hemlock Bones Is Man Who Found Benno de Elbe." Anonymous. *The High Point Enterprise* (Jan. 26, 1917). In a humorous conclusion to a true-crime scandal in the small city of High Point, North Carolina, Hemlock Bones, "the famous gum shoe artist and detective," was given credit for apprehending de Elbe, a German baker who secretly left town after leaving bad checks and other debts all over town. The once-respectable businessman was caught in Washington, D.C.
5) Hemlock Bones, "the great saw mill detective," encounters "the asphyxiating ozone which has made our city famous" in "Passed

by the Censor," an anonymously-written item in *The Leavenworth (Washington) Echo* (Jan. 4, 1918).

6) "Troubles in a Pawn Shop," featuring Hemlock Bones, was a two-scene burlesque skit staged by the Scouts Minstrels (a combined Boy and Girl Scout effort) at St. Rose's Hall in Scranton, Pennsylvania (Dec. 10, 1919). Francis Coon portrayed Hemlock Bones.

7) "The Great Detective Caper: Hemlock Bones—Who He?" *Sam Slade: Robo-Hunter*, No. 26 (Quality Comics, Nov. 1988). Jack Adrian (writer) and John Higgins (artist). Aliens searching for "the greatest detective genius of all time" instead abduct an incompetent actor who appears in a television program, "Hemlock Bones—Master Sleuth." A comic book appearance.

8) Hemlock Bones is a one-time corruption of Sherlock Holmes' name in *The Baker Street Boys: The Case of the Stolen Sprinklers* by Anthony Read (Walker Books, 2008). "You ought to be a detective, like that Mr. Whatsisname—Hemlock Bones, is it?"

9) *Murder of the Mystery Detective* (2009), a play by Penny Warner, features Hemlock Bones as one of six famous detectives summoned as a challenge by Sir Arthur Conan Hoyle, who is then murdered in his own library. An audience participation production, often staged as a fundraiser for local libraries.

Hemlock Booms

Hemlock Booms is one of seven parody names in "Prize Detective Story." Anonymous (*The Weekly Magazine*, May 8, 1897). Retitled "Holmes and the Startled Banker" in *As It Might Have Been: A Collection of Sherlockian Parodies from Unlikely Sources* (Robert C.S. Adey, ed.; Calabash Press, 1998). Hemlock Coombs repeatedly changes his name as he makes a series of trivial deductions.

Hemlock Coombs

Hemlock Coombs is a famous detective who appears in "Prize Detective Story." Anonymous (*The Weekly Magazine*, May 8, 1897). Retitled "Holmes and the Startled Banker" in *As It Might Have Been: A Collection of Sherlockian Parodies from Unlikely Sources* (Robert C.S. Adey, ed.; Calabash Press, 1998). Coombs changes his name six different times as he makes a series of trivial deductions about suspender buttons, a servant girl, and a lost bank president.

Hemlock Foames
"The Murder of Conan Doyle," a play featuring Hemlock Foames and Squatson. Ray Russell (*Playboy*, May 1955). Reprinted in *The Game Is Afoot: Parodies Pastiches and Ponderings of Sherlock Holmes* (Marvin Kaye, ed.; St. Martin's Press, 1994). A satire in which Foames and Squatson match wits with Professor Goryarty.

Hemlock Hoax
Hemlock Hoax, the Detective (1910). A short silent comedy film. Produced by Lubin Manufacturing Co. Released Apr. 11, 1910. Presumably lost; the cast is unknown. Hemlock Hoax tries to solve a murder, but is actually the victim of a practical joke.

Hemlock Holmes
1) "Lady Honiton's Diamonds," featuring detective Hemlock Holmes. Maitland Leroy Osborne (*National Magazine*, Oct. 1898). A series of irrelevant "deductions" allows Hemlock Holmes to discover what happened to some missing jewelry.
2) "Sherlock Holmes Up-to-Date," featuring Hemlock Holmes. A syndicated cartoon by Claude Eldridge Toles. Widely distributed in 1900 by the International Syndicate of Baltimore. Hemlock Holmes, "the king of detectives," matches wits with Gladys Kanbee, "queen of the opera."
3) *The Fall of a Star*, featuring Hemlock Holmes, was a play staged by the junior class for the annual "Pug Ugly" at Stanford University (Oct. 30, 1903). Written by M.H. Thorpe; Hemlock Holmes was portrayed by S.C. Haver. A musical farce concerning students who have fallen into trouble and are called before the faculty committee.
4) Hemlock Holmes is sarcastically invoked in "The Machine Was Nicely Lubricated," a political report by J.W. Grant in *The Scranton Republican* (May 18, 1906). "Hemlock Holmes, the detective, was unable to discover the master hand that controlled the convention which nominated the Democratic candidates for the legislature."
5) "Mystery of the Cigars," featuring Hemlock Holmes. In the regular "Stories of Daily Life/Whirl of the Town" column of the *El Paso Herald* (June 11, 1907). Hemlock Holmes, "a brother of

Sherlock's," investigates "why an inferior brand of cigars, strong enough to kill a horse were substituted and distributed" on a club excursion.

6) Hemlock Holmes makes a number of erroneous deductions about a sleeping train passenger based on the idea that "the eyelashes of the upper lid of his left eye slant toward the left." Anonymous, but credited to *The Washington Post*. The story was published in several newspapers under different titles, including "As Plain As a Nose" (Dec. 29, 1907) and "By His Left Eyelashes" (May 25, 1908).

7) *The Adventure of the Eleven Cuff Buttons*. "Being the Exciting Episodes in the Career of the Famous Detective Hemlock Holmes, as Recorded by His Friend Dr. Watson." James Francis Thicrry (The Neale Publishing Co., 1918). The constantly-imbibing Earl of Puddingham has suffered the theft of eleven of his twelve cuff buttons. A novel-length parody, also featuring Inspector Lestrayed.

8) Hemlock Holmes was a Cockney police bulldog with a "Cary Grant accent" frequently featured in *The Dick Tracy Show*, a syndicated animated television series produced by United Productions of America (UPA), 1961-62. The voice was provided by Jerry Hausner.

9) "The Adventure of the Artissium Murderer," featuring Hemlock Holmes and Dr. Watts. John McGoldrick. *Sidelights on Holmes*, Vol. 1, No. 3 (1967).

10) "The Mystery of Hemlock Farms," featuring Hemlock Holmes, a three-foot-high puppet. Presented at Lafayette Plaza in Bridgeport Connecticut (Aug. 27-Sept. 1, 1973). Holmes and Watson go to the country and encounter a magician of surprising skill.

11) "Hemlock Holmes and Datson: The Empty Cash Box" (Feb. 20, 1981) and "Hemlock Holmes and Datson: The Case of the Stolen Diamonds" (May 8, 1981) appeared in the *Scholastic News Citizen*. Children's stories, illustrated by Sanford Hoffman.

12) Hemlock Holmes, "the botanist detective," drawn by Koko Gonzales, appeared in *The K-Zone Bulletin*, the on-line publication of *K-Zone: Where Kids Rule*, produced by Summit Media of the Philippines. He was one of the 18 Holmes parody characters to take part in "Crisis of Infinite Holmes" (Aug. 2008), an adventure involving Sherlockian characters working together to save their concurrent universes.

13) *Home Sweet Homicide*, featuring Hemlock Holmes. Written by Tony Schwartz and Marylou Ambrose (Tonylou Productions 2016). A comedic audience-participation murder mystery. Assisted by Whatson.

Hemlock Jones
1) "The $10,000 Robbery: Hemlock Jones as a Detective Discovers the Culprit." Anonymous, but credited to *The New York Journal*. The short humorous tale was reprinted in numerous other American newspapers between 1892 and 1899. A stopped clock helps Hemlock Holmes discover which of nine young women working as bookkeepers stole money from a large department store.
2) "The Fatal Gas Bill," featuring Hemlock Jones. Anonymous (*The Buffalo Evening News*, May 15, 1897). While investigating thefts from a jewelry shop, Hemlock Jones uses the cost of gas to help nab the culprit.
3) "The Missing Letter," featuring Hemlock Jones. Opie Read. Originally published in about 1899 in *The Arkansas Traveler*, a weekly humor and literary journal. Reprinted in other newspapers, including *The Riverina Recorder* of Australia (Oct. 31, 1900). Jones helps a jealous "middle-aged banker" find a love letter written by his young wife.
4) "The Stolen Cigar Case," featuring Hemlock Jones. Bret Harte. *Condensed Novels: Second Series—New Burlesques* (Houghton Mifflin, 1902). Reprinted in *The Misadventures of Sherlock Holmes* (Ellery Queen, ed.; Little, Brown & Co., 1944). A graphic/comic adaptation by Bob Versandi appeared in *The Bank Street Book of Mystery* (Pocket Books, 1989). Jones falsely accuses Watson of theft, thus ensuring the doctor's success in life.
5) "The Mystery of the Missing Man," featuring Hemlock Jones. Anonymous. *The Binghamton Press* of New York (May 26, 1905). A short tale written as an advertisement of Atlas Compound, "the greatest tonic on earth," a product of Jeremiah MacDonald.
6) Hemlock Jones, Jr., appeared in *Stanford—The Life Strenuous*, a three-act farce produced by the junior class of Stanford University (Mar. 30, 1906). A student is arrested for "lifting" silverware from a San Francisco Hotel, but is finally cleared by his fraternity brothers. Written by W.G. Bateman. Jones was portrayed by H.W. Taft.

7) "The Plutonians," featuring Hemlock Jones, was the annual hundred-night performance of the cadets at West Point (Feb. 23, 1907). Hemlock Jones is engaged to track down a thief who took a magic Egyptian locket from an American heiress and journeyed with it to the Elysian Fields in search of treasure. Written by Charles Dunbar Rogers, who also portrayed Jones.

8) Hemlock Jones and chorus performed a musical number, "The Man with the Hidden Star," as part of *The Plaid Mackinaw*, a two-act production of the Micomi Club of the Michigan College of Mines (now Michigan Tech) in Houghton (April 1914). The Micomi Club was a student-run dramatic group that staged an annual musical comedy.

9) Hemlock Jones, "mastermind of the twentieth century," explains to his obese assistant Elmer Fatson that girls attend the University of North Carolina "to pursue learning or learn pursuing." In "Etcetera: From the Exchange Desk" by Ben Dixon. *The Daily Tar Heel*, the university's student newspaper (Oct. 27, 1937).

10) Hemlock Jones was a one-time sarcastic corruption of Sherlock Holmes' name in *Dance of Death* by Helen McCloy (William Morrow & Co., 1938). Her detective hero, psychologist Dr. Basil Willing, is taunted: "Cigarette Stumps and Match Ends from Floor of Palace Theater, Mr. Hemlock Jones?"

11) Flip Wilson (in full Sherlockian costume) portrayed Hemlock Jones with Johnny Brown as Dotson in Season 1, Episode 11, of *The Flip Wilson Show* on NBC. A woman (Connie Stevens) has lethal intentions for her elderly husband. Directed by Tim Kiley. First aired Dec. 3, 1970.

12) Hemlock Jones is a one-time corruption of Sherlock Holmes' name in *Sherlock Holmes: Gods of War* by James Lovegrove (Titan Books, 2014). Sherlock Holmes encounters a gamekeeper, who threatens: "Hoy! Quiet you, Mr. Hemlock Jones or whatever your name is… Any more of your lip and it won't go well with you."

Hemlock Shears

1) Hemlock Shears is another version of the name given to the antagonist of Arsène Lupin, originally the creation of Maurice LeBlanc, in some English translations of *The Exploits of Arsène Lupin* (1907), *The Fair-Haired Lady* (1909), and *The Hollow*

Needle (1911). Herlock Sholmes (the original French version) and Holmlock Shears (in most English translations) are more common. 2) Hemlock Shears is used in "The What's It All About Dept." panel of "The Roundup," a full-page regular local feature of *The Arizona Republican* drawn by Webb Smith, the staff cartoonist (May 29, 1921). "If you ever had the idea you were descended from Hemlock Shears, now is the time to prove it."

Hemlock Shoals
"The Maltese Cockroach," featuring Sir Hemlock Shoals, an "inter-dimensional detective." Bill Mantlo (writer), and Gene Colan and Dave Simons (artists). *Howard the Duck*, No. 4 (Marvel Comics, March 1980). Shoals journeys from his home world of Maltesia in search of a powerful "cosmic key."

Hemlock Sholmes
"Hemlock Sholmes & the Case of the Klunky Klues" was a children's program for grades 4 and up at the Bound Brook (New Jersey) Library. "Clue sheets" were distributed on Aug. 16, 1982, to be returned by Aug. 20. Part of the "Bound Brook Book Adventurers" series of activities.

Hemlock Shomes
Hemlock Shomes appeared in *Mystery Men Comics* (Fox Publications) in such short adventures as "Hemlock Shomes and Dr. Potsom: The Case of the Missing Molars" by Fred Filchock (No. 3, 1939) and "Hemlock Shomes" by Al Weine (No. 20, 1940). Shomes is a current-era private eye.

Hemlock Soames
Hemlock Soames was the disguise of Boris Badenov in the "Box Top Robbery" episodes of the first season of the animated television series *The Rocky and Bullwinkle Show* (Apr.9-May 7, 1960). Produced by Jay Ward Productions for ABC. Voiced by Paul Frees. Assisted by Natasha Fatale as Dr. Watchme.

Hemlock Stones
1) *The Tale of the Giant Rat of Sumatra*, featuring Hemlock Stones, is a comedy album recorded by The Firesign Theatre (Columbia Records, 1974). Philip Proctor portrays Hemlock Stones, with David Ossman as Flotsom. The script by Philip Austin appears

in written form in *The Firesign Theatre's Big Mystery Joke Book* (Straight Arrow Books, 1974). Subtitled "A Thrilling Mis-Adventure from the Cheque-Book of Hemlock Stones." Both Stones and his client, Miss Violet Dudley, need a fix.

2) *The Bronze Medal Murders*, featuring Hemlock Stones and Dr. Snotson, was a play presented at the Milano Inn of Indianapolis on Mar. 9, 2002. They solve a murder at the Winter Olympics.

Herblock Stones

Herblock Stones and Witsno appeared in two stories by Paul D. Herbert, privately produced in very limited editions in 1983: "The Adventure of the Musical Disaster" and "The Enigma of the Surprise Package." Both are reprinted in his collection *Unmitigated Bleat* (Wessex Press, 2017).

Herlock Domes

Herlock Domes is a recurring character in *Supersnipe Comics*, a Street & Smith comic book publication which appeared from 1942 to 1949. Ed Grushkin (writer) and Herbert Marcoux (artist). Herlock Domes is a boy detective, in full Sherlockian costume, who is assisted by Koppy (Supersnipe) McFad. They solve cases and capture criminals, usually in spite of themselves.

Herlock Holmes

1) "Herlock Holmes." Episode 2 of *Chum Per Hour*, an internet series about struggling actors who try to make ends meet by starting a friend-for-hire company. One of the business partners, portrayed by Christina Cuffari, is nicknamed "Herlock Holmes" by a strange customer because she is a "a real little detective." Produced by MoreCowbell/Finnegan Productions for YouTube; written by Tim Finnigan; directed by Michael Anthony Horrigan. Posted Sept. 28, 2011.

2) *Herlock and Swatson in the Mystery of the Royal Goose*, featuring Herlock Holmes. An interactive children's program, presented by the Paper Planes & Daisy Chains Theatre at the Edinburgh Fringe Festival, Aug. 19-23, 2014. Stuart Freestone portrayed Herlock Holmes.

Herlock Olmes
"Fuller Spunk and Company Detective Agency" was a feature in *Hyper Mystery Comics*, No. 1 (May 1940) and the subsequent issue. Fuller Spunk is a retired actor and inventor turned detective, known for having portrayed "Herlock Olmes" in stage productions.

Herlock Shoames
Herlock Shoames is another version of the name given to the antagonist of Arsène Lupin, originally the creation of Maurice LeBlanc, in some European translations of *The Exploits of Arsène Lupin* (1907), *The Fair-Haired Lady* (1909), and *The Hollow Needle* (1911), although Herlock Sholmes (the original French version) is more common.

Herlock Sholem
"The First Scoop or the Last." Anonymous (as "Herlock Sholem"). *The Dame: Yearbook of the University of Notre Dame*, 1914.

Herlock Sholmes
1) Herlock Sholmes appeared in several anonymous short sketches syndicated to American newspapers in the late 1890s, including: "The Genius of Herlock Sholmes" (*Detroit Free Press*, Mar. 3, 1895); "He Solves Another" (*The New York Sun*, Aug. 23, 1896); "Another Mystery Solved" (*Sacramento Daily Record-Union*, Nov. 29, 1896); and "Perspicacity of Herlock Sholmes" (*The Buffalo Evening News*, Mar. 17, 1897). The stories often appeared in various other newspapers with different titles.
2) "One Against Our Old Friend Sherlock," featuring Herlock Sholmes. Anonymous. (*Tit-Bits*, June 26, 1897). Reprinted in *My Evening with Sherlock Holmes* (John Michael Gibson and Richard Lancelyn Green, eds.; Ferret, 1981). Sholmes makes a series of deductions about an old tramp, without even looking at him.
3) "Met His Match: Herlock Sholmes Had a Trying Interview with a Reporter." Anonymous, but attributed to the *St. Paul Dispatch*. Reprinted in various newspapers, including the *Brooklyn Daily Eagle* (July 11, 1897). Nobody other than a newspaper reporter "ever got ahead of a detective."
4) "Miss Smartleigh's Gloves," featuring Herlock Sholmes. Anonymous (*Suderland Daily Echo and Shipping Gazette*, Oct. 4, 1902). A short joke in the "Grave and Gray" column.

5) "Herlock Sholmes Again." Anonymous. *Snap-Shots*, June 20, 1903. Reprinted in *As It Might Have Been: A Collection of Sherlockian Parodies from Unlikely Sources* (Robert C.S. Adey, ed.; Calabash Press, 1998). Herlock Sholmes makes a long series of clever, but wrong, deductions about the owner of a woman's glove found by his friend Swatson.

6) "Herlock Sholmes and the Strange Adventure of the Earl of Sethwick's Goose Liver." Anonymous (*Cincinnati Enquirer*, Apr. 10, 1904). Herlock Sholmes tells Dr. Votson about his search for the stolen liver of a talking goose, and he traps Moriarty, who visits his apartment in Butcher Street.

7) "A Hitherto Unrecorded Conversation Between Dr. Watson and Mr. Herlock Sholmes." S.T. Ewart. *The Library World* (April, 1906). Sholmes makes elaborate deductions about a cryptic message found by Watson at his club, only to find himself embarrassingly wrong.

8) Herlock Sholmes is the original French-edition name given to the antagonist of Arsène Lupin in three novels by Maurice LeBlanc: *The Exploits of Arsène Lupin* (1907), *The Fair-Haired Lady* (1909), and *The Hollow Needle* (1911). English language versions published in America by Harper most often changed the name to Holmlock Shears. Other variations in translation have included Hemlock Shears and Herlock Shoames.

9) "The Return of Herlock Sholmes: The Case of the Missing Name Plate." Anonymous (as "A. Donan Coyle"). *The University Missourian* (Feb. 21, 1911). Sholmes and Watson, with lodgings in Caker Street, solve the case of a stolen crest bearing the Greek Letters Pi Beta Phi.

10) "The Chicago Adventures of Mr. Herlock Sholmes." Richard Henry Little (*The Chicago Daily Tribune*, May 26, 1911). Assisted by Dotson. A parody entry in Little's "Round About Chicago" column. On a visit to Chicago, Sholmes and Dotson consider the account of "many sluggers engaged in a desperate fight."

11) *The Amateur Sleuth* (1913), featuring Herlock Sholmes. A short silent comedy film, produced by the Gaumont Studios of France. The cast members are unknown. Released Mar. 27, 1913. Sholmes tracks down unlikely villains who have sent a threatening note demanding money.

12) Herlock Sholmes concocts some fanciful theories about the murder of a Chinese man in "How the Great Detective-Editor Solves a Chinese Murder Mystery." Anonymous (as "Ole Doc Watson"). *The Day Book* (Sept. 9, 1913).

13) "Water Water Everywhere and Not a Drop for Tea," featured Sherlock Holmes in a World War I German prison camp publication, *In Ruhlben Camp* (1915). Men are disappearing from the barracks at night, but Sholmes discovers them sleeping upright out of habit from standing in line.

14) Herlock Sholmes is the creation of Charles Hamilton, who wrote a series of stories under the pen name of Peter Todd, beginning with "The Adventure of the Diamond Pin." Using a liberal dose of humor, satire, and puns, Hamilton produced a total of 93 Sholmes stories between 1915 and 1925 in *The Greyfriars Herald*, *The Magnet*, *The Gem*, and *Penny Popular*. Two additional stories were published many years later, in 1950 and 1952, in *Tom Merry's Own Annual*. Two anthologies of note are *The Adventures of Herlock Sholmes* by Peter Todd (The Mysterious Press, 1976) and *The Complete Casebook of Herlock Sholmes* by Charles Hamilton (Hawk Books, 1989). Assisted by Dr. Jotson.

15) "Herlock on the War: An Interview," featuring Herlock Sholmes. Anonymous (as "The Bark"). *The Sporting Times* (Feb. 5, 1916). While Watson is serving in Flanders, a reporter visits Sholmes on Pastrycook Street to solicit "an opinion of this rotten war."

16) Herlock Sholmes was a character in "The Bell Boy" in 1918, a musical comedy revue staged as part of The Scarlet Gaieties, a frequent production in Adelaide, South Australia. Ernest Parkes portrayed Herlock Sholmes.

17) "The Lost Professor," featuring Herlock Sholmes and Dr. Potson. Anonymous (as "Sir Arthur Donan Coyle"), in *The Shriek and Other Stories* (Stanley Paul & Co., 1923). Reprinted by Magico Magazine in 1986. Sholmes begins his case only after "pulling at a hookah, chewing hashish and playing a plaintive violin concerto."

18) "Herlock Sholmes Catches Reds." Anonymous (as "A Donan Coyle"). *The Daily Worker* (Oct. 18, 1924). Sholmes, "the great New York Detective," is ridiculed for his pursuit of communists, and is eventually put into a padded cell along with Watson. "One…

thinks he is a detective and the other one seems just plain ordinary dumb."

19) Herlock Sholmes was a witness in a mock trial conducted by the Methodist Young People's Guild of South Australia (Oct. 21, 1926). Herlock Sholmes' cigar was "an important piece of evidence in the case."

20) *The Limejuice Mystery, Or Who Spat in Grandfather's Porridge?* (1930), featuring Herlock Sholmes and Anna Went Wrong. A short silent film featuring marionettes performing to a musical score. Produced by Joseph Seiden for Associated Sound Film Industries; directed by Jack Harrison. Herlock Sholmes pursues a Tong assassin, who entraps himself.

21) "The Six O'Clock Mystery" doubled as a very short anonymously-written tale featuring Herlock Sholmes and Batson and as an advertisement for Ivory Soap, a product of Procter & Gamble. It appeared in 1930, with an illustration of Sholmes in the bathtub. A copy was reproduced by Peter E. Blau in his 2017 edition of "The Compliments of the Season," a handout for the BSI Weekend in New York.

22) "The Bound of the Haskervilles: An Unpublished Memoir of Herlock Sholmes, the Famous Detective, As Told By Dr. Jotson." Anonymous (as "T.P.J."). *Mirage*, Oct. 1930. Reprinted in *As It Might Have Been: A Collection of Sherlockian Parodies from Unlikely Sources* (Robert C.S. Adey, ed.; Calabash Press, 1998). Sholmes and Jotson, who live in Shaker Street, are called upon to help the heir of the Haskervilles meet a traditional family challenge.

23) "The South Sea Soup Co." featuring Herlock Sholmes. John Ross Macdonald (as "Kenneth Millar"). *The Grumbler* (Kitchener-Waterloo Collegiate and Vocational School, 1931). Assisted by Sotwun. Sholmes investigates the murder of Oswald Ox-Tailby and becomes head detective of the South Sea Soup Co., but "never succeeded in finding an oyster in the oyster-soup."

24) *Herlock Sholmes and Mr. Batson: A Comedy in Three Acts* was copyrighted Jan. 11, 1934, by Dan Benson (Donato Alfred Boccio) of Brooklyn, New York, but apparently was never staged.

25) "The Missing Whisky Case," featuring Herlock Sholmes and Wactor Dotson. Anonymous (*Bits of Moss*, Spring 1950). Reprinted in *As It Might Have Been: A Collection of Sherlockian*

Parodies from Unlikely Sources (Robert C.S. Adey, ed.; Calabash Press, 1998). Sholmes silently congratulates the burglar who successfully stole a quantity of top-shelf whiskey as he enjoys his own nightcap.

26) "The Case of the Missing Treaty." Roger Jenkins. *The Collector's Digest*, May 1960. A parody of Charles Hamilton's parodies, featuring Herlock Sholmes and Dr. Jotson.

27) "The Boy Who Lost His Foot" and "The Tragedy of the Little Side." Eric Fayne. *The Collector's Digest Annual*, 1960 and 1961 respectively. Parodies of Charles Hamilton's parodies featuring Herlock Sholmes and Dr. Jotson.

28) Herlock Sholmes appeared in four episodes of the French television series *Arsène Lupin*, once in 1971 and three times in 1973. Lupin's rival Herlock Sholmes was portrayed by Henri Virlojeux.

29) *Herlock Sholmes* was a Yugoslavian parody comic strip by Julio (Jules) Radilović and Zvonimir Furtiner in the mid-1970s. One of them, "Herlock Sholmes: The Master of Disguise" appeared in *Cartoonist Profiles*, No. 20 (Dec. 1973).

30) Herlock Sholmes is a famous CorSec (Corellian Security Force) detective appearing in *Young Yoda Campaign*, fan-made online fiction for "*Star Wars* Fanon" on Wikia (about 2014). Sholmes investigates the murder of a trillionaire, implicates various heirs, and is discovered to himself be the culprit. He is transported to Endor, where he becomes a serial killer of Ewoks.

Herlock Shomes

1) "A Few Adventures of Mrs. Herlock Shomes." Anonymous (as "Ka"). *The Student: A Journal for University Extension Students* (1894). Julia Shomes, the widow of Herlock Shomes, pursues his work in two stories: "The Adventure of the Tomato on the Wall" and "The Identity of Miss Angela Vespers." Both are reprinted in *The Affair of the Lost Compression and Other Stories* (Ferret Fantasy, 1975).

2) "Beyond His Income: Evidence Which Settles a Bank Cashier's Guilt," featuring Herlock Shomes. Anonymous, but credited to the *St. Louis Republic* and reprinted in various newspapers throughout America (May-Aug. 1895). A bank employee is proved guilty beyond doubt because he has been able to eat "beef—beef for dinner" four nights in one week. The story is a reflection of the ongoing

effects of the Panic of 1893, an economic depression that caused widespread unemployment and near-starvation through 1897.

3) "Another Victory for Herlock Shomes." William Henry Siviter. *Harper's Bazaar*, Dec. 19, 1896. Herlock Shomes sees through a bearded lady's disguise.

4) "How He Did It: Herlock Shomes Explains the Way to Detect a Bride and Groom." Anonymous. *Harper's Bazaar*, Jan. 30, 1897. Shomes deduces that a young couple on his train are newlyweds.

5) Herlock Shomes, "the boy detective," offered testimony in a comic "mock trial" staged by the Young Men's Hebrew Association of St. Louis (June 13, 1901). In a case of embezzlement, Fred Abrams portrayed Herlock Shomes.

6) "Herlock Shomes' Farewell: The Reason Related by Dr. Potson." Anonymous (*The Strand Magazine*, Dec. 1904). A short story written as an advertisement for Catesby & Sons, manufacturers of cork linoleum.

7) "Conclusive Evidence," featuring Herlock Shomes and his wife, was a short joke attributed to the *Detroit Tribune* and reprinted in various newspapers in 1906. Shomes deduces that his wife trimmed her corns by the state of his razor.

8) "The Weirdly Thrilling Adventure of the Lost Bathing Suit," featuring Herlock Shomes and Dr. Rotson. L.C. Hopkins. *Uncle Remus' Home Magazine* (Nov. 1908).

9) Herlock Shomes and Poston appeared in a short joke concerning a "tender hearted" farmer. Attributed to the *Boston Transcript* and reprinted in various newspapers including *The Pittsburg Press* (Nov. 16, 1908), where it was titled simply "Herlock Shomes."

10) "Herlock's One Mistake," featuring Herlock Shomes. Henry A. Hering (St. Paul's Church of Sketty, 1910). Reprinted in a special limited edition by Ferret Fantasy in 1980. Shomes is tricked into allowing a treaty to be stolen. Assisted by Dr. Spotson.

11) "The Mystery of the Missing Pawn: An Adventure of Herlock Shomes." H.T. Dickinson. *The British Chess Bulletin* (Jan. 1911). Shomes comes to the aid of Edwin Basker of Basker Hall, who is missing a piece from his personal chess set.

12) "She Took the Commission," featuring Mrs. Herlock Shomes, "the famous female detective," who disdains a $10,000 reward unless it is offered at a discount. Reprinted in various American

newspapers including the *Fort Gibson (Oklahoma) New Era* (Mar. 23, 1911) and the *Mattoon (Illinois) Journal Gazette* (May 2, 1911).

13) "The Mystery of the Missing Shirt," featuring Herlock Shomes and Fatson, by Alfred Edward (A.E.) Swoyer appeared in *The Black Cat*, No. 193 (Oct. 1911). A fatuous Shomes is retained to solve the mystery of his client's undershirt, which disappeared while he was wearing it.

14) Herlock Shomes, "the great detective," solved the case of the murder (or suicide) of a fat man who was "asked if it was hot enough for you" in "Justifiable Homicide," a segment of "Bits of Byplay," the humor column of *The Cincinnati Enquirer* (July 16, 1912).

15) Herlock Shomes appeared in three serials in *The Wipers Times* (renamed *The B.E.F. Times* for the third story), produced in London for the troops fighting in the Great War (World War I): "Herlock Shomes at It Again" (six chapters, Feb. 12-May 1, 1916); "Narpoo Rum" (nine chapters, 1916-17); and "Zero! Or The Bound of the Baskershires" (three chapters, Dec. 25, 1917-Feb. 26, 1918). All anonymously written, perhaps by the same author. Assisted by Capt. Hotsam, a doctor, who was also called Plotsam and Flotsam by the careless Herlock Shomes in the text.

16) In "Honeymooners Abroad," a story by journalist and novelist Zoe Beckley of the *Washington Times' Herald* and published in serial form in several American newspapers in 1922, a newlywed couple is sent to Europe to investigate a corrupt business manager. The bride promises her husband that she will "help you solve the mystery, Mr. Herlock Shomes!"

17) Herlock Shomes and Dr. Gottsom were characters in *Step This Way*, a high school musical mystery-comedy play presented at Canonsburg (Pennsylvania) High School (Nov. 12-13, 1936). Valuable pearls are stolen, and the young detectives encounter a pirate ghost, secret panels, and a savage wild man.

18) "Herlock Shomes: A Case of Indemnity" by Simon Paul Travaglia is a parody retelling of the canonical Sherlock Holmes story "A Case of Identity" posted on the Google Groups "Tasteless Jokes" site (June 25, 2001). The client, with a "preposterous hat and vacuous face" consults Shomes, who concludes that the problem is a split personality. Assisted by Whatnot.

19) "Herlock Shomes and Swatson: The Movie" was a short film produced by and starring child actors as part of the Movie Magic Film Camp of Victoria, British Columbia, and posted on YouTube (Aug. 29, 2016). Shomes, assisted by Juan Swatson, investigates the theft of a valuable bracelet.

Herlock Soames
The Arsene Lupin-Herlock Soames Affair. S. Beach Chester (The Aspen Press, 1976). Assisted by Dr. Watts. "A comic duel of wits between the world's greatest detective, Sherlock Holmes, and the world's master criminal, Arsene Lupin (herein masquerading under the aliases Herlock Soames and Arsene Lupine), before the bewildered eyes of a much oppressed headwaiter."

Herlock Solmes
Herlock Solmes, the great detective, appears in "The Adventures of Sherlock Mario." Season 1, Episode 18, of *The Super Mario Bros. Super Show!*, an animated television series (one of three series based on the video game). Produced by DiC Animation for syndication by Viacom Enterprises. Mario assumes the identity of Sherlock Mario to find the missing Herlock Solmes, encountering Professor Kooparity and the Killer Kitty of the Kaskervilles along the way.

Hermlock Holmes
Hermlock Holmes and Ronald Weistson appear as minor characterizations in "Harry Potter and the Magic of Fairy Tail" (2012), an Italian online fan fiction crossover story between Harry Potter and Fairy Tail. Published on the Makelele Forum Community website.

Herr Lock Shömes
Herr Lock Shömes and Matson appear in two anonymously written stories in *The Student* (Edinburgh University): "The Adventures of Herr Lock Shömes: The Mystery of the Elastic Band" (March 6, 1914), in which a black rubber band betrays Matson; and "The Adventures of Herr Lock Shömes: The Mystery of the Acetylene Lamp" (May 20, 1914), which features the Hound of the Caskervilles. Both are reprinted in *My Evening with Sherlock Holmes* (John Michael Gibson and Richard Lancelyn Green, eds.; Ferret, 1981).

Hodiah Twist
Hodiah Twist is a Sherlockian character in Marvel Comics publications: "The Praying Mantis Principle" by Don McGregor (*Vampire Tales*, No. 2, Oct. 1973); "Monster of the Mind Machine" by Don McGregor (*Amazing Adventures*, No. 32, Sept. 1975); and "The Hero Killer Principle" by Richard Marschall (*Marvel Preview*, No. 16, Fall 1978).

Holmlock Blake
"Tit for Tat," featuring Holmlock Blake, the master detective. Walter Holton. *The Golden Book of Comics* (Oldhams Press, n.d.). A poetic appearance.

Holmlock Shears
1) Holmlock Shears is the name of the antagonist of Arsène Lupin in English-language editions of three novels by Maurice LeBlanc: *The Exploits of Arsène Lupin* (Harper & Bros., 1907); *Arsène Lupin vs. Holmlock Shears* (Grant Richards, 1909—originally *The Fair-Haired Lady*, and retitled *The Blonde Lady* in America); and *The Hollow Needle* (Doubleday, Page & Co., 1910). The last chapter of the first book, "Holmlock Shears Arrives Too Late" is reprinted in *The Misadventures of Sherlock Holmes* (Ellery Queen, ed.; Little, Brown & Co., 1944).
2) Holmlock Shears appeared in two stories by Anthony Armstrong in *Gaiety*. "The Scarlet Pimple" (Nov. 1926) finds Shears in the wrong story. "The Reigate Road Murder" (Dec. 1926) features Shears' assistant Watnot and some bicycle-riding murderers. Both are reprinted in *As It Might Have Been: A Collection of Sherlockian Parodies from Unlikely Sources* (Robert C.S. Adey, ed.; Calabash Press, 1998).

Homelock Sherles
"The Arch Criminal Slinker," featuring Homelock Sherles. Anonymous (*Whistable Times and Herne Bay Herald*, Aug. 5, 1911). A one-paragraph joke in which the criminal cannot prove his own confession.

Homelock Shermes
Homelock Shermes is an alternative title for the 1913 short silent comedy film *Homlock Shermes* starring Pearl White as "Pearl, the

girl detective." Directed by Phillips Smalley. White, the "Queen of the Serials" was best known for *The Perils of Pauline*.

Homlock Shermes

Homlock Shermes (1913). A short silent comedy film starring Pearl White as "Pearl, the girl detective," who goes undercover to help rescue a falsely-imprisoned young man, only to find out he is being confined because of his drunkenness. Released by the Crystal Film Company on May 18, 1913. Directed by Phillips Smalley. Also known as *Homelock Shermes*.

Horlock Shem

"The Bounder of Camberville." Julius Herman (as "Herbert Skimpole"). *The Granta*, May 13, 1921. Reprinted in *As It Might Have Been: A Collection of Sherlockian Parodies from Unlikely Sources* (Robert C.S. Adey, ed.; Calabash Press, 1998). Assisted by Dr. Westcott, who brings Shem the problem of an ancient mummy that interrupted a dance party.

Hoskell Chomers

"The Adventure of the Solitary Bride," featuring Hoskell Chomers. Anonymous (as "E. Alson Canoy"). *Ellery Queen's Mystery Magazine* (Feb. 1993). Hoskell Chomers is an anagram of Sherlock Holmes. Assisted by Sandwort (an anagram of Dr. Watson).

Hurlock Shoams

"Hurlock Shoams—One of His Adventures." Walter Ferguson (as "Sir Arthur Cannon Ball"). *Sturm's Oklahoma Magazine*, Sept. 1907. Shoams and his friend Dr. Squatson live in Beaker Street. They investigate the theft of cigars tied with pink ribbons.

Hurlock Sholmes

1) *R.F. and M.F.; or the Two Are One*, featuring Hezekiah Hurlock Sholmes, was a one-act play, first staged June 25, 1900, at the New Theatre Royal in Croydon, England. A melodrama; Clarence Hague portrayed the "warm-hearted detective."
2) "A Mouse in the Room," featuring Hurlock Sholmes. Anonymous. A short joke credited to *London Opinion* and widely distributed to American newspapers, which reproduced it between 1911 and 1913. One of the first to do so was *The Charlotte News* (Oct. 19, 1911).

3) "Hurlock Sholmes, Detective" appeared in the *Felix the Cat* Sunday comic strip by Pat Sullivan, Oct. 7, 1923. While pursuing milk thieves, Felix (Hurlock Sholmes) captures Pretty Pete, a career criminal.

Kerlock Shomes

The Adventures of Kerlock Shomes and Dr. Warsaw. Tudor Gross (Magico, 1980). A collection of nine stories that originally appeared in *Stamps* magazine between June 5, 1943, and Sept. 28, 1946. All of the mysteries relate to stamp collecting. A much earlier story by the same author, "The Great Philatelic Mystery," was published in *The American Philatelist* (Aug. 1922), in which Shomes lives in Paker Street.

Kermlock Holmes

"The Strange Case of the Missing Mermaid Costume," featuring Kermlock Holmes (Kermit the Frog). Laura Hitchcock (writer) and Marie Severin (artist). *Muppet Babies*, No. 13 (Marvel/Star Comics, May 1987). In Victorian England, Kermlock encounters a ship's crew of Miss Piggy fans and a real mermaid.

Kreplock Holes

Kreplock Holes appeared in stories by Gary Louis Wakshul in five consecutive issues of the annual *Holmeswork*: "A Study in Red" (1974), "The Pound of the Basketballs" (1975), "The Peradventure of the Player Piano Player" (1976), "The Misadventure of the Footprint" (1977), and "The Vandal with Anemia" (1977). Narrated by Ormand Gesundheit Sacker.

Laugh-a-Lock Holmes

Laugh-a-Lock Holmes, a clown detective, drawn by Koko Gonzales, appeared in *The K-Zone Bulletin*, the on-line publication of *K-Zone: Where Kids Rule*, produced by Summit Media of the Philippines. He was one of the 18 Holmes parody characters to take part in "Crisis of Infinite Holmes" (Aug. 2008), an adventure involving Sherlockian characters working together to save their concurrent universes.

Lockjaw Bones

1) "From the Adventures of Lockjaw Bones" was a short humorous sketch, attributed to the *New York Sun* but otherwise anonymous,

that appeared in several American newspapers (Aug-Sept. 1903). Bones, assisted by Swatson, tracks a one-legged criminal.

2) "Dimmock Turns Detective," using the name Lockjaw Bones as an alias. *The Escapades of Mr. Alfred Dimmock* by Fox Russell (Everett & Co., 1906). Reprinted in *The Armchair Detective* (Winter 1984).

3) Lockjaw Bones appears in two stories by "Ben Eath" (Herman Charles Bosman) in *The Jeppe High School Magazine* of his native South Africa: "The Mystery of the Ex-M.P." (July 1921) and "The Mystery of Lenin Trotsky" (Dec. 1921). Assisted by Jotson.

Lockley Soames

The Adventure of the Missing Brother. Eugene Edmund Snyder (Binford & Mort, 1994). A novel featuring Professor Lockley Soames and Dr. Henry Schultz. Members of a college town Sherlockian society put the methods of the world's foremost consulting detective to good use.

Loufock-Holmès

The Adventures of Loufock-Holmès. Pierre Henri Cami (Flammarion-Marpon, 1926). A comic novel by Cami, considered by Charles Chaplin to be "the greatest humorist in the world," and featuring Loufock-Holmès. "No mystery resists him." Reissued by L'Atalante in 1997, with 110 illustrations by Nicholas de la Casinière. Both editions are in French.

Lovelock Holmes

Lovelock Holmes, a romantic detective, drawn by Koko Gonzales, appeared in *The K-Zone Bulletin*, the on-line publication of *K-Zone: Where Kids Rule*, produced by Summit Media of the Philippines. He was one of the 18 Holmes parody characters to take part in "Crisis of Infinite Holmes" (Aug. 2008), an adventure involving Sherlockian characters working together to save their concurrent universes.

Matchlock Holmes

Matchlock Holmes, "the Survival Expert," drawn by Koko Gonzales, appeared in *The K-Zone Bulletin*, the on-line publication of *K-Zone: Where Kids Rule*, produced by Summit Media of the Philippines. He was one of the 18 Holmes parody characters to take part in "Crisis of Infinite Holmes" (Aug. 2008), an adventure involving Sherlockian characters working together to save their concurrent universes.

Mereluck Holmes
Mereluck Holmes is one of ten "alternative names for Sherlock Holmes" proposed by Mrs. Hudson in *Nursing Holmes*, a two-act play by Cenarth Fox (Fox Plays, 2009). Holmes discovers the list in his landlady's personal scrapbook.

Mereluck Tombs
"The Adventure of the Missing Group." A.S. Reeve. *Carry On: The Armstrong Munition Workers' Christmas Magazine*, Dec. 1916. Reprinted in *As It Might Have Been: A Collection of Sherlockian Parodies from Unlikely Sources* (Robert C.S. Adey, ed.; Calabash Press, 1998). Mereluck Tombs and Dr. Dotson search for missing military recruits.

Merlock Jones
Merlock Jones, the "world famous detective," appeared in most of the *Popeye* daily comic strips, by E.C. Segar and distributed by King Features Syndicate, from Aug. 24 to Oct. 3, 1932. They are collected in *E.C. Segar's Popeye, Vol 3: Let's You and Him Fight*. Kim Thompson, ed. (Fantagraphic Books, 2008). Merlock Jones is hired by Castor Oyle to bodyguard King Blozo.

Molar Vons
"The Adventure of the Svedborg Strangler," featuring Molar Vons. Frank Thomas. *The Pontine Dossier* (Mar. 1978). Assisted by Dr. Lydecker Larker. A parody of a parody, in this case of the Solar Pons stories of August Derleth. Assisted by Larker.

Momlock Holmes
Momlock Holmes is the designation awarded to amateur sleuth Jennifer Shannon (as portrayed by Lori Laughlin) by her teenage son in *Garage Sale Mystery: All That Glitters*, a television movie produced by Bargain Street Productions for the Hallmark Channel. Written by Walter Klenhard; directed by Peter DeLuise. First aired Oct. 26, 2014.

Mooch Sheckls

"The Adventure of the Boing! Ritual," featuring Mooch Sheckls and Tweany. Robert L. Fish (as "Rif H. Lobster"). *The Anagram Detectives* (Norma Schier, ed.; The Mysterious Press, 1979). Reprinted in *Ellery Queen's Mystery Magazine* (Feb. 1993). Mooch Sheckls and Tweany are anagrams of Robert L. Fish's parody characters, Schlock Homes and Watney.

Morecock Bones

Morecock Bones is a one-time corruption of Sherlock Holmes' name in *Holmes on the Range* by Steve Hockensmith (St. Martin's Minotaur, 2006). "I thought they'd still be off playin' Sheerluck Jones or Morecock Bones or whatever the hell that feller's called."

Morelock Holmes

Morelock Holmes, "the zombie detective," drawn by Koko Gonzales, appeared in *The K-Zone Bulletin*, the on-line publication of *K-Zone: Where Kids Rule*, produced by Summit Media of the Philippines. He was one of the 18 Holmes parody characters to take part in "Crisis of Infinite Holmes" (Aug. 2008), an adventure involving Sherlockian characters working together to save their concurrent universes.

Morlock Tomes

Morelock Tomes appeared in four literature-oriented stories by George Locke: "The Bookcase of Morelock Tomes" in *Science Fiction First Editions* (Ferret Fantasy, 1978); "Some Variations on a Time Machine" in *Antiquarian Book Monthly Review* (Oct. 1978); "A Nineteenth Century Debacle" (Ferret Fantasy, 1979); and "The Channel Tunnel Mystery" (Ferret Fantasy, 1990). Assisted by Dr. Clotson.

Mukluk Gnomes

"The Adventure of the Purloined Pastiche," featuring Mukluk Gnomes. Robert Eckfcldt. *Venture: The Student Literary Arts Magazine* (Suffolk University, Fall 1976). Assisted by Dr. Watsup.

Mycock Bones

Mycock Bones is a character name in *Sherlock Bones* (2012), a British pornographic film featuring Mark Sloan as Sherlock

Bones/Mycock Bones, with Lucy Love as Hotson. Produced by Kaisenxxx; directed by Rick Bush.

Mylock Bloodstalker

1) Mylock Bloodstalker appeared in *Kamandi: The Last Boy on Earth*, Nos. 52-59 (DC Comics, 1977-78), including "The Sign of Three" in No. 56 (April/May 1978). Jack C. Harris (writer) and Dick Ayers, Alfredo Alcala, and Danny Bulandi (artists). Mylock Bloodstalker is a canine detective in post-apocalyptic Earth, assisted by Doile.
2) Mylock Bloodstalker and Doile also appeared in *Karate Kid*, No. 15 (DC Comics, July/Aug. 1978). Bob Rozakis (writer) and Juan Ortiz (artist).

Myron Honize

Myron Honize is a grandson of Sherlock Holmes and Irene Adler in "The Adventure of Stormy Cleopatra" by Thomas J. Limoli in *The Baker Street Journal*, Vol. 19, No. 1 (March 1969). His identity is revealed in the midst of a hurricane in Florida.

Naughton Jones

Gentlemen of Crime, featuring Naughton Jones. Arthur Gask (Herbert & Jenkins, 1932). Naughton Jones and Professor Mariarty help a millionaire battle racketeers in an old castle.

Nerdslock Combs

Nerds Coloring Book: Case of the Fading Nerds, featuring Nerdslock Combs and Dr. Whatsit. S.M. Ballard (Sunmark/Marvel Books, 1987). Illustrated by Terry Kolvalcik.

Neville Boyles

Neville Boyles appeared in two stories by Jon Wilmunen. The first was "The Adventure of Sir Edward Pins: An Adventure of Neville Boyles and Dr. Watchpot by Acorn N. Doyle" in *The Baker Street Journal*, Vol. 15, No.3 (Sept. 1965). This was followed by "The Adventure of the Tarred Captain: A New Watchpot-Neville Boyles Story" in *The Gamebag*, No. 2 (1966).

Oilock Combs

"More Adventures of Oilock Combs: The Succored Beauty." William B. Kahn. *The Smart Set*, Oct. 1905. Reprinted by the Beaune

Press in a stand-alone pamphlet (1964), and in *The Game Is Afoot: Parodies Pastiches and Ponderings of Sherlock Holmes* (Marvin Kaye, ed.; St. Martin's Press, 1994). The recently-divorced Dr. Spotson visits Oilock Combs, and a lost duchess seeks their help.

Old Cap Jones
Old Cap Jones appears in "The Modern Sherlock," a combination of a rhyming mystery by Carlton Fitchett and a five-panel comic strip, written by Alton McConkey and drawn by Paul Fung, in *The Seattle Post-Intelligencer* (Nov. 6, 1924). Jones, in deerstalker, apprehends the thief of a valuable necklace.

Ozone Holmes
"Ozone Holmes: Deducer of the Inexplicable—Tracer of Lost Mysteries." Bill Skurski. *Harpoon*, No. 2 (Histrionic Publications, Nov. 1974). In a photo-comic appearance, Ozone Holmes and Flotsam are called to the Mediums Club to solve the disappearance of an astral body.

Padlock Bones
1) "The Adventures of Padlock Bones." Sol Cohen (*The Jewish Messenger*, Mar. 16 and 23, 1900). Padlock Bones explains cases involving a German baker in search of a missing 14-year-old boy and a dog suspected of murder and arson to his friend Hotson.
2) "Padlock Bones." Mabel McGinnis (*Life*, Sept. 5, 1901). Chumpson, who narrates the story, is reunited with Padlock Bones in Switzerland, where they help rescue a child who has been hiding in a tree for six months.
3) "Padlock Bones, the Dead-Sure Detective." H.A. MacGill. A syndicated series of seven comic strips that appeared over the course of three weeks in Hearst afternoon newspapers in 1904. Three of the strips are reprinted in *Sherlock Holmes in America* (Bill Blackbeard, ed.; Harry N. Abrams, 1981).
4) "The Return of Padlock Bones." Anonymous. *Every Where Magazine* (June 1905). Assisted by Wattsey. Readers are assured that the short tale is "not by Conan A. Doyle, Sir."
5) Padlock Bones and his companion Dr. Watdaughter were the subjects of a short sketch titled "Sherlock Undone" by James W. Babcock in *Lippincott's Magazine* in 1905. Bones makes a number of deductions about an intruder with muddy feet who stole cigars

from his rooms, but Watdaughter informs "your royal loftiness" that all of them are incorrect. Reprinted in various American newspapers (Nov. 1905-Jan. 1906).

6) Padlock Bones locates a singer whose whereabouts are "unknown, even to a lyceum bureau route clerk" in "The Spotlight," a regular column by Ralph Bingham in *The Luyceumite and Talent* magazine (Nov. 1911).

7) *Saving the Child* (1914), featuring Max Asher as "Padlock Bones, detective," was a short silent comedy film. Produced by the Universal Film Manufacturing Co.; directed by Allen Curtis; released Jan. 14, 1914. Bones pursues a villain and his evil cohorts who have kidnapped a baby from a wealthy family.

8) *Jerry and the Smugglers* (1916), featuring Padlock Bones, was one of 56 short silent comedy films in the "Jerry" series, written and directed by Milton J. Fahrney in 1916-17. Produced by Cub Comedies. Gordon McGregor performed the role of Padlock Bones. Released Apr. 1, 1916. After finding Padlock Bones' detective manual and disguises, Jerry goes in search of a band of Mongolian smugglers.

9) Padlock Bones was the humorous invention of Mary E. Bostwick, a reporter for *The Indianapolis Star* in her account of a convention of the International Secret Service Association: "Men, Who Make Life Unhappy for Crooks, Discuss Evil Doings" (May 7, 1924). Bones investigates an "embargo on false whiskers" and a waiter's thumbprint on his soup plate.

Padlock Booms

Padlock Booms is one of seven parody names in "Prize Detective Story." Anonymous (*The Weekly Magazine*, May 8, 1897). Retitled "Holmes and the Startled Banker" in *As It Might Have Been: A Collection of Sherlockian Parodies from Unlikely Sources* (Robert C.S. Adey, ed.; Calabash Press, 1998). Hemlock Coombs repeatedly changes his name as he makes a series of trivial deductions.

Padlock Domes

"Padlock Domes, or Who Stole the Japanese Paper Basket" was a comedy skit produced at the Rehearsal Theatre in London (Jan. 7, 1913). Charles Leftwich wrote the skit and portrayed Padlock Domes. Assisted by Dr. Jotson; also featuring Prof. Notoriety.

Padlock Holmes

1) "Deductive Reasoning," featuring Padlock Holmes. Anonymous. *The Atchison (Kansas) Daily Champion* (June 7, 1897), and other newspapers of the time. A short joke in which Padlock Holmes unmasks a former member of the police force.

2) *Padlock Holmes* was a three-act comedy spoof of William Gillette's *Sherlock Holmes.* Presented by The Jesters, a dramatic club, at the Park Theatre in New York, May 17-19, 1900; written by Theodore Banta Sheldon and Robert B. Smith. Guy H. Hubbard portrayed Padlock Holmes, assisted by Doctor Whatson, with Prof. Yuraliarty.

3) "A New Padlock Holmes Story." Anonymous (as "A. Coining Doyle"). *The Washington Post*, May 7, 1905. Padlock Holmes investigates nine murders "committed in the immediate neighborhood" of Watson's house, and all the circumstantial evidence points to the doctor.

4) Padlock Holmes, in full Sherlockian regalia, was featured in two sports cartoons by Harold Russell in *The Cincinnati Enquirer* (May 29 and June 2, 1914).

5) *Padlock Holmes* (1918), was a two-reel western short film starring Shorty Hamilton. Probably produced by the W.H. Clifford Photoplay Co. and released before Sept. 1, 1918. Clifford had been production manager for the Monogram Film Co. when it produced a long series of Shorty Hamilton westerns (1914-1917) before forming his own company and continuing the series. *Padlock Holmes* was described as "a sensational western drama, full of thrilling stunts. A punch in every foot." Presumably lost; not listed in Hamilton's filmography, but advertised by movie houses throughout the US.

6) Padlock Holmes is mentioned in the *Broncho Bill* daily comic strip by Harry O'Neill (May 1, 1943). As the search for a bandit known only as The Ghost continues, Broncho Bill's sidekick Tornado exclaims, "Barbecue my carcass and cover me with gravy if this ain't a mystery for Padlock Holmes!" Distributed by United Feature Syndicate.

7) Padlock Holmes, drawn by Koko Gonzales, appeared in *The K-Zone Bulletin*, the on-line publication of *K-Zone: Where Kids Rule*, produced by Summit Media of the Philippines. He was one of the 18 Holmes parody characters to take part in "Crisis of

Infinite Holmes" (Aug. 2008), an adventure involving Sherlockian characters working together to save their concurrent universes.

8) *Padlock Holmes & Wendy Watson in The Case of the Disappearing Willie*. John Denison (Why Knot Books, 2015). A children's book, intended to be the first in a series.

Padlock Homes

"The Adventures of Padlock Homes" was a recurring feature in *Champ Comics* and *Speed Comics* (Ed Whelan, writer and artist), publications of Family Comics, from 1942 to 1945. Assisted by Dr. Watsis, Padlock Homes matches wits with Axis agents led by his "archenemy, the Professor."

Padlock Jones

1) "An Easy Case for Padlock Jones." Anonymous. *Snap-Shots*, (Sept. 26, 1903). Reprinted in *As It Might Have Been: A Collection of Sherlockian Parodies from Unlikely Sources* (Robert C.S. Adey, ed.; Calabash Press, 1998). Padlock Jones recovers a pampered four-year-old snatched from a colonel's garden.

2) "The Adventures of Padlock Jones" were three stories by W.L. Riordan in *The New York Times Magazine Supplement*: "A Bedlamite" (Oct. 11, 1903); "The Stolen Diamonds" (Oct. 15, 1903); and "Beet Sugar and Reciprocity" (Oct. 25, 1903). Assisted by Jotson.

3) Padlock Jones appeared in the Sunday comic strip *The Imaginary Adventures of Little Orvy* by Rick Yager (Mar. 26-Apr. 16, 1961). Jones investigates the case of the Hound of the Daffodils. Syndicated to newspapers throughout the United States.

Padlocked Homes

Padlocked Homes, was featured in *Dr. Jekyll and Mrs. Hyde*, "a deadly drama in three acts," which was part of a Minstrel Jubilee Benefit staged at Sherman, Clay & Co. Hall in San Francisco (Nov. 9, 1901). Clarence Colman portrayed the detective Padlocked Homes. The story involved a murder at Lady Danver's castle, a pursuit to Africa and San Francisco, and the revelation of a "gigantic swindle."

Parrot Holmes
"The Case of the Lost Lorikeet," featuring Parrot Holmes and Dr. Macawson. Laurie Fraser Manifold (*The Serpentine Muse*, Fall 2016). A one-panel cartoon appearance.

Persnurlock Holmes
Persnurlock Holmes appeared in a long-running series of anonymously-written humorous short sketches in two newspapers in New South Wales, Australia, including: "The Fall Mystery" (*Sydney Sun*, Sept. 9, 1920) with Sroliver Coyle; "The Mysterious Tomsky" (*Newcastle Sun*, Apr. 8, 1925) concerning a missing Tom tied to the Russians; "Roadside Mystery" (*Sydney Sun*, Dec. 28, 1929) about a missing lorry and a floating hat; "Loose Description" (*Newcastle Sun*, Jan. 29, 1936) concerning a "typical underworld figure" with heavy makeup; and "Palonaise" (*Newcastle Sun*, Nov. 21, 1945) about a Polish man found with a bullet through his heart.

Petcock Holmes
"A Mystery in Circles," featuring Petcock Holmes. Paul Braczyk. *Stock Car Racing* (Sept. 1976). Assisted by Dr. Warsaw. The hero's name is an allusion to a petcock, a small shut-off valve to control the flow of gasoline.

Pharaoh Jones
Pharaoh Jones is the alias assigned to Sherlock Holmes in "The Disappearance of Lady Frances Carfax" as published in *Challenge to the Reader: An Anthology* (Ellery Queen, ed.; Blue Ribbon Books, 1940). In each of the 25 stories, Queen altered the name of the famous literary detective featured, and the "challenge to the reader" was to figure out who that detective was. Narrated by Dover, rather than Watson.

Philo Combs
"The Affair of the Sussex Cyclist: The Exploitation of Philo Combs." Ronald Goulart (as "Samuel Josep and Peter Dawson"). *The California Pelican* (University of California-Berkeley, Nov. 1953). Assisted by Dr. Flotsam.

Philo Gubb
Philo Gubb, Correspondence School Detective. Ellis Parker Butler (Houghton Mifflin Co., 1918). One Sherlockian themed chapter

was included in the magazine serialization of the novel, but left out of the printed book. That chapter, "Watson, Once Epaminondas, Joins Detective Gubb," is reprinted in *Sherlock Holmes in America* (Bill Blackbeard, ed.; Harry N. Abrams, 1981).

Philo Holmes
My Grandfather's Clock (1934), featuring Philo Holmes. A short musical comedy film. Produced by MGM; directed and co-written (with Richard Goldstone) by Felix E. Feist. Released Oct. 27, 1934. Charles Judels appeared as Philo Holmes, with Franklin Pangborn as Dr. Watkins. Suspects are brought from a nightclub to discover a murderer in Phwitterby-on-Thames, England.

Picklock Bones
"Henry's Latest Thriller: Another Escapade of Picklock Bones, the Great Defective." Bertram Lamb (as "Uncle Dick"). *Pip & Squeak Annual* (The Daily Mirror, 1932). Picklock Bones tries to avoid the "clutches of the sinister figure" stalking him.

Picklock Holes
The Adventures of Picklock Holes: A Sherlockian Parody Cycle by R.C. Lehmann (Bradbury, Agnew & Co. 1901), consisted of eight stories from 1893-94. Seven additional stories from 1903-04 and one from 1918 were collected in *The Return of Picklock Holes* (Magico, 1980). All originally appeared in *Punch* under the pseudonym "Cunnin Toil." Assisted by Dr. Samuel Potson.

Picklock Holmes
Picklock Holmes is a one-time corruption of Sherlock Holmes' name in Chapter 24 of *All at Sea: A Fleming Stone Detective Story* by Carolyn Wells (J.B. Lippincott, 1927). "Oho! You are a detective? Hello, Mr. Picklock Holmes!"

Picklock Homes
"Picklock Homes' Last Case." Anonymous (as "Yaffle"). In: *Pity the Poor Rich* (George Allen & Unwin, 1947). In this left-leaning political satire, Picklock Homes cannot "register the difference between financiers and confidence men, between business men and safe breakers."

Picklock Soles

Picklock Soles is a one-time corruption of the name Smallpox Soles, the Holmes parody character featured in "The Marischal Manor Mystery." Anonymous (*Alma Mater*, Oct. 31, 1923). A play, reprinted in *As It Might Have Been: A Collection of Sherlockian Parodies from Unlikely Sources* (Robert C.S. Adey, ed.; Calabash Press, 1998).

Pocklock Holmes

Pocklock Holmes is a Pokemon character who "worked at Her Majesty's government, lives in London," as conceived by Aleksas Pielikis of Vilnius, Lithuania on GooglePlus (Feb. 22, 2014).

Pollack Hmms

Pollack Hmms investigates a case of possible murder in "The Old Russian Woman" by Cathy McCarthy. *Mycroft's Messenger*, No. 15 (Oct. 1979). Assisted by Dr. Notsaw.

Poplock Holmes

The Grand Adventures of Poplock Holmes is a "Victorian-flavored hip-hop" musical album, geared toward the steampunk genre, originally released Feb. 14, 2016. Lead singer Jerrold Ridenour is Poplock Holmes, while Frank Langley is DJ Watson. The final cut on the album is "Pound of the Basskervilles."

Porlock Moans

"The Adventures of Porlock Moans." Nicholas Utechin. *Shades of Sherlock Annual*, No. 4 (July 1970). Assisted by Dr. Potsdam, and residing on Bacon Street.

Potluck Bones

"Why Musical Comedy Has No Plot," featuring Potluck Bones and Dr. Cotson. Anonymous (as "C O'M"). Mrs. Budson announces the client, a theatrical manager who wants Bones to "discover the plot of a musical comedy," supposedly an impossible task. *The Playgoer* (Apr. 1904).

Psylock Holmes

Korean Gangnam-style pop star Psy (Park Jae-sang) took on the role of "Psylock Holmes" in exposing an impostor impersonating him at the Cannes Film Festival, according to a post by Mike Janela on the Guiness World Records website (May 23, 2013).

Puglock Holmes

1) "Puglock Holmes Solves the Brown Blanket Mystery" is a short live-action video produced by Christine Lorraine. A dog discovers "who was lurking beneath the brown blanket that fateful night." Posted on YouTube (July 22, 2012).

2) Puglock Holmes, a bulldog in Sherlockian costume, is the creation of the artist Suz Roach of Asheville, North Carolina (2015). "Puglock Holmes is excellent at sniffing out the clues and solving the most difficult mysteries."

3) "I am Puglock Holmes," featuring a pug with hat and pipe, is the subject of a series of products created by artist Philip Monero of India and marketed online at posterguy.in. Items include a poster, magnets, t-shirt, coffee mug, phone case, pillow, and mousepad.

Pureluck Holmes

1) Pureluck Holmes is featured in a humorous poster for a fictional film, *The Curious Incident of the Dog in the Night-time... The Hound*. "Based on a novel by Sir Arthur Donut Hole. Starring Barrymore Duck as Pureluck Holmes. Nigel Brute as Dr. Whatsup." *Mediascene*, No. 24 (May-June, 1977).

2) Pureluck Holmes is a feline consulting detective in the *Streethounds* series of downloadable video games, created by Richard Hoover for SeaLeft Studios: "The Unlocked Room" (Mar. 2015), "The Cursed Cannon" (Nov. 2015), "The Valentine's Vendetta" (Feb. 2016), and "The Halloween Deception" (Oct. 2016). Assisted by freelance-writer mouse Jane Ampson, Pureluck Holmes solves "confounding crimes baffling police forces the world over."

Pureluck Jones

"The Speckled Hatband, Not by Sherlock Holmes," featuring Pureluck Jones. Written by John Dighton. A BBC regional broadcast of Feb. 20, 1935. Pureluck Jones was portrayed by Bobbie Comber.

Purlock Hone

"Our Mr. Smith," featuring Purlock Hone. Introduction to *The Revelations of Inspector Morgan*. Oswald Crawfurd (Dodd, Mead

& Co., 1907). Reprinted in *The Misadventures of Sherlock Holmes* (Ellery Queen, ed.; Little, Brown & Co., 1944). Hone's friend Jobson expects Purlock Hone to reach astonishing deductions about international intrigue from a mysterious visitor named John Smith, but "the plain truth" is less impressive.

Purrrlock Holmes
Purrrlock Holmes: Furriarty's Trail is a deduction-based board game designed by Stephen Sauer (San Diego: IDW Games, 2017). Purrrlock Holmes is a cat detective, in Sherlockian costume, associated with Scotland Pound. The object of the game is to successfully stop Furriarty, who is "terrorizing London" before his scheme is completed. Art by Jacquie Davis.

Quarrelrock Hums
Quarrelrock Hums is a corruption of the name Sherlock Holmes in *Wilde About Holmes* by Milo Yelesiyevich (Comic Masque, 2008), one of many names used within a bizarre hallucination that occurs when "a delirious Holmes" suffers from "a cocaine frenzy."

Radford Shone
Radford Shone. Headon Hill (Ward, Lock & Co., 1908). A collection of stories spoofing Sherlock Holmes' methods. Shone, the "much-talked-of solver of mysteries" is attended by a "wooly-brained admirer… who lives with him." One of the stories, "The Tenth Green," is reprinted in *I Believe in Sherlock Holmes* (Douglas G. Greene, ed.; Dover Publications, 2015).

Raffles Holmes
R. Holmes & Co.: Being the Remarkable Adventures of Raffles Holmes, Esq., Detective and Amateur Cracksman by Birth. John Kendrick Bangs (Harper & Bros., 1906). Raffles Holmes is the descendant of both Sherlock Holmes and A.J. Raffles, the gentleman thief.

Rex Homes
"Tha Grate Fur Koat Mistery," featuring Rex Homes. *Showshoe Al's Bed Time Storries (and Uther Times)*. Albert J. Bromley (Minton, Balch & Co., 1926). Assisted by Dr. Hotbun, "the famus detektiff" Rex Homes is visited by a waitress. Her fur coat has been stolen by her boyfriend, a poet.

Rockhard Scones

Rockhard Scones is one of the "great made-up detectives," as conceived by James Parker in his review of Sherlockian volumes in *The New York Times Sunday Book Review* (Oct. 26, 2015).

S. Herlock Holmes

"S. Herlock Holmes." An anonymously drawn cartoon appearing in *Life* (Dec. 1902). Holmes tracks a Cockney, who drops his Hs.

Sa Haapu

The Locked Tomb Mystery, featuring Sa Haapu and Wadjsen. Elizabeth Peters. *Sisters in Crime* (Marilyn Wallace, ed.; Berkeley Books, 1989). Reprinted in *The Year's Best Mystery and Suspense Stories* (Edward D. Hoch, ed.; Walker & Co., 1990). Sa Haapu functions as a detective in ancient Egypt.

Saeloc Holmes

"The Case of the Scandalous Starship," featuring Saeloc Holmes. Brad Keefauver. *The Holmesian Federation*, No. 4 (1983). In a *Star Trek* tale, Saeloc, a descendant of Sherlock Holmes, solves a murder on the *Enterprise*. Assisted by Chon Omston.

Sanford Haus

"A Scandal in Hobohemia," featuring Sanford Haus. Jamie Wyman. *Two-Hundred and Twenty One Baker Streets* (David Thomas Moore, ed.; Abbadon Books, 2014). Sanford "Crash" Haus—"Vagabond. Owner. Performer. Owner and Proprietor of Siggiorno Brothers Traveling Wonder Show"—enlists former soldier Jim Walker to help him find a killer.

Saurian Holmes

"Kiss: The Land of Khyscz," featuring Saurian Holmes. Ralph Macchio (writer) and John Romita, Jr. (artist). *Marvel Super Special*, No. 5 (Marvel Comics, Sept. 1978). Trapped in the Land of Leftovers, the band members enlist the help of lizard-like detective Saurian Holmes, who vies against his rival Professor Maharishi to help them escape.

Scherlock Holmes

The Scherlock Holmes *risto-pub-birreria* (restaurant-pub-brewery) was the name of a now-closed establishment in Naples, Italy. The street sign, still standing in 2018, features a silhouette of Holmes and a scene of London. "Since 1978." A photograph was featured in *Ineffable Twaddle*, newsletter of the Sound of the Baskervilles of Seattle (Feb. 2018).

Schlock Holmes

1) "A Cracked Look at Young Schlock Holmes." Joe Catalano (writer) and Walter Brogan (artist). *Cracked*, No. 220 (Globe Communications, July 1986). A satirical look at what Steven Spielberg "was afraid" to reveal in his 1985 film, *Young Sherlock Holmes*.

2) Schlock Holmes is a one-time corruption of Sherlock Holmes' name in *And Then There Was No One: The Last of Evadne Mount* by Gilbert Adair (Faber and Faber, 2009). The reference, "the bogus Holmes," is to Sherlockian pastiche characters.

Schlock Homes

1) Schlock Homes is the creation of Robert L. Fish. Beginning with "The Adventure of the Ascot Tie," Fish produced a total of 32 stories between Feb. 1960 and June 1981. All originally appeared in *Ellery Queen's Mystery Magazine*. Collections include *The Incredible Schlock Homes* (Simon & Schuster, 1966); *The Memoirs of Schlock Homes: A Bagel Street Dozen* (Bobbs-Merrill Co., 1974); and *Schlock Homes: The Complete Bagel Street Saga* (Gaslight Publications, 1990). Assisted by Dr. Watney, Schlock Homes misinterprets everything he sees, but somehow muddles his way to a solution for each case. Also featuring his brother Criscroft Homes, Inspector Balustrade, and rivals Prof. Marty, Col. Moron, and Irene Addled.

2) Schlock Homes made an appearance in "The Adventure of the Boing! Ritual" by Norma Schier in *The Anagram Detectives* (Mysterious Press, 1979), a collection of mysteries involving anagrams.

Sedgewick Hawk-Styles

Sedgewick Hawk-Styles: Prince of Danger was the title of the 1966 pilot episode of a proposed television series for ABC. The series itself, a spoof starring Paul Lynde as a Sherlock Holmes-type character in the Victorian era, was never produced. Written by Bud Freeman.

Sellem Jones

Sellem Jones, a book agent, was the disguise identity of Surelock Holmes in *A Case of Mix-Up*, a two-scene musical comedy play. Written by Fred W. Rath, who performed as Holmes/Jones for Class Day at the Manual Training High School of Brooklyn, New York (Feb. 2, 1912). "A burlesque on Sherlock Holmes and on wireless telegraphy."

Semloh

"The Other Side of Reason." John Lutz. *Mike Shayne Mystery Magazine* (Dec. 1974). Reprinted in Lutz' anthology *Until You are Dead* (Five Star, 1998). Semloh is Holmes spelled backward. An amateur detective utilizes the "process of illogicality," the reverse of deduction and logic.

Seol-ok

In *Queen of Mystery*, a South Korean television series, Yoo Se-ol-ok, who wants to be a police officer, teams with detective Ha Wan-Seung to solve mysteries in 16 episodes that aired on KBS2 (Apr. 5-May 25, 2017). Written by Lee Seong-min; directed by Kim Jin-woo and Yoo Yeong-eun. Seol-ok was portrayed by Choi Kang-hee.

Shadlock Bones

"S.S. Penmanship," featuring Shadlock Bones. Isabel Manning Hewson (writer) and Olive Bailey (artist). *Land of the Lost Comics*, No. 8 (L.L. Publishing Co., Dec. 1947). A comic book fish detective in Sherlockian costume.

Shadrach Chomes

"The Adventure of the Spackled Bend," featuring Shadrach Chomes and Vasser. Eli M. Liebow. *Pathfinder of Congregation Solel*, Highland Park, Illinois (March 9, 1990).

Shadrach Holmes

Double Trouble Squared. Katherine Lasky (Harcourt, Brace & Co., 1991). A mystery novel for teen readers. Shadrach Holmes is a ghost who reveals the existence of a missing Conan Doyle story.

Shadrach Voles
Shadrach Voles is one of the "great made-up detectives," as conceived by James Parker in his review of Sherlockian volumes in *The New York Times Sunday Book Review* (Oct. 26, 2015).

Shagbark Jones
Shagbark Jones, a medicine-faker and detective, appeared in a series of six stories by Ellis Parker Butler in *Red Book* in 1917. The first of them, "The Mystery Man," is reprinted in *I Believe in Sherlock Holmes* (Douglas G. Greene, ed.; Dover Publications, 2015).

Shallock Holmes
"The Adventure of the Wisbech Werewolf, by Sir Aether Colin Dolc," featuring Shallock [Holmes]. John Jacobson. *The Rosslyn Review* (Mar. 16, 1974).

Shamlock Bones
One for Tooty (1913), featuring Shamlock Bones. A short silent comedy film. Released by the Éclair American Film Co. on Nov. 30, 1913. An unknown actress portrays Tooty as Shamlock Bones, in full Sherlockian attire, who pursues suspicious men into a saloon.

Shamrock Bones
Shamrock Bones was a recurring character in *Walt Disney's Mickey Mouse* and *Walt Disney's Comics and Stories* from 1952 to 1972. He was often called upon to assist Mickey Mouse and Goofy in solving cases. His first appearance may have been in "The Shattered Glass Mystery, Part I" in *Walt Disney's Comics and Stories* (Dell Comics, Mar. 1952). Shamrock Bones occasionally appeared in other Disney comic books such as *The Beagle Boys*, No. 17 (Gold Key, July 1973).

Shamrock Cohen
Shamrock Cohen and Dr. John Wetsuit appeared in two stories by Bob Lynn (writing as "Bud Buonocore"): "Shamrock Cohen and the Amorous Doppelganger" in *Invocation*, No. 8 (Apr. 1976) and "Shamrock Cohen and the Case of the Faithful Dagger" in *Invocation*, No. 12 (Apr. 1977). Both were reprinted in a pamphlet by Magico Magazine in 1981.

Shamrock Ferret

The Last War: Detective Ferrets and the Case of the Golden Deed, featuring Miss Shamrock Ferret. Richard Bach (Scribner, 2003). Assisted by Burrows. With a reputation as a successful sleuth, Shamrock Ferret considers a problem from her "cases unsolved chair," leading to an important lesson about war and peace. From the *Ferret Chronicles* series of books.

Shamrock Holes

Shamrock Holes is a one-time corruption of the name Smallpox Soles, the Holmes parody character featured in "The Marischal Manor Mystery." Anonymous (*Alma Mater*, Oct. 31, 1923). A play, reprinted in *As It Might Have Been: A Collection of Sherlockian Parodies from Unlikely Sources* (Robert C.S. Adey, ed.; Calabash Press, 1998).

Shamrock Holmes

1) Shamrock Holmes and Dr. Mike Watson were members of a jury of historical and literary characters in *The Wearing of the Green*, a play produced at the Paducah, Kentucky, High School in honor of St. Patrick's Day (Mar. 17, 1909). Holmes and Watson were portrayed by brothers Edward and McClain Mitchell.

2) Shamrock Holmes is one of ten "alternative names for Sherlock Holmes" proposed by Mrs. Hudson in *Nursing Holmes*, a two-act play by Cenarth Fox (Fox Plays, 2009). After finding the list in his landlady's personal scrapbook, Holmes makes particular note of it, since it is an Irish name, and goes on to read a list of her "alternative names for Dr. Watson," including Dr. Flotsam, Dr. Flopson. Dr. Rotson, Dr. What's-it, Dr. What's-on, and Dr. What's-up.

3) *The Adventures of Shamrock Holmes: Troubles in Toronto*. Angus McDonald (CreateSpace, 2014). Shamrock Holmes is a 10-year-old detective assisted by his English bulldog Farticus.

4) *Shamrock Holmes* was a play written and directed by Penny Kohut and presented at the TheatreNOW Dinner Theatre of Wilmington, North Carolina (Feb. 24-Mar. 25, 2017). In an "Irish wake-meet-murder mystery," local historian and armchair detective Shamrock Holmes (portrayed by Ron Hasson) solves a case in Shenanigan's Pub.

Shamrock Homes

1) Shamrock Homes appeared in two chapters of *A439: Being the Autobiography of a Piano* (Incorporated Society of Musicians, 1900), a round-robin novel, with each chapter written by a different member of the Society. Homes, who had been disguised as "Mr. Strong," is revealed in Chapter 20, written by H. Chilver Wilson.

2) Shamrock Homes, Miss Maple and Samuel Slade help Chief Detective Albert the Duck in *Albert's Halloween: The Case of the Stolen Pumpkins*. Leslie Tryon (Atheneum, 1998). A children's book in which clues are followed from the pumpkin patch to the library.

Shamrock Houses

Not Another Murder Mystery, featuring Shamrock Houses. A play by Steve Caverno, presented by the Guerilla Theatre of Wilmington, North Carolina (Jan. 24-Feb. 2, 2008). Shamrock Houses was portrayed by Kevin Wilson.

Shamrock Jolnes

Shamrock Jolnes appeared in three stories by O. Henry: "The Sleuths" and "The Adventures of Shamrock Jolnes" in *Sixes and Sevens* (Doubleday, Page & Co., 1911); and "The Detective Detector" in *Waifs and Strays* (Doubleday, Page & Co., 1917). In the three often-reprinted stories, Jolnes respectively takes second place to a detective named Juggins, makes deductions about a Southerner and his daughters, and is himself pursued by a master criminal. Assisted by Dr. Whatsup.

Shamrock Jones

"The Mysterious Tracks," featuring Shamrock Jones. *The Arrow Book of Brain Teasers*. Martin Gardner (TAB Books, 1959). Reprinted by Scholastic Book Services in 1962.

Shamrock Wolmbs

"The Singularge Experience of Miss Anne Duffield," featuring Shamrock Wolmbs. John Lennon. *A Spaniard in the Works* (Simon & Schuster, 1965). Assisted by Doctored Whopper. A stage version, co-written by Lennon, Adrienne Kennedy, and Victor Spinetti, was first performed by the National Theatre Company in 1967. "Ellafitzgerald, my dear Whopper."

Shamshock Phones
"Shamshock Phones, Detective" appeared in a total of ten comic strips by Sam Green of Rockville, New York, in 1979. They were published in two limited editions of 100 signed copies.

Shamus Homes
"Shamus Homes: The Return of the Ripper." Lou Silverstone (writer) and Jack Rickard (artist). *The Mad Book of Mysteries* (Warner Books, 1980). "From the records of Doctor Whatso, we present…another adventure in the life of Shamus Homes," with his "archenemy" Professor Mortuarity and Inspector La Strada.

Sharl Homes
Sharl Homes is a corruption of the name Sherlock Holmes in *Wilde About Holmes* by Milo Yelesiyevich (Comic Masque, 2008), one of many names used within a bizarre hallucination that occurs when "a delirious Holmes" suffers from "a cocaine frenzy."

Sharlock Holmes
"A Study in Stagnation," featuring Sharlock Holmes and Nigel Watson. Tom Mengert. *The Victorian Journal*, No. 2 (March 1971).

Sharlowe Com's
Sharlowe Com's by John Paul Cabot is a comic creation which appeared in a series for The Literary Circle of the Blue Carbuncle of Toulouse, France, an organization which was active from 1997-2011.

Shaw La Coombs
"How the Ancient British Borrow: From *A Study in Shaggy*." Walter Murphy. *Prescott's Press*, No. 7 (Sept. 1990). Shaw La Coombes and Dr. John H. Benwat discuss a case of international importance with a confused Inspector Stanley Hopeless.

Shayluck Hums
Shayluck Hums is a corruption of the name Sherlock Holmes in *Wilde About Holmes* by Milo Yelesiyevich (Comic Masque, 2008), one of many names used within a bizarre hallucination that occurs when "a delirious Holmes" suffers from "a cocaine frenzy."

Shearlock Combs

"The Kimberley Diamond Mine Substitution Scandal," featuring Shearlock Combs. Steve Clarkson (Privately Printed, 1970). Assisted by Dr. Witsend.

Shearlock Hollmes

"Perfectly Simple, Watson," featuring Shearlock Hollmes. Wilbur S. Boyer. *Boys' Life: The Boy Scouts' Magazine*, Vol. 8, No. 4 (April 1918). One of a series of stories featuring Johnnie Kelly. In this case, he assumes to role of "Shearlock Hollmes, the detectif" to solve a mystery.

Shedlock Combs

"The Coming Back of Shedlock Combs by Woctor Dotson." Leavitt Corning (*The Razoo*, 1909). Reprinted in *A Book by Sauntering Silas & Co.* (Corning Advertising Agency, 1911). A retelling of "The Empty House," with a reference to Yotland Scard and an attempt on the life of Shedlock Combs by an associate of Mofessor Proriarty with "a slingshot with an expanding bullet." Apparently, one of several Shedlock Combs stories.

Shedlock Holmes

"Shedlock Holmes and Louisiana Raffles" and "Shedlock Holmes and Louisiana Raffles: The Great Sausage Mystery." Ed Carey. *The Pittsburgh Gazette* (July 13 and July 20, 1902). Small time crook Louisiana Raffles uses such tricks as shoes on a dog and a heated penny to elude Shedlock Holmes.

Shedlock Homes

Shedlock Homes is mentioned in the novel *Finnegans Wake* by James Joyce (Viking Press, 1939). "I should like to ask that Shedlock Homes person who is out for removing the roofs of our criminal classics by what *deductio ad domunum* he hopes *de tacto* to detect anything unless he happens of himself, *movibile tectu*, to have a slade off." The book also has references to Conan Boyles and Moriartsky.

Shedlock Jones

"Dr. Jekyll & Mr. McDuck," featuring Shedlock Jones. Season 1, Episode 60, of *Duck Tales*, an animated television series. First aired Dec. 23, 1987. Produced by the Walt Disney Co.; written by

Margaret Osborne and Michael Keyes; directed by Terence Harrison. Shedlock Jones helps find an antidote for a potion making Uncle Scrooge give away money.

Sheer Look Holmes

Sheer Look Holmes, a musical play by Godfrey Shipp, presented by the West Bridgford Baptist Revue Group of Nottinghamshire (Apr. 29-May 1, 1976). Keith Winter portrayed Sheer Look Holmes.

Sheer Luck Holmes

1) *Sheer Luck Holmes and the Pithtenstein Sword* (1978), an amateur film written and directed by Dennis Wickline, premiered at the Grosse Pointe South High School, Michigan (Sept. 11, 1978). A famous film producer, assisted by Jimmy Witson, searches for the elusive Pithtenstein Sword. A spoof on the film industry.

2) *Sheer Luck Holmes! Or the Ghastly Secret of Greystone Manors*. Ian Dorricott and Simon Denver (Maverick Musicals and Plays, 1980). A musical play, often produced by high schools. Premiered in Bisbane, Australia, in 1979. Frequently titled more simply as "Sheerluck Holmes."

3) *Sheer Luck Holmes: The Panto* (2012). Written by Bob Heather and Cheryl Barrett. A musical pantomime. Sheer Luck Holmes, assisted by Dotty Watson and his dog Baskerville, solves a mysterious case of missing art. With Mary Arty and three policemen named "Arthur, Cone and Oil."

Sheer-Luck Holmes

1) "Alias Sheer-Luck Holmes." *The Danny Thomas Show*, No. 1249 (Dell Four-Color Comics, Nov.-Jan. 1961/62). In London, Danny Williams captures a notorious jewel thief and is dubbed Sheer-Luck Holmes. A comic book appearance.

2) Sheer-Luck Holmes is a one time corruption of Sherlock Holmes' name in *The 6 Messiahs* by Mark Frost (William Morrow, 1995). Narrated by a bitter Conan Doyle: "Nearly a year now since Sheer-luck took the plunge, and public outrage at his demise shows no signs of slacking off."

3) Sheer-Luck Holmes appeared in two features, both by Terry Fletcher (as "Fletch") in *Knockout*, a British comic book: "The Case of the Trapper's Return" (1972) and "The Music Eater: Another Great Sheer-Luck Holmes Adventure" (1973). The latter,

along with Sheer-Luck's Quiz" appeared in *Superbook: A Super Collection of Fun, Fact, Fiction, and Fantasy* (Barron's Educational Series, 1977), which was compiled for the Children's Writers and Illustrators Workshop.

4) "Sheer-Luck Holmes." Season 1, Episode 7, of *Whizziwig*, a live-action children's science fiction television program, produced by Carlton Television for CITV of Britain. An extraterrestrial grants wishes to a boy, often with tragic results. Created by Malorie Blackman, and written by Jim Eldridge. First broadcast Feb. 18, 1998.

5) Sheer-Luck Holmes is a one-time corruption of the name Sherlock Holmes in *The Master Sleuth on the Trail of Edwin Drood* by Robert F. Fleissner (Xlibris, 2002). On the golf course, Holmes makes a "perfect drive" and a hole-in-one, inspiring this jealous designation.

6) *Sheer-Luck Holmes: Clueless Again*, a musical mystery play by Ben E. Millett, produced at the Desert Star Playhouse in Murray Utah, Apr.-June 2011. Scott Holman portrayed the title character, who investigates the murder of a famous archaeologist.

Sheer-Luck Hums

Sheer-Luck Hums is mentioned briefly in *The Spy Who Fell Off the Back of the Bus* by Marc Lovell (Doubleday Crime Club, 1988). The spy, Appleton Porter, finds himself "wondering what was so special about… Sheer-Luck Hums."

Sheerbach Tones

Sheerbach Tones and Bopson appeared in two stories by J.N. (Jerry Neal) Williamson: "The Adventure of the Bugged Bird: A Christmas Story Like without Slush" (*Baker Street Journal Christmas Annual*, 1960), and "Bopping It in Bohemia, or Sheerbach Tones in Basin Street" (*Ellery Queen's Mystery Magazine*, Jan. 1961).

Sheercheek Holmes

"Sheercheek Holmes—An All-Too-Human History of Stage & Screen Variations on a Name." Howard Ostrom and Ray Wilcockson (No Place Like Holmes, Sept. 22, 2014). An online essay.

Sheercrocked Moans

Sheercrocked Moans and Dr. Watsdotter appeared in two stories by Gayle Lange Puhl: "The Adventure of the Stocksen Bonds" in *The Baker Street Journal*, Vol. 18, No. 2 (June 1968), in which he brings about the downfall of Professor Artymore; and "The Adventure of Rasil Bathbone" in *Shades of Sherlock Annual*, No. 6 (Jan. 1972).

Sheerflop Soames

"Sheerflop Soames and Bottson" were comic strip characters who appeared in an entire series drawn by D.C. West for the British *Comicolour Album* (Gerald G. Swann, Ltd.) in about 1948.

Sheerlock Holmes

Sheerlock Holmes is the name adopted by the title character in *T. Haviland Hicks, Junior* by J. Raymond Elderdice (D. Appleton & Co., 1916). Chapter 7, "Introducing Sheerlock Holmes" and Chapter 10, "Sheerlock Holmes Deduces!"

Sheerlock Omes

Sheerlock Omes and Doctor Watnot were comic strip characters who appeared in "Rivals of Sheerlock Omes," which was drawn by Denis Gifford for *Rex Magazine* in 1972.

Sheerluck Bones

1) Sheerluck Bones, "the great detective" appeared in "The Daily Novelette," a regular syndicated column appearing in various American and British newspapers between 1915 and 1919. The short humorous tales by anonymous authors were published with such titles as "The Green Lane Murder Mystery" and "The Spook Glen Robbery."

2) Sheerluck Bones, a "dud detective," appears in "Funniosities of Carrie and Company" by Roy Wilson. *Merry and Bright*, No. 68 (July 20, 1918). A comic strip, in which Sheerluck Bones unsuccessfully tries to regulate fishing at the beach.

3) "Really No Problem at All: Case Presented to the Great Sheerluck Bones Hardly Worthy of His Wonderful Brain." *The Highland Recorder* of Highland County, Virginia (May 27, 1921), but attributed to *London Answers*. A man consults Bones about his wife, who is acting in a peculiar manner.

4) *The Island of Treasure* (1922), featuring Sheerluck Bones, private detective. A musical comedy play, written by George Court. Assisted by Dr. Whatsome, "friend and confidant of the famous detective."

5) "The Adventures of Sheerluck Bones: The Mystery of the Stolen Bootlace." Anonymous (as "A.J.P."). *The Alcester Grammar School Record*, No. 22 (Dec. 1925). Assisted by Watsup, Sheerluck Bones bungles the search for a priceless diamond-studded bootlace.

6) *That's All There Is* (1934), featuring Sheerluck Bones. A stage comedy review by Adam Brown, performed at Aird's Castle in Crail, Scotland (Feb. 14-15, 1934). Sheerluck Bones was portrayed by W. Beattie.

7) "The Case of the Baffled Boss" was a short theatrical revue in which "the great detective Sheerluck Bones" investigates a factory strike, but places all the blame on the proprietor. Staged at London's Communist-oriented Unity Theatre Club (Mar.-May, 1938).

8) "The Bash Street Pups in Sheerluck Bones!" *Beano Comic Library*, No. 364 (1997). A comic publication of D.C. Thompson & Co.

9) "Murder at the Oriental Express" was an on-line story by D.M. Robertson (writing as "The Warrior in Jet and Gold") for the Speculative Vision website (Apr. 27, 2003). It features "Sheerluck Bones, crime fighting undertaker, and his overweight sea-going partner in brine, Capt. Wantbun" battling Bones' nemesis Sgt. Morearteries.

10) Sheerluck Bones and Doctor Spotson are characters in the play "Who Dun It? A Magatha Mystrie" by Kevin Hallewell (Dakzn Publications, 2010). Bones and Sposton join Miss Marble to investigate the theft of a diamond necklace.

Sheerluck Bonkers

"Sheerluck Bonkers." Season 1, Episode 2, of *Raw Toonage*, an animated television series. Produced by the Walt Disney Co. for CBS; directed by Larry Latham. Sheerluck Bonkers searches for a priceless pendant stolen from a princess. Voiced by Jim Cummings. First aired Sept. 26, 1992.

Sheerluck Brown
Visitors from Oz: The Wild Adventures of Dorothy, the Scarecrow, and the Tin Woodman. Martin Gardner (St. Martin's Press, 1998). Sheerluck Brown, a bear detective, appears in Chapter 12.

Sheerluck Coames
"The Modern Radio Sleuth." Jay Coote (*Amateur Wireless*, Dec. 7 and Dec. 14, 1929). Reprinted in *As It Might Have Been: A Collection of Sherlockian Parodies from Unlikely Sources* (Robert C.S. Adey, ed.; Calabash Press, 1998). When a radio is installed in Dacre Street, Sheerluck Coames and Botson identify mysterious foreign transmissions.

Sheerluck Combs
"Sheer Luck Again," featuring Sheerluck Combs. Stanley Rubinstein (*The Detective Magazine*, April 13, 1923). Reprinted in *As It Might Have Been: A Collection of Sherlockian Parodies from Unlikely Sources* (Robert C.S. Adey, ed.; Calabash Press, 1998). Combs investigates the theft of Whatson's records of unpublished cases.

Sheerluck Cones
"The Monchu Mystery," featuring Sheerluck Cones, Famous Detective. *Bugs Bunny*, No. 208 (Gold Key Comics, May 1979). Bugs Bunny hopes to become the new assistant to Sheerluck Cones when the Monchu Mansion is burglarized.

Sheerluck Coombes
Sheerluck Coombes was a character in a short play titled *The Elusive Lydia* staged for various Y.M.C.A. and church groups in Britain between 1928 and 1930. Assisted by Whatson, with Sgt. Lessergrade and Prof. Mortuary.

Sheerluck Cracky
The Wacky Adventures of Cracky, Nos. 1-10 (Gold Key Comics, 1972-1975), included a story featuring the wise and thoughtful Sheerluck Cracky (Cracky the Parrot) and the bumbling Dr. Watsup (Caws the Crow) in every issue, except No. 3.

Sheerluck Gnomes

"Misadventures of Sheerluck Gnomes: Misadventure XXCIVL—The Bars of Soap, or The Jew au Jus." T.P. Stafford. *The Modern Detective*, Mar. 9, 1898. Sheerluck Gnomes and Potson are consulted by the managers of a Limehouse boarding house about noisy guards of a shipment of soap. Reprinted in *Baker Street Miscellanea*, No. 1 (April 1975).

Sheerluck Goof

"Sheerluck Goof and the Giggling Ghost of Nottenny Moor." John Blair Moore (writer), and Bill Fugate and Larry Mayer (artists). *Walt Disney's Goofy Adventures*, No. 16 (Disney Comics, Sept. 1991). Sheerluck Goof (Goofy) and Dr. Whatsup (Mickey Mouse) live at 112 Halfbaked Street. They encounter Inspector LaQuacke (Donald Duck), Mrs. Cluckson, and the archenemy Moreorlessity.

Sheerluck Holds

1) Sheerluck Holds of Quaker Street and his assistant Batson appear in "The Mystery of the Point to Point Lace" by J.B. Aiken (*Banba* of Dublin, Ireland, 1921). Holds solves a mystery surrounding the disappearance of "a valuable piece of lace."
2) "Sheerluck Holds' Smartass Caper." Ronald L. Smith (*Fling Magazine*, Mar. 1976). A pornographic parody with Sheerluck Holds, Dr. Witsend, Inspector Latwat, and Morey Arty.
3) Sheerluck Holds reappeared in *Fling Magazine* in pornographic comic strips by David Fell: "Sheerluck Holds in the Case of the Diddled Divorce" (Mar. 1981), "Sheerluck in the Case of the Missing Maidenhead" (Sept. 1981), and "Sheerluck: The Night of the Living Zipper" (Nov. 1982).

Sheerluck Holmes

1) *Sheerluck Holmes* was a Sunday half-page comic strip by Jacob Myer, distributed by the Keystone Syndicate (1906-07). After a dispute with the American representatives of Arthur Conan Doyle, the title of the comic strip was changed to *Sheerluck Homes*.
2) "The Man Wore Rubbers," featuring Sheerluck Holmes, was a short joke distributed to American newspapers, including *The Charlotte (North Carolina) News* (Mar. 3, 1910). The villain "succeeded in erasing his footprints." Assisted by Dr. Buttsin.

3) "The Great Circus Mystery," featuring Sheerluck and Blotzo. *Bugs Bunny*, No. 281 (Dell Four-Color Comics, 1950). Detectives Sheerluck [Holmes] and Blotzo, both dressed in Sherlockian costume, lose the case of missing circus animals to Bugs Bunny and Porky Pig.

4) "Copscotch," featuring Sheerluck Holmes and Dr. Potson, was a musical comedy play written by Barbara Swan and staged by the Women's College of the University of Rochester, New York (Mar. 11, 1950). Three villains are pursued near Cookingham Palace.

5) "The Whitechapel Murders: A Tale of Sheerluck Holmes and Dr. Witsend." Eric Morecombe and Ernie Wise. *Morecombe & Wise Special* (Weidenfeld & Nicolson, 1977).

6) "The Adventures of Sheerluck Holmes." *Tweety and Sylvester*, No. 82 (Gold Key Comics, June 1978). Sheerluck Holmes (Sylvester the Cat) and Watson (Tweety Bird) investigate a murder and encounter a Sherlock Holmes impersonator along with Sherlock Holmes himself.

7) "Sheerluck Holmes and the Lost Teddy Bear." Hal Ober. *McDonaldland Fun Times*, No. 3, (1983). Published by McDonald's Restaurants of Canada.

8) "The Bruhaha Reunion," featuring Sheerluck Holmes, was a play staged by the Murder Unlimited Mystery Theatre in Chilliwack, British Columbia (Nov. 20, 1999). Sir Percival Bruhaha convenes his conniving relatives to announce his sole heir, with predictable results.

9) *Sheerluck Holmes and the Hounds of Baker Street*. Doug Peterson (Big Idea Books, 2005). A children's book in the "Veggie Tales" series. Larry the Cucumber as Sheerluck Holmes is assisted by Bob the Tomato as Dr. Watson.

10) *Sheerluck Holmes and the Golden Ruler* (2005) is an animated film in the "Veggie Tales" series, again featuring Larry the Cucumber as Sheerluck Holmes and Bob the Tomato as Dr. Watson. Directed by Mike Nawrocki, who also voices Sheerluck; written by Robert G. Lee. The story teaches children to treat others as they would like to be treated.

11) Sheerluck Holmes is one of ten "alternative names for Sherlock Holmes" proposed by Mrs. Hudson in *Nursing Holmes*, a two-act play by Cenarth Fox (Fox Plays, 2009). Holmes discovers the list in his landlady's personal scrapbook.

Sheerluck Homes

1) *Sheerluck Homes* was the second title of a Sunday half-page comic strip by Jacob Myer, distributed by the Keystone Syndicate (1906-07). Originally titled *Sheerluck Holmes*, the feature's name was changed after a dispute with the American representatives of Arthur Conan Doyle.

2) "The Disappearance of Dunn-Browne," featuring Sheerluck Homes. Charles Hamilton (as "Hector Hutt"). *The Magnet*, No. 1651 (Oct. 7, 1939). Assisted by Dr. Spotson. One of four such stories under this pseudonym; for the remaining three, the name was changed to Sheerluck Jones.

3) "Sheerluck Homes" is mentioned in the *Archie* daily comic strip by Bob Montana of June 13, 1965. Archie rehearses for the play *Sheerluck Homes* by Sir Archibald Andrews. Distributed by King Features Syndicate.

4) Sheerluck Homes is a comic book character by Freddy Milton, appearing in *Seriemagasinet*, published in Bagsvaerd, Finland, 1978-79. A full volume, *Sheerluck Homes* (Interpresse, 1982), collected Milton's Sheerluck Homes tales.

5) Sheerluck Homes was one of eight "Acme Detective Agency" licenses available to players of *Stop, Thief!*, an "electronic game of cops and robbers" produced by Parker Brothers (1979). Players act as detectives pursuing an invisible thief.

Sheerluck Houses

"The Case of the Cracked Cruncher," featuring Sheerluck Houses. Written by Joanna Humphrey. Produced for the Vallecito Middle School of San Rafael, California, in 1980. Assisted by Dr. G. Whatsup.

Sheerluck Hums

Sheerluck Hums is a character in a series of stories by 14-year-old Larry Yust of Winnetka, Illinois, who produced his own arts and letters journal, *Hullabaloo*, in 1945.

Sheerluck Jones

1) *Sheerluck Jones, or Why d'Gillette Him Off?* By Malcolm Watson and Edward La Serre. An hour-long parody of William Gillette's play, *Sherlock Holmes*. The spoof opened at Terry's Theatre of London (Oct. 29, 1901) and ran for 138 performances, with

Clarence Blackiston in the title role. Assisted by Dr. Rotson. Printed as *Sheerluck Jones: A Dramatic Criticism in Four Paragraphs and As Many Headlines* (Peter Schoffer, 1982).

2) "Sheerluck Jones, or The Encyclopaedia Brittanica." Edward S. Blair (*The Grotonian*, 1907). Assisted by Spitzen. Jones solves the disappearance of a 32-pound book from the school library.

3) Sheerluck Jones appeared in a short joke as part of the syndicated "Most Anything" column in American newspapers (Nov. 1908). Coming across a man's bloody body, a revolver on the floor, and a note "in the writing of the deceased," Jones comes to an astonishing conclusion: "Watson… there has been a suicide."

4) Sheerluck Jones, "the great detective," appeared in "Why I Jilted Nan" by Helen Gillespie in *The Omega*, the annual of Ann Arbor (Michigan) High School (1910). Jones solves the disappearance of a girl pursued by two rivals for her affection, one not particularly bright and the other "a villain."

5) *A Victim of Circumstance*, featuring Sheerluck Jones, a comedy play written by Grenville P. Jones, who also appeared as the detective, at the St. Mark's Church schoolroom of Walsall, England (Feb. 4, 1915).

6) "The Model T Mystery," featuring Sheerluck Jones. E.H. Soans. (*The Ford Times*, Aug. 1916). Assisted by What's On. "The only woman that Sheerluck Jones had ever betrayed the slightest affection for" has disappeared.

7) *Lost in Limehouse* (1933), featuring Sheerluck Jones, a comedy short film. Produced by the Masquers Club of Hollywood for RKO Radio Pictures; written by Harrington Reynolds and Walter Weems; directed by Otto Brower. Released Apr. 7, 1933. Olaf Hytten portrayed Sheerluck Jones, and Charles McNaughten appeared as Hotson. A heroine is rescued from a classic villain and Chinese gangsters.

8) Charles Hamilton, writing as "Hector Hutt" wrote three stories for *The Magnet* under the collective title of "The Adventures of Sheerluck Jones," featuring his assistant Dr. Spotson: "Bagging the Bombster" (No. 1659; Dec. 2, 1939), "Jones—The Master Spy" (No. 1660; Dec. 9, 1939), and "The Ruffstuff Rhythm Boys" (No. 1665; Jan. 13, 1940). These were among four such stories under this pseudonym; in the first, the name was Sheerluck Homes.

9) "Sheerluck Jones in the Case of the Missing Heir." *Wonder Comics*, No. 6 (Great Comics, Oct. 1945). Sheerluck Jones (a canine detective) and his assistant Dr. Fatson (a pig) uncover a kidnapping plot planned by their own client.

10) "Inspector Bonehead," featuring Sheerluck Jones. *The Wizard* (D.C. Thomason & Co), Apr. 28, 1973 and May 5, 1973. The two detectives search for a jewel thief. A British comic appearance.

11) Sheerluck Jones is a one-time corruption of Sherlock Holmes' name in *Holmes on the Range* by Steve Hockensmith (St. Martin's Minotaur, 2006). "I thought they'd still be off playin' Sheerluck Jones or Morecock Bones or whatever the hell that feller's called."

Sheerluck Ohms

1) *The Adventures of Sheerluck Ohms: As Related by Doctor Watts Ion*. Anonymous (Magico Magazine, 1980). A collection of 15 short tales that originally appeared in *The Anaconda Wire*, an advertising publication of the Anaconda Copper Co. between June 1947 and Nov. 1951.

2) "The Case of the Curious Contest!" featuring Sheerluck Ohms. Willie Hines. *The Electric Company Magazine*, No. 69 (Oct. 1980). Assisted by Wattsun. Geared toward young readers.

Sheerluck Roams

Sheerluck Roams and Doctor Whats-on Investigate the Case of the Missing Minute. Anthony Aikman (CreateSpace, 2010). A cartoon mystery, attributed to "Sir Arthur Go-on Foil." Sheerluck Roams has "lodgings in Barker Street."

Sheeur-Loque Holmes

Sheeur-loque Holmes was the first attempt at pronouncing Sherlock Holmes' name by a flower girl in Paris in "The Comfort of the Seine" by Stephen Volk. Included in *Gaslight Arcanum* (J.R. Campbell and Charles Prepolec, eds.; Edge, 2011). Holmes enlists an aged C. Auguste Dupin in the investigation of her death.

Sheila Holmes

Sheila Holmes, Kid Detective: The Case of the Missing iPad, written by Ashlynn Walker. A children's production at Northwestern Oklahoma State University (Nov. 21-23, 2011). Assisted by Waffles, a dog. Sheila Holmes was portrayed by Natalie Sacket.

Sheila-Locke Holmes

"The Last of Sheila-Locke Holmes." Laura Lippman. *A Study in Sherlock* (Laurie R. King and Leslie S. Klinger, eds.; Bantam Books, 2011). A young girl, who idolizes Sherlock Holmes, opens a "detective agency" and solves a case, but learns a disturbing secret about her parents.

Shelby Holmes

The Great Shelby Holmes (2016) and *The Great Shelby Holmes Meets Her Match* (2017) by Elizabeth Eulberg (Bloomsbury USA Children's Books), feature a nine-year-old sixth-grader who is "the best detective her Harlem neighborhood has ever seen." Assisted by 11-year-old John Watson (whose Army doctor mother was wounded in Afghanistan) and her dog Sir Arthur.

Shellac Holmsburg

Shellac Holmsburg appeared in the Aug. 26 and 27, 1926, editions of the comic strip *Barney Google and Spark Plug* by Billy Debeck. They are reprinted in *Sherlock Holmes in America* (Bill Blackbeard, ed.; Harry N. Abrams, 1981). Shellac Holmsburg, "private detective from Oscaloosa," is asked to find the missing Barney Google.

Shellack Homes

"The Case of the Missing Pearls," a play featuring Shellack Homes. Earl J. Dias. In: *Plays* (Mar. 1957). Assisted by "his faithful companion" Dr. Jon Whoopson, Shellack Homes pursues a case at the home of a wealthy retired British diplomat.

Shelley Gomez

Shelley Gomez is a one-time corruption of Sherlock Holmes' name in "Art, Crime and Enlightenment" by Vithal Rajan, one of the stories in *Holmes of the Raj* (Writer's Workshop, 2006). "Mr. Shelley Gomez and the Doctor... are here to advise me, yes, on how best to make this most magnificent palace a home."

Shelley Holmes

The Adventures of Shelley Holmes. Neil J. Stone. Fearon Education (David S. Lake Publishers), 1988. Shelley Holmes, assisted by Jimmy Watson, pursues at thief at Barnett High School and clears her brother's name. A mystery novel for teen readers.

Shellshock Sloan

"The First Adventure: From the Adventures of Shellshock Sloan." Joel Monka. *The Illustrious Clients' News* (June 1984).

Shelly Holmes

1) *The Adventures of Shelly Holmes*. Cass Lewis (Family Vision Press, 1993-1994). A series of three books for young readers, including *Dead Man's Confession*, *Till Death Do Us Part*, and *Deadly Nightshade*. The great-granddaughter of Sherlock Holmes can "see what others don't see" and "discover what others pass by."
2) Shelly Holmes is a South Carolina transgendered woman who uses a vape pipe and has a deep devotion to Sherlock Holmes in "The Adventures of the Melted Saint" by Gail Z. Martin. *Baker Street Irregulars* (Michael A. Ventrilla and Jonathan Mayberry, eds.; Diversion Books, 2017).

Shelook Holmes

"Shelook Holmes." Stanley A. Franklin (*The Daily Mirror*, Apr. 30, 1968). An editorial cartoon in which "Barbara Castle is the only man in the cabinet." A reference to the prominent member of the British Labour Party who served several roles in the cabinet of Prime Minister Harold Wilson.

Sher Lok Holmes

"A Scandal in Manchuria," featuring Sher Lok Holmes and Wat Sun. Alan Coren. *Punch*, No. 255 (July 17, 1968). Also featuring Mrs. Hud Son, Plofessor Molly Arty, and Eileen Adler.

Sherbert Cones

"The Adventures of Sherbert Cones" is a series of eleven stories by Eric Grevstad in *The Trinity Tripod* (Trinity College of Hartford, Connecticut) from Oct. 25, 1977, to Apr. 29, 1980. Assisted by his friend Wheaton, Sherbert Cones is beset by his nemesis Mary Ardie in his on-campus life.

Sherbert Foams

"The Mystery of the Tortoise and the Hare," featuring Sherbert Foams. Charles Mears (*Child Life Magazine*, Aug.-Sept. 1978). Assisted by Dr. Proctor.

Sherbert Scones
Gub Gub's Book, featuring Sherbert Scones, the Icebox Detective. Hugh Lofting (Jonathan Cape, 1932). Scones, famous for solving such cases as "the Case of the Missing Eggs," pursues the Mexican Pantry Bandit in a "Food Mystery Story."

Sherbet Foams
"Fatty Fudge as Sherbet Foams in The Hound of the Picnic Basket." Anonymous. *The Beano* (Oct. 28, 1989). The "giant slavering hound" after the picnic basket is Sherbet Foams in disguise. Assisted by Dr. Bon-Bon.

Sherbet Jones
Sherbet Jones; or Who Stole the Roller Skates (1911), a play. Hugh Robinson portrayed Sherbet Jones, with Ernest Thesiger as Dr. What's On and Miles Malleson as Professor Goryarty, at the Kingsway Theatre in London for two performances on Sept. 20, 1911.

Sherbourne Rath
Druid's Blood. Esther M. Friesner (New American Library, 1988). A fantasy novel set in Victorian England. Detective Sherbourne Rath is assumed dead, but he reappears under the name Brihtric Donne. Assisted by Dr. John H. Weston.

Shercock Bones
1) "A Game at Chess: A Vacuosity in One Gasp," featuring Shercock Bones. Edwin A. Greig (*British Chess Magazine*, Oct. 1918). Assisted by Whatson. A chess problem, in which Bones' life is forfeit to Professor Moratorium if he fails to solve it.
2) "Shercock Bones and Dickter Watson in The Case of the Mighty Manhood," a pornographic on-line comic. *That's Not Sexy* (Jan. 18, 2011).

Sherdog Bones
Sherdog, the family pet, uses a pipe that gives him the powers of Sherlock Holmes. His assistant is his owner, Takeru (Wa To Son) They appear in *Sherlock Bones*, Vols. 1-7. Yuma Ando (writer) and Yuki Sato (artist). Manga graphic novels produced in English by Kodansha Comics (2013-14).

Sherdog Holmes

Sherdog Holmes, featuring the comic character Snoopy in full Sherlockian costume, examining the front door of his "Snoopy Holmes" dog house at 221B, is featured on several products, including prints, a pillow case, t-shirts, iPod and iPad cases, and a shower curtain. Produced by 3Second Design and Art. Featured on various on-line marketing sites.

Sheridan Haynes

In two novels by Julian Symons, *A Three-Pipe Problem* (Collins, 1975) and *The Kentish Manor Murders* (Viking, 1988), Sheridan Haynes is an actor who portrays Sherlock Holmes on television, but who assumes the role in a more direct manner.

Sheridan Hume

Herlock (2015), featuring Sheridan Hume and Jonny Watts, a proposed mystery-drama web series. The pilot episode, "Silver Blade," featured Gia Mora as Sheridan Hume, a brilliant detective, and Alana Jordan as Jonny Watts, her student assistant. Written by Lee Eric Shackleford; directed by David E. Duncan.

Sherk Oms

"The Greatest Tertian," featuring Sherk Oms. Anthony Boucher. In: *Invaders of Earth* (Groff Conklin, ed.; Vanguard press, 1952). Reprinted in *The Science Fictional Sherlock Holmes* (Robert C. Peterson, ed.; The Council of Four, 1960). Sherk Oms, "unquestionably the greatest Tertian of all time," was "a pursuer of offenders against society." His biographer was Wa Tsn. As reported by a Martian historian of the future, who confuses Sherk Oms (Sherlock Holmes) with Sherk Sper (Shakespeare).

Sherlark Holmes

"Sherlark Holmes" is the subject of a digital-sculpture figurine design of a lark with deerstalker, pipe and magnifying glass examining a young bird, just hatched and ready to go to school. Designed by Victoria Barranco, an animation student at Northeastern University in Boston. Posted on Vimeo, a video-sharing website (Jan. 2017).

Sherlark Honed

"The Master." Jeffrey R. Huddleston. A series of cartoons featuring Sherlark Honed in *Wheelwrightings*, the journal of The Hansoms of John Clayton, the Sherlock Holmes Society of Peoria (1981-82). Assisted by Wiston, with Professor Mire Arty.

Sherlaw Combs

"The Missing Miss Miller: A Comedy in Three Acts," featuring Sherlaw Combs. Harold Asa Clark (Walter H. Baker & Co., 1907). A farcical play, often staged in the first quarter of the 20th Century.

Sherlaw Kombs

"Detective Stories Gone Wrong: The Adventures of Sherlaw Kombs." Robert Barr (as "Luke Sharp"). *The Idler* (May 1892). Retitled "The Great Pegram Mystery" in *The Face and the Mask* (Frederick A. Stokes, 1895). Reprinted often, most notably in *The Misadventures of Sherlock Holmes* (Ellery Queen, ed.; Little, Brown & Co., 1944). Assisted by Dr. Whatson, Sherlaw Kombs explains a mysterious shooting death on a train, but turns out to be completely wrong in his conclusions.

Sherlhock Holmès

"The Last Adventure of Sherlhock Holmès" by Georges Avryl was a satirical story appearing in *La Revue Limousine*, No. 63 (Jan. 1, 1929). On a visit to Paris, a landlord asks Sherlhock Holmès to investigate "horrible, inexplicable cries" eminating from an apartment. He discovers them to be a recording of a session of the Chamber of Deputies.

Sherlick Holmes

Sherlick Holmes is a 1975 pornographic film starring Harry Reems in the title role, with Zebedy Colt appearing as Watson. Produced by Taurus Productions; written by Victor Milt, and directed by Bear Wilson.

Sherlie Holmes

The Pipe (1912), featuring Sherlie Holmes. A short silent comedy film. Produced by Vitagraph Company of America. Released Apr. 15, 1912. Sherlie Holmes is portrayed by Marshall P. Wilder.

Sherlimerick Holmes
"The Adventures of Sherlimerick Holmes." Jane E. Hinckley (*Prescott's Press*, June 1992). He appears in two of the 60 limericks written for the canonical tales.

Sherloc Holmes
"Sherloc Holmes's Queerer Brother" by R.C. Vallarian (*Blueboy Magazine*, June 1978). A pornographic story in which Oscar Wilde appears as an associate of Holmes.

Sherlock Abodes
Sherlock Abodes is among the "pastiche Sherlock Holmeses," as conceived by Michael Szymanski in his review of *The Adventures of Solar Pons* for the specialty publication *Different Worlds: Journal of Adventure Gaming* (July-Aug. 1986).

Sherlock Ambrose
Sherlock Ambrose (1918), a short silent comedy film. Produced by the L-KO Company; directed by Walter S. Fredericks. Released Mar. 27, 1918. Mack Swain portrays Sherlock Ambrose, an immigrant mistaken for a detective who nevertheless finds a lost diamond ring.

Sherlock Baffles
Sherlock Baffles was a character in the three-act vaudeville musical *The Ham Tree*. Book by George V. Hobart; music by Jean Schwartz; lyrics by William Jerome. The play was performed 90 times at the New York Theatre (Aug. 28-Nov. 11, 1905). W.C. Fields, in his Broadway debut, portrayed Sherlock Baffles.

Sherlock Blake
1) *The Terrible Tec* (1916), a short silent comedy film, presumably lost, featuring Billy Merson as Sherlock Blake. Produced by Homeland Films of Britain; written by Reuben Gilmer; directed by W.P. Kellino. Released Jan. 1916. A detective dons disguises to catch diamond thieves.
2) "The Terrible Tec," featuring Sherlock Blake. Sydney Drew. *Puck* (Feb. 19, 1916). Assisted by Wrotten-clew. Apparently, an adaptation of the film in written form.

Sherlock Bonds

"Bonds, Sherlock Bonds" is featured in *Punch Club: The Dark Fist, Part 1*, an extension of the *Punch Club* boxing simulation video game developed by Lazy Bear Games and published by TinyBuild Games on Mar. 8, 2016.

Sherlock Bonehead

Sherlock Bonehead (1914), a short silent comedy film, featuring Lloyd V. Hamilton as Sherlock Bonehead. Produced by the Kalem Co.; written and directed by Marshall Neilan. Released Aug. 21, 1914.

Sherlock Bones

1) Sherlock Bones was among the guests invited to "Merry Andrew's Box Car Party," an episode of the regular "Merry Andrew's Jest and Jingle" column of the *Chicago Daily Tribune* (Nov. 10, 1901). Sherlock Bones "can detect the earmarks of authorship without any difficulty."

2) Sherlock Bones, a skinny dachschund described as a "faithful attendant," was one of the characters in the 1906-07 Sunday comic strip *The Kin-der-Kids*, created by Lyonel Feininger for the *Chicago Tribune*.

3) "Sherlock Bones, Editor: He Applies Deduction to Manuscripts and Surprises Watson." Anonymous (*The New York Sun*, Jan. 16, 1910). Sherlock Bones demonstrates that he can tell by the look, touch, or smell of a manuscript if it is suitable for his magazine.

4) "All the Symptoms," featuring Sherlock Bones. Anonymous (*Judge Magazine*, Aug. 13, 1921). Attributed to *The Pittsburg Chronicle*, where it was titled "Decoding an Adolescent Daughter." Sherlock Bones reveals that a young woman "in a highly nervous state" was actually "training herself to be a movie actress."

5) *Spooky Spooks* (1925), featuring Sherlock Bones. A short silent comedy film. Produced by Samuel Bischoff productions; written and directed by Al Herman. Released Oct. 20, 1925. Jack Cooper portrays Sherlock Bones, who pursues villains in a haunted house.

6) "Toy Talkies," often featuring Sherlock Bones, was a regular feature written and drawn by Walter Quermann for the Sunday Magazine section of the *St. Louis Post Dispatch*. The first Sherlock Bones feature appeared Aug. 24, 1932, running weekly with

this character at least through Oct. 29, 1933. A paper-dolls style cut-out game for children with a short play script featuring animal characters, including the canine Sherlock Bones.

7) "The Return of Sherlock Bones" was one of the skits in the "1938 Varieties" presented by students of the Roosevelt Junior High School of Appleton, Wisconsin (Apr. 21, 1939). Sherlock Bones was portrayed by Edwin Blackman, Jr. Assisted by Potson.

8) Sherlock Bones, "Dogtective," appeared in *The Case of the Stolen Pearls* by Erva Merow (James & Jonathan, 1961), a "Peek-a-Book" for small children in which holes are punched out for Sherlock Bones' eyes. "Sherlock Bones and His Many Disguises" is credited for his success.

9) *Sherlock Bones: Tracer of Missing Pets*. John Keane (J.B. Lippincott Co., 1979). Sherlock Bones is the alias of the author, who opened what he claimed was the first "canine detective agency" in Oakland, California, in 1976 and described his work in this autobiography. Avon issued the paperback version in 1980. His partner was Paco, a sheepdog.

10) *Dot and the Koala* (1985), featuring Sherlock Bones. An Australian animated feature film. Produced by Yoram Gross Films; written by Greg Flynn; directed by Yoram Gross. Voiced by Keith Scott.

11) *The Mysterious Disappearance of Ragsby*, featuring Sherlock Bones. Barbara Alexander (Oak Tree Publications, 1985). A beloved teddy bear has been "bear-napped" by the dreaded Slime-beast. Assisted by Whatsit.

12) "In Pups We Trust," featuring Sherlock Bones. Season 1, Episode 7, of *Pound Puppies*, an animated television series. First aired Oct. 25, 1986. Produced by Hanna-Barbera for ABC; written by June Patterson and Wendy West.

13) Sherlock Bones, a hound in Sherlockian costume, was the subject of an advertising campaign launched on Mar. 11, 1990, by Milk Bone, a dog treat product of Nabisco. Children were encouraged to find clues in Milk Bone boxes to help solve "The Case of the Vanishing Flavor Snacks." Prizes included $10,000 in gold or one of 1,000 "Sherlock Bones t-shirts."

14) Sherlock Bones was a character in "Her Wicked Ways," a play performed at the Footloose Dinner Theatre in Thornleigh (near Sydney), Australia (Oct. 1991). John Faassen portrayed Sherlock

Bones, who attempts to foil a woman who is plotting to murder her fifth wealthy husband.

15) Sherlock Bones, a pipe-smoking skeleton sporting a trench coat, deerstalker, and magnifying glass, is the mascot of the Los Angeles Coroner's Department. To meet a budget shortfall, the character was developed in 1993 for a line of accessories including t-shirts, mugs, tote bags, beach towels, and other items. *Skeletons in the Closet* was the title of the catalogue.

16) *The Adventures of Sherlock Bones* by Kate Mellenten and Tim Wood (Index, 1997), a "lift a flap book" for children. When Tommy starts school, his "faithful companion" Sherlock Bones sets out in search of a new job.

17) *Sherlock Bones: The Case of the Broken Time Machine* was a mystery play for young people presented by the National Parks Service and the Ohio Erie Canal Coalition at the Akron, Ohio, city hall council chambers (Dec. 1997). This "youth theatre entertains with an educational twist."

18) "The Case of Vamberry, the Wine Merchant." *The Elementary Cases of Sherlock Holmes.* Ian Charnock (Breese Books, 1999). In the story, Sherlock Holmes' fellow students called him "Sherlock Bones, the vampire bat of Bart's."

19) Sherlock Bones is the artistic name of a British hip-hop producer, video director, and "sound designer" who released *No Rulers*, a 13-cut digital album, on Aug. 1, 2005. A second collection of 16 cuts, *The Funeral of Sherlock Bones*, was released on June 2, 2015.

20) Sherlock Bones is one of ten "alternative names for Sherlock Holmes" proposed by Mrs. Hudson in *Nursing Holmes*, a two-act play by Cenarth Fox (Fox Plays, 2009). Holmes discovers the list in his landlady's personal scrapbook.

21) *Sherlock Bones* (2012), a British pornographic film featuring Mark Sloan as Sherlock Bones/Mycock Bones, with Lucy Love as Hotson. Produced by Kaisenxxx; directed by Rick Bush.

22) *Sherlock Bones and the Missing Cheese* by Susan Stevens Crummel with illustrations by Dorothy Donohue (Amazon Children's Publishing, 2012), for preschoolers. Cheese from a "cantankerous cow," the Cowabunga cheese, has gone missing, and Sherlock Bones must find it.

23) *Sherlock Bones*, Vols. 1-7. Yuma Ando (writer) and Yuki Sato (artist). Manga graphic novels produced in English by Kodansha Comics, 2013-14. The family pet, Sherdog, uses a pipe that gives him the powers of Sherlock Holmes. His assistant is his owner, Takeru (Wa To Son).

24) Sherlock Bones, a great dane detective, and Dr. Jane Catson, a war-wounded surgeon, solve murders in two books by Lauren Baratz-Logsted published by Tantrum Books in 2017: *The Adventures of Sherlock Bones: Doggone* and *The Adventures of Sherlock Bones: Dog Not Gone!* They are assisted by the Baker Street Regulars and their leader, Waggins.

25) Sherlock Bones and Dr. Catson appear in *Sherlock Bones and the Times Table Adventure* (Buster Books, 2018) and *Sherlock Bones and the Addition and Subtraction Adventure* (Flash Kids, 2018) by Jonny Marx with illustrations by John Bigwood. Children use mathematics to solve problems and help Sherlock Bones "foil Professor Moriratty's evil plans."

Sherlock Boob

1) *The Sherlock Boob* (1914), a short silent comedy film. Produced by Rex Motion Picture Co.; written by Bruce M. Mitchell; directed by Robert Z. Leonard. Released June 14, 1914. Robert Z. Leonard portrays Sherlock Boob, who captures two swindlers with the help of the mayor disguised as a reporter.

2) *Sherlock Boob, Detective* (1915), a short silent comedy film. Produced by Crown City Film Manufacturing Co.; written by Anthony Coldeway; directed by Bruce M. Mitchell. Released Jan. 9, 1915. Frank Moore portrays Sherlock Boob, who winds up arresting a burro.

Sherlock Brown

Sherlock Brown (1922), a silent comedy film. Produced by Metro Pictures Corp.; written and directed by Bayard Veiller. Released June 26, 1922. Bert Lytell portrayed Sherlock Brown, who investigates the theft of a secret formula for a powerful explosive from the U.S. government.

Sherlock Bug

Another Tale (1914), featuring Sherlock Bug. A silent cartoon. Produced by Lubin Manufacturing Co.; written and directed by

Vincent Whitman. Released Apr. 28, 1914. Sherlock Bug, the great detective, traps a dangerous gang in Bugland.

Sherlock Chick
Sherlock Chick appeared in four children's books by Robert Quackenbush, all published by Parents Magazine: *Sherlock Chick's First Case* (1986), *Sherlock Chick and the Peekaboo Mystery* (1987), *Sherlock Chick and the Giant Egg Mystery* (1988), and *Sherlock Chick and the Case of the Night Noises* (1990). Sherlock Chick was hatched from his egg already wearing a deerstalker and holding a magnifying glass.

Sherlock Clones
1) "Sherlock Clones" is a science fiction story by Alex Boyd, published by Wattpad, an on-line site (Nov. 2012). The story is reported to have been taken "from the journal of a single-clone Watson."
2) Sherlock Clones is the identity assumed by Sherlock Holmes when "Sherlock meets Sherlock" in a science fictional setting as described on the Tumblr site of "Miniature Bucky" in 2014.

Sherlock Cohen
"Cohen, the Detective," featuring Sherlock Cohen and Wasserman. A skit on NBC's *Sneak Preview* program (July 11, 1943), which eventually became a short-lived series on the NBC Blue Radio Network for 10 episodes (Aug. 17-Oct. 18, 1943). Two partners in the clothing business solve mysteries. Sherlock Cohen was portrayed by John Brown.

Sherlock Combs
1) Sherlock Combs, "a defective detective," was a character in an adapted version of *Savageland* by Walter Ben Hare, a two-act musical comedy originally produced at Cornell University in 1912 (with a character named Shylock Bones) and performed by numerous community theatres in the 1920s and 1930s.
2) Sherlock Combs, "a great bumblebee detective," appeared in four episodes of "Toy Talkies," written and drawn by Walter Quermann for the Sunday Magazine section of the *St. Louis Post Dispatch*: "Sherlock Combs on the Job" (June 25, 1933), "Captured" (July 2, 1933), "The Judgment of Queen Buzz" (July 9, 1933),

and "Court Martialed" (Aug. 6, 1933). A paper-dolls style cut-out game for children with a short play script. Assisted by Dr. Dragon, a "snake doctor."

3) "The Adventure of the Sculptor's Arm," featuring Sherlock Combs. Robert R. Pattrick. *Sherlock in L.A. Catalogue*, No. 7 (1989). Assisted by Dr. J.H. Voltson.

4) Sherlock Combs was a recurring character in the opinion columns of Harry Reynolds, editor of the *Journal Gazette* of Mattoon, Illinois, beginning with "Elementary, My Dear" (June 1, 1970) and continuing through "Fat Democrat Behind Murder, Says Sherlock" (Mar. 13, 2004). In the earlier columns, Sherlock Combs is assisted by Dr. Vatson, who is replaced in later years by Dr. Clodson. In a typical column, "Sherlock Combs and the Hound of Dumpsterville" about a landfill issue (June 2, 1999), Combs consults Inspector Lastromie.

5) Sherlock Combs is the identity assumed when "Sherlock styles his hair," as suggested by Tumblr's "Knight of Time" in 2013.

Sherlock Cones

1) "Sherlock Cones" by Roy Messina was a winning artistic creation for "Construction 2003," an art contest sponsored by the Middletown, New Jersey, Department of Parks and Recreation. The sculpture, with deerstalker, pipe and magnifying glass, was on display in March 2003.

2) Sherlock Cones is the identity assumed when "Sherlock serves ice cream," as suggested by "John Watlock" on Tumblr (June 10, 2015).

Sherlock Dale

Sherlock Dale is the identity assumed by the chipmunk character in full Sherlockian dress when he decides to become a detective. In "The Defective Detective," in *Walt Disney's Chip 'n' Dale*, No. 17 (Dell Comics, Mar.-May 1959), he claims that "Sherlock Dale always nabs his mouse, even the hoppy kind." In "Sherlock's Last Case," in *Walt Disney's Chip 'n' Dale*, No. 50 (Gold Key Comics, Jan. 1978). Dale is determined to be a detective; but after a series of flops, Chip plots to get him to "quit Sherlockin' forever."

Sherlock Dalek

"The Sherlock Dalek," given the name Dalock Holmes was designed by the artist known as Adrienne D. as a combination of Sherlockian and Dr. Who themes. Daleks are an extraterrestrial race of mutants in the *Doctor Who* television series. The image is featured on various products, including prints, a throw pillow, t-shirts, hoody, wall clock, and laptop sleeve. Featured on Society6, an on-line marketer.

Sherlock Dodo

"Sherlock Dodo." Season 1, Episode 9, of *Animal Crackers*, an animated television series. Produced by Cinar Children's Entertainment for Alphanim; broadcast on Teletoons in Canada and Fox Family in the USA. First aired Nov. 1997. Voiced by Teddy Lee Dillon.

Sherlock Domes

Sherlock Domes and Dr. Watkins were characters appearing in at least two episodes of *Uncle Croc's Block*, a short-lived live action/animated series on ABC. Carl Ballentine portrayed Domes, and Stanley Adams portrayed Watkins.

Sherlock Doyle

Some Hero (1914), featuring Sherlock Doyle. A short silent comedy film. Produced by the Crystal Film Co.; directed by Phillips Smalley. Released May 31, 1914. Charles de Forrest portrayed Sherlock Doyle, who protects an heiress from her greedy uncle.

Sherlock Drones

1) Sherlock Drones is the identity assumed by *Star Wars'* C-3PO, with R2D2 as his Watson, in original on-line illustrations by an artist known as Mr. Broom of New California Republic (NCR) in 2014 (iFunny.com).

2) Sherlock Drones is a nickname "when someone who talks a lot tells you something inherently obvious" (inherentlyfunny.com, Apr. 27, 2015). Similarly, Sherlock Drones is the identity assumed by Sherlock Holmes when he "goes on and on about a case" as described on the Tumbler site of "Miniature Bucky" in 2014.

Sherlock Droopy

Droopy, Master Detective, an animated television series, featured "Sherlock Droopy" (Episode 2) and "Sherlock Droopy Gets Hounded" (Episode 6). Both first aired in 1993 on the Fox Television Network. Produced by Hanna-Barbera for Turner Entertainment. Assisted by Dr. Dripple. One segment has them protecting Becky Baskerveil from a family curse.

Sherlock Duck

"Sherlock Duck: The Adventure of the Animated Government." Robert A. Smith. *Star Reach*, No. 4 (Mar. 1976). Sherlock Duck assumes a disguise to pursue the case. "Evil was afoot, but then, it rarely takes the bus."

Sherlock False

They Came to Rob Hong Kong (1989), featuring Sherlock False, a slapstick film produced in Hong Kong by Cinema City & Films Co.; directed by Clarence Yiu-leung Fok. Dean Shen portrays Sherlock False.

Sherlock Ferret

The Adventures of Sherlock Ferret. Hugh Aston (Inknbeans Press, 2014). A collection of four stories featuring Sherlock Ferret and Watson Mouse, M.D., who live in the basement of Mrs. Hudson's bakery.

Sherlock Fink

"Wedding Detective," featuring Jerry Lewis as Sherlock Fink, was a skit on *The Colgate Comedy Hour* on NBC (Sept. 21, 1952). Detective Fink appears at Dean Martin's wedding, causing predictable disruption.

Sherlock Foams

1) "Swiped Sweets," an episode of *Lazy Town*, a children's television program produced in Iceland. Sherlock Foams is the name given to Robbie Rotten's detective character. Original airdate: Aug. 20, 2004.

2) Sherlock Foams is the identity assumed when "Sherlock shampoos," as suggested by "John Watlock" on Tumblr (June 10, 2015). Alternatively, Sherlock Foams is the identity assumed when

"Sherlock dyes his hair," as suggested by Nealee Fisher of "Nerds R Us" in response.

Sherlock Fumes

Sherlock Fumes was the subject of a joke submitted to the "Laugh Lines" blog column of *The New York Times* by Paul Seaburn on Jan. 24, 2008: "Scotland Yard is investigating the video that allegedly shows British singer Amy Winehouse smoking crack. They've got their best crack expert on it—Sherlock Fumes."

Sherlock Gnomes

1) "Sherlock Gnomes in South Africa" was a series of eight anonymously-written stories. They appeared in *Scraps* (James Henderson's Penny Weekly), a South African publication (Mar. 10-May 26, 1900). Assisted by Dr. Totson.
2) Sherlock Gnomes is the identity assumed by Sherlock Holmes when he "buys a large variety of common garden decorations," as described on the Tumblr site of "Miniature Bucky" in 2014.
3) Sherlock Gnomes is the identity assumed by a Hobbit-like Sherlock Holmes, as suggested by Nealee Fisher of "Nerds R Us" on Tumblr in response to similar puns posted on June 10, 2015.
4) *Sherlock Gnomes* (2018) is an animated film written by Andy Riley, Kevin Cecil, and Ben Zazove; directed by John Stevenson; and produced by Rocket Pictures, Metro-Goldwyn-Mayer, and Paramount Animation. "Garden gnomes Gnomeo and Juliet recruit renowned detective Sherlock Gnomes to investigate the mysterious disappearance of other garden ornaments." Gnomes is voiced by Johnny Depp. Released March 23, 2018.

Sherlock Goof

"Sherlock Goof." Season 2, Episode 11, of *Goof Troop*, an animated series on the Disney Channel and ABC. First aired Nov. 21, 1992. Produced by the Walt Disney Co.; written by Stephen Levi. Sherlock Goof is one of Goofy's ancestors, battling Professor Inferiority. Voiced by Bill Farmer.

Sherlock Groans

1) *Clancy and Company* was a local children's television program, set in a small detective agency, which aired on WCCO-TV,

Minneapolis, from 1963-67. Sherlock Groans, the founder of the agency, appeared only in a portrait.

2) Sherlock Groans is one of ten "alternative names for Sherlock Holmes" proposed by Mrs. Hudson in *Nursing Holmes*, a two-act play by Cenarth Fox (Fox Plays, 2009). Holmes discovers the list in his landlady's personal scrapbook.

3) Sherlock Groans is a character used for English as a Second Language (ESL) programs, including such exercises as "Sherlock Groans and the Lost Cat" and "Sherlock Groans Finds the Dog." Developed in 2009.

4) Sherlock Groans is the identity assumed by Sherlock Holmes when he "reacts to a (presumably very bad) joke," as described on the Tumblr site of "Miniature Bucky" in 2014.

Sherlock Guck

"Sherlock Guck, the Eskimo Detective," made eight appearances in *The Katzenjammer Kids* Sunday comic strips by Rudolph Dirks (Apr. 28-June 30, 1907). Distributed by the Hearst Newspaper Syndicate. Two are reprinted in *Sherlock Holmes in America* (Bill Blackbeard, ed.; Harry N. Abrams, 1981). Guck has his offices in an igloo and frequently disguises himself as polar animals. In the text of the comic strip, he refers to himself as Shurlock Guck.

Sherlock Haggis

Sherlock Haggis appeared in *The Glen Michael Cavalcade Annual* (1974), both on the cover and in a four-page comic strip, "Sherlock Holmes and Dr. Neeps." Sherlock Haggis appears in traditional Sherlockian costume, but with a kilt. The Scottish publication featured games, puzzles, cartoons, and stories for young people.

Sherlock Hams

1) "Sometimes I Think He Should Have Been Called Sherlock HAMS!" (Cartoon). Eric D. Clark. *The Evening Times* of Glasgow, Scotland (Dec. 28, 1968).

2) "The Hog of the Baskervilles," featuring Sherlock Hams and Dr. Whatswine. Lew Stringer (writer) and Ron Tiner (artist). *Oinki* (Fleetway Publications, Jan.-Feb. 1988). A British comic appearance.

Sherlock Harms

"Mister [Sherlock] Harms" is a one-time corruption of Sherlock Holmes' name in "The Adventure of the Eminent Collector" in *The Lost Stories of Sherlock Holmes* by Tony Reynolds (MX Publishing, 2010). Holmes and Watson try to ransom a priceless letter.

Sherlock Hawkshaw

The Mysterious Mystery! (1924), a short silent "Our Gang" comedy film, in which Mickey Daniels assumes the role of Sherlock Hawkshaw, who is searching for a wealthy kid being held for ransom. Produced by Hal Roach Studios; written by Hal Roach and H.M. Walker; directed by Robert F. McGowan. Released Dec. 14, 1924.

Sherlock Haymes

"The Great Superboy Doublecross," featuring Sherlock Haymes. *Adventure Comics*, No. 263 (DC Comics, Aug. 1959). Pa Kent, in disguise, hires the private detective Sherlock Haymes to find "the secret home and foster parents of Superboy" in an elaborate plan to repay a debt.

Sherlock Helms

1) "As American as Apple Spies," featuring Sherlock Helms. Arthur Hoppe. *The San Francisco Chronicle* (Jan. 16, 1974). In a Watergate scandal-related column, Sherlock Helms is "the incredible masterspy... in charge of spying on Government spies."
2) Sherlock Helms is a one-time corruption of Sherlock Holmes' name in "The Curse of Edwin Booth" by Carol Buggé. *Sherlock Holmes: The American Years* (Michael Kurland, ed.; Minotaur Books, 2010). "Blushing prettily," a young woman originally "from the slums of the Lower East Side" mistakenly greets Mr. Helms.

Sherlock Hemlock

1) Sherlock Hemlock, self-described "world's greatest detective," is one of Jim Henson's Muppets appearing on the *Sesame Street* television series between 1970 and 2012. The character was portrayed by Jerry Nelson. Sherlock Hemlock also appears in various printed forms, including the children's books *Sherlock Holmes and the Great Twiddlebug Mystery* by Betty Lou (Whitman Publishing,

1972), *The Case of the Missing Duckie* by Linda Hayward (Western Publishing, 1981) and *Sherlock Hemlock and the Creature from Outer Space* by Ray Sipherd (Western Publishing, 1981).

2) "If Sesame Street Branched Out into Specialized Avenues of Education," featuring Sherlock Hemlock on "Medical Street." Frank Jacobs (writer) and Jack Davis (artist). *Mad*, No. 203 (E.C. Publications, Dec. 1978).

3) "Wax Museum Mystery," featuring Sherlock Hemlock. *Walt Disney's Comics and Stories*, No. 460 (Gold Key Comics, Jan. 1979). At the Crime Wax Museum, "the newly acquired wax figure of Sherlock Hemlock was completely melted down."

Sherlock Hoax

"Sherlock Hoax with Dr. Puton in The Final Problem." Jon V. Wilmunen. *The Gamebag*, No. 4 (Dec. 1968).

Sherlock Hochmes

Sherlock Hochmes (1908), a lost Hungarian silent comedy film featuring Károly Baumann as Hochmes. Presumably lost, the plot satirized Holmes' ability to "know everything."

Sherlock Höek

"The Case Book of Sherlock Höek: As Told by Dr. S.J. Stupid, M.D." Scott Benson (writer) and Ken Mitchroney (artist). *The Ren & Stimpy Show*, No. 29 (Marvel Comics, Apr. 1995). An experimental scientist has disappeared, and Sherlock Höek needs Dr. Stupid's help to find him.

Sherlock Hoelms

Sherlock Hoelms is a one-time corruption of Sherlock Holmes' name in *The Secret Diary of Dr. Watson* by Anita Janda (Allison & Busby, 2001). Watson is irritated by a newspaper account of the deaths of "the eminent professor James Moriarty and his compatriot… S. Hoelms" and the reporter's refusal to use the first name, Sherlock.

Sherlock Hohms

Sherlock Hohms is the name utilized by Kenny Reese of Pennsylvania, who builds "limited edition exotic coils," which, for legal reasons, he has marketed as artistic jewelry "not intended for use in vape [vapor smoking] equipment" since 2017. He also posts tutorials and reviews on YouTube.

Sherlock Holmz

Sherlock Holmz and Doktor Watson appeared in four separate privately-produced short parodies by Vincent Stephani of Rochester, New York, in 1978. They were "The Adventure of the Twelve Celestials" (1 and 2), "The Curious Case of the Continuing Accumulator," and "The Poser of the Palpitating Panhard."

Sherlock Homeboy

1) P. Diddy portrayed Sherlock, and Will Smith appeared as Watson in a 2011 movie poster parody titled *Sherlock Homeboy*, a takeoff of the 2009 film *Sherlock Holmes*.
2) *Sherlock Homeboy* (July 26, 2012) and *Sherlock Homeboy, Part II* (Mar. 4, 2014, written by Dion Lack) are episodes in the comedy web series *King Bachelor's Pad*, starring Andrew Bachelor. Sherlock Homeboy "solves crimes with swag."

Sherlock Homeless

1) Sherlock Homeless is a recurring character in the British adult spoof/comic magazine *Viz*, which was founded in 1979. Sherlock Homeless solves crimes for the reward money, which is inevitably spent on beer.
2) Sherlock Homeless appears in a single cartoon by Richard Jolley: "Watson, I detect that we're totally skint." Jantoo Cartoons (June 25, 2012).

Sherlock Homely

Sherlock Homely appears in "A-Ha!" Season 2, Episode 7, of *Beetlejuice*, an animated television series. First aired Oct. 20, 1990, on ABC. Produced by Warner Brothers Television in cooperation with Tim Burton, Nelvana Ltd. and the Geffen Film Co.; directed by Robin Budd. Beetlejuice becomes the famed Netherworld detective Sherlock Homely to track down the missing car character Doomie.

Sherlock Homerun

Sherlock Homerun: A Whodunit Puppet Musical (2015). An interactive program for children performed in the greater Los Angeles region. Produced by Noteworthy Puppets. Music and lyrics by Kevin Noonchester and Jerry Reynolds.

Sherlock Homes

1) Sherlock Homes is mentioned in "Hashimura Togo—Detective," one of a series of stories about the Japanese character written by Wallace Irwin and distributed by the Associated Press (Oct. 30, 1910). Pursuing a case for the Slinkerton Detective Co., Togo decides that "now is the time to surround him with our Sherlock Homes abilities."

2) Sherlock Homes is the identity assumed when "Sherlock builds houses," as suggested by Tumblr's "Knight of Time" in 2013.

Sherlock Homes and Gardens

"In Hot Pursuit: A Study in Harlots," featuring Sherlock Homes and Gardens. Fran Lebowitz. *Metropolitan Life* (Dutton Studio Books, 1978). A gay-themed parody. Originally published in *Andy Warhol's Interview Magazine* (Feb. 1977).

Sherlock Homie

1) *Sherlock Homie: The Case of Isabella the Maneater* (1995), a pornographic film starring Sean Michaels as Sherlock Homie, "the greatest sleuth in the hood," and Julian St. Jox as Dr. Watsup. Michaels also directed.

2) *Sherlock Homie* was a fictitious film starring Tracy Jordan, the character portrayed by Tracy Morgan in *30 Rock*, a situation comedy on NBC from 2006 to 2013. The only reference to the film is the image of a poster on the NBC website.

Sherlock Homey

Sherlock Homey is the identity assumed by Skyler in the *Shoe* Sunday comic strip by Chris Cassatt and Gary Brookins (Sept. 21, 2008). Distributed by King Features. Two baseball caps are required for the transformation.

Sherlock Homo

1) Sherlock Homo is the detective in the anonymously-written pornographic tale "The Affair of the Disappearing Dildo" (*Hustler*, Nov. 1975).

2) Sherlock Homo is a character in a feature in the British adult spoof/comic magazine *Viz*, which was founded in 1979. He is an

outrageously gay version of Sherlock Holmes. Without evidence of any wrongdoing, he has well-built men stopped and searched using a ruse to investigate their backsides sighing "someday my prince will come."

3) *Sherlock Homo* was a three-episode gay-themed webcast featuring Andrew Laurich as Sherlock Homo and Craig Gaynier as Watson. Produced by White People TV. Episodes: "A Study in Lavender" (Aug. 16, 2009), "The Second Stain" (Oct. 7, 2009), and "The Confirmed Bachelor" (Jan. 31, 2010).

Sherlock Hones

Sherlock Hones Spy Gadgets and Gear is an online company offering such products as a "spy pen" for capturing hidden photos and videos, invisible ink pens and a UV flashlight. "The modern day Sherlock Hones is into the powers of deductive reasoning and gets the techno savvy spy gear and gadgets to help him along his way to solving the crime."

Sherlock Hong

Sherlock Hong is the hero of four children's novels by Don Bosco, all published by Marshall Cavendish International: *The Immortal Nightingale* (2012), *The Peranakan Princess* (2012), *The Scroll of Greatness* (2014), and *The Legend of Lady Yue* (2014). Sherlock Hong is a teenage detective working with the International Order of Young Seekers.

Sherlock Hoomes

Sherlock Hoomes is a deliberate corruption of Sherlock Holmes' name in "The Record of the Tarleton Murders," one of *The Elementary Cases of Sherlock Holmes* by Ian Chernock (Breese Books, 1999). An overbearing Count insists on addressing Sherlock Hoomes. "His manner was becoming annoying," but Sherlock Holmes is "completely unruffled."

Sherlock Hot Stuff

Hot Stuff in Sherlockian costume is featured in a story cycle including "Sherlock Hot Stuff," "What Happened to Santa," and "It's Elementary" in *Hot Stuff, the Little Devil*, No. 58 (Harvey Comics, Feb. 1954).

Sherlock Hound

1) *The Adventures of Sherlock Hound*. Brenda Sivers (Abelard Books). A series of five books for young readers, including *The Case of the Baffling Burglary* (1980), *Hound and the Witching Affair* (1980), *Hound in the Highlands* (1981), *Count Doberman of Pinscher* (1981), and *Hound and the Curse of Kali* (1982). Canine detective Sherlock Hound is assisted by Dr. Winston.

2) *Sherlock Hound* is a Japanese animated television series featuring an all-canine cast of characters. The 26 episodes first aired Nov. 6, 1984-May 21, 1985. Produced by Yoshimitsu Takahashi for Tokyo Movie Shinsha and for Italian public broadcasting corporation RAI. Directed by Hayao Miyazaki and Kyosuke Mikuriya. Sherlock Hound is a genius and an expert in many fields. Released in six DVD sets by Pioneer Entertainment in 2002. Voiced in English by Larry Moss.

3) *Sherlock Hound and the Case of the Foul Smell* and *Sherlock Hound and the Mysterious Missing Pumpkin*. Scott Ross (Unicorn Publishing House, 1993). Illustrated books for children.

4) *Sherlock Hound*. Karen Wallace (Scholastic Children's Books, 2002). A series of four books for young readers, including *The Case of the Disappearing Necklace*, *The Case of the Fiendish Dancing Footprints*, *The Case of the Gulping Bluebells*, and *The Case of the Howling Armour*. Sherlock Hound battles his enemy, Dr. Ha Ha Hyena.

5) "The Dog Detective," featuring Sherlock Hound and Dr. Westieson. Laurie Fraser Manifold (*The Serpentine Muse*, Summer 2016). A cartoon appearance, with Waggins (posing as a paper boy) at 221B Biscuit St.

Sherlock Hounds

Bitsy the dog assumes the role of "the world's greatest detective Sherlock Hounds" in the *Marvin* comic strip by Tom Armstrong distributed by North American Syndicate, Inc., in 12 daily strips (Apr. 4-14, 2001). In full Sherlockian costume, Sherlock Hounds helps Marvin track the Easter Bunny.

Sherlock Hums

1) "B-Men: The Adventures of Sherlock Hums." A children's story, set in the Bee Detective Bureau. *Mickey Mouse Weekly*, Holiday

Special 1936, a British publication. Reprinted in *As It Might Have Been: A Collection of Sherlockian Parodies from Unlikely Sources* (Robert C.S. Adey, ed.; Calabash Press, 1998). Assisted by Watson Bee.

2) Sherlock Hums is the subject of a short joke in "You're Telling Me" by William Ritt, a syndicated feature of the Central Press Association in July 1964. "Ha! The Adventure of the Burgled Bees. Sounds like a perfect case for that grand old detective Sherlock Hums."

3) Sherlock Hums is mentioned in *Gordo*, a daily comic strip by Gus Arriola, on Oct. 24, 1982. Distributed by United Feature Syndicate. A hummingbird likes "anything by Papa Hummingway or Sherlock Hums."

Sherlock Jones

1) "Sherlock Jones and the Telephone." A short, anonymously written sketch, credited to the *San Francisco Post* and reprinted in various American newspapers (June 1896). Sherlock Jones makes deductions about a law clerk originally from "the agricultural districts."

2) Sherlock Jones is a corruption of Sherlock Holmes' name in *The Whims of Erasmus* by W. Carter Platts (Digby, Long & Co., 1902). The reference is made in Chapter 13, "Mr. Sherlock Holmes Tuttlebury."

3) Sherlock Jones appeared in two anonymously-written short sketches in *The American Hatter*: "Sherlock Jones's Waterloo" (Aug. 1902) and "Sherlock Jones's Advice" (Dec. 1902). Both were credited to *The Hatman*, a publication of The Crofut & Knapp Co.

4) Sherlock Jones, detective, made two appearances in "The Adventures of Sleepy Sam," a one-panel cartoon series in the *Wilkes-Barre (Pennsylvania) News* (July 23 and 25, 1907). Written and drawn by an artist known only as Caffrey.

5) "A Dark Mystery Laid Bare: Sherlock Jones, the Boy Detective, Gets on the Job and Discovers the Plot." Anonymous, but credited to the *Kansas City Star* and reprinted in various American newspapers (Nov. 1909). Revised and retitled "Foiled Again by Sherlock Jones," with the hero transformed into a "new reporter fresh from the big university." Sherlock Jones pursues suspects who are exchanging "mysterious papers."

6) Sherlock Jones was a character in *Picalilli*, a three-act musical comedy written by Margaret Vaughn and presented ay the Mason City (Iowa) High School (Apr. 13, 1936). Sherlock Jones, "a famous detective" portrayed by Arch Gamm, searches for a missing pickle recipe.

7) Sherlock Jones was an often-sarcastic, yet apt, nickname for the heroine of the syndicated *Tallulah/Jezabelle Jones* comic strip by Ira "Yar" Yarbrough (Feb. 6, Feb. 23, and Mar. 19, 1952). "I gave you more credit than you deserve, Miss Sherlock Jones," sneers a mobster just prior to his downfall.

8) *The Case of the Aluminum Crutch: The Casebook of "Sherlock" Jones*. Lester Heath (Dell Publishing Co., 1963). A young man with polio comes to Sherlock Jones with a threatening note, then disappears.

9) Sherlock Jones was a one-time nickname for the hero of *Davy Jones*, a sea adventure comic strip by Al McWilliams (Aug. 16, 1963). "Elementary, my dear Marino," responds Jones as he searches for a suspect in the sabotage of a marina.

10) Sherlock Jones, a monkey, twice appears in mathematics puzzles for children: "Number Trail" in *The Big Book of Puzzles* and "Snow Tracks" in *The Second Big Book of Puzzles*. Michael Holt and Ronald Ridout (Alfred A. Knoph, 1972).

11) "Sherlock Jones," a Victorian-era comedy sketch with Sammy Davis, Jr., in the title role, was featured on *NBC Follies* (Dec. 27, 1973). Peter Lawford portrayed Dr. Watson.

12) "The Adventures of Sherlock Jones." Sol Weinstein and Howard Albrecht (*Playboy*, July 1975). Sherlock Jones, the "ebony master of deduction," and Dr. Datsun, "the Japanese martial arts king," investigate the theft of a revolutionary new automobile engine.

13) Sherlock Jones and his sister Amanda were featured in four "Hidden Clue Mysteries" for young people age 7-11, written by Andrew Bromberg and published by Greenwillow Books in 1982: *Computer Overbyte*, *Rubik's Ruse*, *The House on Blackthorn Hill*, and *Flute Revenge*. Readers use a "clue sheet" to help them solve the cases themselves.

14) "Sherlock Jones, Wrestling Detective" appeared in *Steel Pulse: Pro Wrestling Adventures*, including "Death Grip" by Dennis J. Pimple (writer) and Richard W. Florence (artist) in No. 1 (Spring

1986); and "The UWC Honors Guild" by T. Motley (writer and artist) in No. 3 (Summer 1987).

15) *The Real Adventures of Sherlock Jones and Proctor Watson* (1987), a series of ten half-hour programs for children using puppets and child actors to address everyday problems. Mark Ritts voiced Sherlock Jones. Produced by the Southwest Texas Public Broadcasting Council and distributed by PBS. Directed by Leo Eaton. Originally aired Jan. 4-Mar. 8, 1987.

16) "The Mall and the Night Visitor," featuring Sherlock Jones, was a musical comedy play presented at the Hibberd Middle School of Richmond, Indiana (Dec. 15, 1988). An angel is sent to earth disguised as Sherlock Jones to find "the true Christmas spirit" in a shopping mall. Sandy Bhangoo portrayed Sherlock Jones.

17) *The Adventures of Sherlock Jones* was an original half-hour television comedy written and produced by Pat Basara and performed by the Monroe Township (New Jersey) Youth Theatre (Sept. 1996), and subsequently aired on the local cable system. A 10-year-old detective solves mysteries with his classmates.

18) *Sherlock Jones.* Ed Dunlop (Journey Forth, 2005). A series of four books for young people, including *The Assassination Plot*, *The Missing Diamond*, *The Phantom Airplane*, and *The Willoughby Bank Robbery*. Christian fiction for young readers, featuring a crime-fighting young detective with brilliant powers of deductive reasoning.

19) *No Sh*t Sherlock: A Sherlock Jones Mystery* by Randy Moore (Privately Published, 2018). A modern-day hard-boiled detective at the low end of the profession, Sherlock Jones gets the chance to investigate an actual murder in Atlanta's gritty underworld.

Sherlock Key

"Claude Debussy Meets Sherlock Key!" was a musical concert for children age six and up, featuring the music of Debussy, who is "arrested for musical anarchy" and rescued by Sherlock Key. Presented by the Chamber Music Society of Lincoln Center in 2012.

Sherlock Klotz

"The Odd Boxes Caper," featuring Sherlock Klotz. Season 1, Episode 3, of *Cool McCool*, an animated television series, first aired Sept. 24, 1966. Produced by King Features Syndicate for NBC;

created by Bob Kane. Sherlock Klotz pursues escaped prisoner Jack-in-the-Box.

Sherlock Kush

The Adventures of OG Sherlock Kush, an animated web series created by Joseph Carnegie in 2015 as part of the *Animation Domination* programming on the FXX Network. The voice of Sherlock Kush is provided by Peter Serafinowicz.

Sherlock Mario

"The Adventures of Sherlock Mario." Season 1, Episode 18, of *The Super Mario Bros. Super Show!*, an animated television series (one of three series based on the video game). Produced by DiC Animation for syndication by Viacom Enterprises. Mario assumes the identity of Sherlock Mario to find the missing Herlock Solmes, encountering Professor Kooparity and the Killer Kitty of the Kaskervilles along the way.

Sherlock Moans

1) "Who was the most famous ghost detective? Sherlock Moans." Included in *Puns Spoken Here: Word Play for Halloween*. Richard Lederer (Wryrick & Co., 2006).
2) "Sherlock Moans" was an episode on *The 313 Show*, a web comedy sketch series, featuring Nicholas Anscombe as Sherlock Moans, as published on YouTube on May 14, 2013. Written by Michael Monkhouse.
3) Sherlock Moans is the identity assumed when "Sherlock has an orgasm," as suggested by Tumblr's "Knight of Time" in 2013. The name is used frequently by the authors of "slash fiction."

Sherlock Monk

Sherlock Monk (a monkey) and his assistant Chuck (a duck) were recurring characters in *Fawcett's Funny Animals*, a comic book which ran for 83 issues, from 1942 to 1954, published by Fawcett Publications, and continued in *Funny Animals*, published by Charlton Comics. The character also appeared as a secondary feature in Charlton's *Hoppy the Marvel Bunny* (1946-47) and *Atomic Rabbit*, No. 2 (Oct. 1955). Created and drawn by Jim Scancarelli.

Sherlock Moose
"Sherlock Moose and the Moose of the Baskervilles." Bob Foster. *Crazy Super Special*, No. 70 (Jan. 1981). An illustration accompanying the feature "The History of Moosekind, Pt. X."

Sherlock Mouse
"The Hound of Basketville: Starring Sherlock Mouse and Dr. Goofy." *Walt Disney's Comics and Stories*, No. 300 (Gold Key Comics, Sept. 1965). The 25th Anniversary Issue of this title, with Mickey Mouse in the leading role.

Sherlock Murphy
Radio Times (Jan. 19-25, 1985) features a cover photo of Les Dawson "as clueless sleuth Sherlock Murphy" in his new BBC Radio 2 program, *Listen to Les*.

Sherlock Oan
Sherlock Oan appeared in full Sherlockian dress as a phony detective in "15 Things That Are Wrong with Identity Crisis," an episode of *Atop the Fourth Wall*, a web series "where bad comics burn." Produced by Lewis Lovhaug; published on YouTube (Apr. 20, 2015). Sherlock Oan is portrayed by Kyle Kallgren.

Sherlock Ohms
1) "The Case of the Unknown Quantity." *Sherlock Ohms and Dr. Watts* (Promotional Publishing Co., 1958). A comic book from "The Better Light Better Sight Bureau."
2) Sherlock Ohms was the disguise of Boris Badenov in the "Missouri Mish Mash" episodes of the third season of the animated television series *The Rocky and Bullwinkle Show* (Nov. 12-Dec. 31, 1961). Produced by Jay Ward Productions for NBC. Voiced by Paul Frees.
3) Sherlock Ohms and Dr. Watts were featured in a series of stories by Steven Tomashefsky: "Doctor Negative: An Adventure of Sherlock Ohms and Dr. Watts" in *Studies in Scarlet*, No. 2 (Dec. 1965); "The Adventure of Isadora Persano" in *The Baker Street Journal*, Vol. 16, No. 4 (Dec. 1966); and "The Colossal Schemes of Baron Maupertuis" in serial form in *Baker Street Pages*, Nos. 9-16 (1966). Two of these appeared under the pseudonym of "S'ian Lemming."

4) Inspector Sherlock Ohms of Standard International Yard appeared in an anonymously-written, pun-filled short adventure "Sherlock Ohm's Law" in the *Boston College Chemical Bulletin* (1988). Ohms suffers a flat tire in Recipro City.

5) A long-standing joke among electricians is "Q: Who solves mysteries involving electricians? A: Sherlock Ohms." Included in *101 Amazing Jokes* by Jack Goldstein (Andrews UK, 2013).

6) Sherlock Ohms is "a hand-made artisan e-liquid" for vapor smoking, developed and manufactured in the United Kingdom since 2015. The product comes in three flavors: Bohemian Scandal, Yellow Face, and Noble Bachelor.

7) Sherlock Ohms and John Watts-On are featured in t-shirts, hoodies, and sweatshirts marketed by Look Human, an on-line merchandising company headquartered in Columbus, Ohio. The products have been available since 2016.

8) Sherlock Ohms and Dr. Wattson are electricity-related comic characters created by Mehul Gupta of New Delhi. Featured in "Science Jokes" on pinterest.com. Posted on that site in 2017.

Sherlock Ol-mes

Sherlock Ol-mes appeared in a long series of fantastic and rollicking early-20th Century pastiches "counterfeited in the pulp factories of Barcelona," according to Ellery Queen. Anonymously written by various hands and distributed throughout the Spanish-speaking world.

Sherlock Oomph

A Villainous Villain (1916), featuring Sherlock Oomph. A short silent comedy film. Produced by the Vitagraph Co. of America; written by G. Graham Baker; directed by Larry Semon. Released Sept. 8, 1916. Hughie Mack portrays Sherlock Oomph, who saves his sweetheart from a dastardly criminal.

Sherlock Otis

"The Case of the Black Feather," featuring Cabbage Patch doll Otis Lee as "Sherlock Otis." *Xavier Roberts' Collector's Dispatch* (Winter 1987). A children's story.

Sherlock Phones

Sherlock Phones is the identity assumed when "Sherlock needs help," as suggested by "John Watlock" on Tumblr (June 10, 2015).

Sherlock Pimple

Flivver's Famous Cheese Hound (1915), featuring Sherlock Pimple. A short silent comedy film, starring Fred Evans. Produced by Piccadilly Film Productions; directed by Charles Weston. Released Jan. 21, 1916. Also known as *Pimple's Million Dollar Mystery*. A detective tracks down a bank robber and fights him on the roof of a train.

Sherlock Pinky

Sherlock Pinky appears in "Pinky Squeaks." Season 2, Episode 15, of *Pinky Pinky Doo*, an animated television series. Created by Jim Jinkins; produced by Sesame Workshop/Cartoon Pizza for Nick Jr. In Victorian England, the famous detective Sherlock Pinky is called to help a renowned composer solve "The Case of the Funny Sound." Voiced by India Ennenga. First aired Nov. 1, 2008.

Sherlock Q. Jones

Sherlock Q. Jones's Casebook of Puzzles, Riddles & Muddles and *More Puzzles, Riddles & Muddles from Sherlock Q. Jones's Casebook*. John Pinkney (Watermill Press, 1992). Sherlock Q. Jones, "the world's sloppiest sleuth," encourages readers to help solve sticky problems and assorted brain teasers. Assisted by his faithful dog Watson.

Sherlock Roams

1) Sherlock Roams was a character in "The Keramos Club Revue," a combination minstrel/comedy program staged at the Ceramic Theatre of East Liverpool, Ohio (Mar. 6, 1919). Sherlock Roams and Dr. Spotzum solve a mystery at the Café Rivoli. The detective was portrayed by Doc Bode.
2) Sherlock Roams is the identity assumed under separate yet similar circumstances on Tumblr: when "Sherlock goes on an adventure," as suggested by "Knight of Time" (2013); when "Sherlock goes on a road trip and gets lost," as described on the site of "Miniature Bucky" (2014); and when "Sherlock travels," as suggested by "John Watlock" (June 10, 2015).

Sherlock Romes

1) "The Affair of the Lost Compression," featuring [Sherlock] Romes and Scotson. Anonymous (as "Croton Oyle"). *The Car Magazine: The Monthly Review of Travel* (1903). Reprinted in *The Affair of the Lost Compression and Other Stories* (Ferret Fantasy, 1975). Romes and Scotson investigate what they suspect is the sabotage of an automobile to be used in an important race.

2) "The Adventure of the Strong Odor," featuring Sherlock Romes and Dr. Rotson. A short joke, attributed to the *Cincinnati Enquirer* and reprinted in various other American newspapers (Mar. 1912). Romes evaluates "the unsuspecting suspect."

Sherlock Rooms

Sherlock Rooms is one of seven parody names in "Prize Detective Story." Anonymous (*The Weekly Magazine*, May 8, 1897). Retitled "Holmes and the Startled Banker" in *As It Might Have Been: A Collection of Sherlockian Parodies from Unlikely Sources* (Robert C.S. Adey, ed.; Calabash Press, 1998). Hemlock Coombs repeatedly changes his name as he makes a series of trivial deductions.

Sherlock Sam

Sherlock Sam is a series children's books featuring Samuel Tan Cher-Lock by A.J. Low (Adan Jimenez and Felicia Low-Jimenez), published by Andrews McMeel Publishing (2013): *Sherlock Sam and the Missing Heirloom in Katong*, *Sherlock Sam and the Ghostly Moans in Fort Canning*, and *Sherlock Sam and the Sinister Letters in Bras Basah*. Set in Singapore, Sam is assisted by his robot, Watson.

Sherlock Shamrock

"The Adventures of Sherlock Shamrock: Table of Contents." Henry W. Gould (as "Patrick O'Conan Donegal"). Supposedly published by the "Erin Go Bragh Irregular Book Co., 1895." A one-page imaginary table of contents for The Scion of the Four of Morgantown, West Virginia (on St. Patrick's Day, Mar. 17, 1976).

Sherlock Shamus

Sherlock Shamus is an alternative name for "*Sesame Street*'s resident detective," as conceived by Chester Alan Marshall in "Horse Sense," a quiz for the *Cincinnati Enquirer* (Jan. 14, 1981).

Sherlock Sholem
Sherlock Sholem made two appearances in "*The New York Magazine* Competition" by Mary Ann Madden. In Competition No. 473 (Apr. 25, 1983) Judy Price suggests "The Adventures of Sherlock Sholem—Memoirs of 221B Baker Street" in response to an earlier anagram challenge. In Competition No. 822 (May 8, 1995), "Sherlock Sholem—Israeli detective in relentless pursuit of his nemesis, Professor Yom Tirra" is the example given for the challenge of the day.

Sherlock Sholom
"Sherlock Sholom, the World's Smartest Detective." *Alefbet Pop-Up and Storybook*. Sol Scharfstein (KATV Publishing House, 1984). An educational aid for learning the Hebrew alphabet.

Sherlock Sleuth
Sherlock Sleuth (1925), a short silent comedy film, starring Arthur Stone. Produced by Hal Roach Studios; written by H.M. Walker; directed by Ralph Ceder. Released July 12, 1925. The house detective of the Hotel Omigosh pursues a notorious thief known as "the Weasel."

Sherlock Slick
"Sherlock Slick, The Schoolboy Dick." Bob Monkhouse (writer and artist). *Smasher Comics*, No. 1 (Themes), 1947. A British comic appearance in which Sherlock Slick stops a bully from stealing deliveries from the butcher's errand boy.

Sherlock Sloans
"Sherlock Sloans Takes the Mystery Out of Food Shopping," a brochure for Sloan's Family Supermarkets. An advertisement promoting the brochure is reproduced in *Communication*, No. 38 (April 4, 1978), the newsletter of the Pleasant Places of Florida.

Sherlock Snoop
Snoop, or The Case of the Yellow Judge, featuring Sherlock Snoop and Dr. Whatsup. A play by Paul Hansard. Performed at Hintlesham Hall in London in Nov. 1975. Snoop and Whatsup live in 221B Grocer Street and encounter Inspector Les Trade.

Sherlock Soames

1) "The Alibi," featuring [Sherlock] Soames and Potson. E.V. Knox (as "Evoe") in his collection *Fancy Now!* (Methuen & Co., 1924). Despite all the evidence against him, a murder suspect establishes an alibi with the help of Soames and Daylight Savings Time.

2) "The Adventure of the Fifty Percent Solution," featuring [Sherlock] Soames and Muffin. Gahan Wilson (*The National Lampoon*, April 1978). Soames and Muffin succeed in saving the Alsatian Submarine Treaty after other famous detectives fail.

Sherlock Sooty

Sooty & Co., a children's television series, featured "Sherlock Sooty Visits" (1995) and "The Return of Sherlock Sooty & Dr. Wosit" (1998). Produced by Granada Television and released on the ITV Network; created by Matthew Corbett. The characters are hand puppets.

Sherlock Stones

"Sherlock Stones: Master Detective of Bedrock," featuring Fred Flintstone as Sherlock Stones and Barney Rubble as Dr. Whetstone. Paul Kupperberg (writer), and Fernando Yache and Mike DeCarlo (artists). *The Flintstones and the Jetsons*, No. 20 (DC Comics, Cartoon Network Series, April 1999). Fred wants to prove that he is "just as good a detective as Sherlock Stones."

Sherlock Thrones

Sherlock Thrones is one of ten "alternative names for Sherlock Holmes" proposed by Mrs. Hudson in *Nursing Holmes*, a two-act play by Cenarth Fox (Fox Plays, 2009). Holmes discovers the list in his landlady's personal scrapbook.

Sherlock Tones

1) Sherlock Tones is an "Electro Pop Hip Hop" band from Oakland, California, active since 2009. Their music is described as "an electric alternative hip hop sound with pop sensibility." Sherlock Tones' first studio album, "Saturn's Return" was released in 2010.

2) Sherlock Tones is the identity assumed when "Sherlock dyes his hair," as suggested by Nealee Fisher of "Nerds R Us" on Tumblr in response to similar puns posted on June 10, 2015.

Sherlock Troll

Sherlock Troll appeared in the Sunday comic strip *Broom Hilda* by Russ Myers (Dec. 6, 1971). Irwin Troll, in Sherlockian costume, is determined to rid the world of the "arch-fiend" Professor Broom-Hilda.

Sherlock Watkins

Sherlock Watkins, "the arm of the law," is a character in *Thompson of the Varsity: A College Comedy in Three Acts*. Edward M. Harris (Penn Publishing Co., 1918). The play was originally staged in 1910.

Sherlock Watson

1) "Sherlock Watson's Last Case." A.F. Arnold. *The Amateur Mart* (March and May, 1935). A mystery in two parts.
2) Sherlock Watson is the identity assumed when "Sherlock gets married" (presumably to Dr. Watson) as suggested by "John Watlock" on Tumblr (June 10, 2015). The idea of a sexual relationship and even marriage of the two characters is a favorite of "slash fiction" authors.

Sherlock Wholmes

"Sherlock Wholmes, the Doctor and Whatson." Sarshi. A comedic crossover mash-up of Sherlock Holmes and *Dr. Who*, posted on fanfiction.com (Aug. 19, 2010). A tale involving space ships traveling through time, exploding universes, and immortal people.

Sherlock Woof

Robbing the Fishes (1916), featuring Sherlock Woof, a short silent comedy film. Produced by the Edison Company; written by Earle Edwards; directed by Will Louis. Sherlock Woof, a supporting character, was portrayed by Raymond McKee. Released May 17, 1916.

Sherlock Yack

1) *Sherlock Yack: Zoo Detective* was a series of seven French children's books written by Michel Amelin and illustrated by Ruth Christelle (Milan Jeunesse, 2006-07), with such titles as *Who Strangled the Tiger?* and *Who Knotted the Python?* The "new zoo puzzles" invited readers to solve the mystery themselves.

2) *Sherlock Yack: Zoo Detective* was an animated children's television series of 52 episodes (13 minutes each) based on the books by Michel Amelin. Produced for Mondo TV of France and distributed throughout Europe (May 4, 2011-Dec. 22, 2012). Directed by Jerome Mouscadet. Voiced by Martial le Minoux. Sherlock Yack is the zoo's manager as well as its detective. Viewers actively join in the investigation.

Sherlock Zones
Sherlock Zones is the identity assumed when "Sherlock gets sleepy," as suggested by "John Watlock" on Tumblr (June 10, 2015).

Sherlocko
The Robbery at the Railroad Station (1912), a silent short comedy film, featuring Sherlocko in full Sherlockian costume. Also known as *Sherlocko and Watso*. Produced by Champion Film Co. Released Feb. 26, 1912. Sherlocko conducts a minute investigation as he pursues a daring robber who has stolen a lantern from a railway official.

Sherlocko Homo
"The Affair of the Disappearing Dildo." John Hegenberger. (*Hustler Magazine*, Nov. 1975). Assisted by Dr. Twatson. Pornographic.

Sherlocko Smith
Miss Sherlocko Smith, a department store detective, appeared in one of four cartoons by T.E. Powers in "When We Have Women Detectives" distributed by the Hearst Newspaper Syndicate on Mar. 17, 1912. Reprinted in *Sherlock Holmes in America* (Bill Blackbeard, ed.; Harry N. Abrams, 1981).

Sherlocko the Monk
Sherlocko the Monk: A Complete Compilation, 1910-1912. Gus Mager (Hyperion Press, 1977). The character first appeared in 1910 with his partner Watso, but was eventually scrapped after Arthur Conan Doyle threatened legal action. Mager based his later character, Hawkshaw the Detective, on Sherlocko the Monk.

Sherlocks Combs

Click, Cluck (1921), a musical comedy for the stage, originally presented at Cornell University in the fall of 1921, then reworked (*i.e.*, cleaned up) for the annual review of the American Legion of Logan, Utah (Dec. 10, 1921). Written and directed by A.B. Cusworth, who also portrayed Sherlocks Combs.

Sherlockz Homz

A Study in Skarlit (1915), featuring Sherlockz Homz. A short silent comedy film. Produced by Comedy Combine for the Sunny South Film Co.; written and directed by Fred Evans and Will Evans. Released Dec. 1915. Sherlockz Homz (portrayed by Fred Evans) faces off against the master criminal Professor Moritorium (portrayed by his uncle, Will Evans).

Sherlog Combes

"When the Spirits Rapped: A Nasty Incident in the Career of Sherlog Combes." Anonymous (*London Opinion*, March 29, 1919). Followed by "Baffled: Another Adventure of the Dear Old Has-Been, Sherlog Combes" (June 7, 1919). Both are reprinted in *As It Might Have Been: A Collection of Sherlockian Parodies from Unlikely Sources* (Robert C.S. Adey, ed.; Calabash Press, 1998). Assisted by Potson. The stories are satirical statements about Arthur Conan Doyle's work in spiritualism.

Sherlook Ohms

"The Case of the Missing Joules: A Chem Gem Necklace," featuring Detective Inspector Sherlook Ohms of Standard International Yard. Gene Doty (*Journal of Chemical Education*, July 1960). Reprinted in *Chemistry* (Sept. 1969). An unusual use of a large number of chemical and scientific terms.

Sherlopp Homes

"The Cannonball Caper," featuring Bugs Bunny in his "Sherlopp Homes hat, which always brings out my detective genius." *Bugs Bunny*, No. 194 (Gold Key Comics, Mar. 1978).

Sherluck Bones

Sherluck Bones Mystery-Detective Book (Volumes 1-6). Jim and Mary Razzi (Bantam Skylark Books, 1981-1984). Followed by *The Search for King Pup's Tomb* (Bantam Books, 1985). Canine detective Sherluck Bones, a reincarnation of Dennis Bones (who was created by the same authors), is assisted by Scotson in presenting mysteries that contain clues that allow young readers to find a solution.

Sherly Holmes
Sherly Holmes was a character on Episode 2 of *Showreel* (Mar. 23, 2013), a web series about the film, television and theatre industries. In a segment titled "Behind the Lens—Writing: An Informative Guide," Amanda Bacchi portrayed Sherly Holmes, with Courtney Becht as Joan Watson. Produced by 31 Digital.

Sherman Holmes
The Return of the World's Greatest Detective (1976), a television movie featuring Larry Hagman as Sherman Holmes, a Los Angeles policeman who hits his head in an accident and wakes thinking he is Sherlock Holmes. Assisted by Dr. Joan Watson (portrayed by Jenny O'Hara). Intended to be a series pilot. Produced by Universal Television for NBC; directed and co-written (with Roland Kibbee) by Dean Hargrove. First aired June 16, 1976.

Sherman Homes
Bride of Frankenstien, featuring Sherman Homes. A play by Tim Kelly (Pioneer Drama Service, 1976). A "comedy-horror show" in two acts, with Sherman Homes, a private investigator and karate expert.

Sherman Horn
"The Singular Affair of the Aluminium Crutch," featuring Sherman Horn and Wilson. Arthur Porges. *Three Porges Parodies and a Pastiche* (Magico Magazine, 1988). Reprinted in *The Adventures of Stately Homes and Sherman Horn* (Battered Silicon Dispatch Box, 2008). The strange circumstances of the death of a wealthy yacht owner who was washed overboard after tossing away his crutch.

Sherman Sherlock
"The Strange Case of Eili Ekaf," featuring Sherman Sherlock. *Bunny*, No. 20 (Harvey Comics, Dec. 1971). Vacationing at the beach, Sherman Sherlock arrests the wrong man in a kidnapping case.

Shermlock Shomes

"Shermlock Shomes!" Harvey Kurtzman (writer) and Bill Elder (artist). *Mad*, No. 7 (Educational Comics, Oct./Nov. 1953). The character reappears in "Shermlock Shomes in The Hound of the Basketballs." Harvey Kurtzman (writer) and Bill Elder (artist). *Mad*, No. 16 (Educational Comics, Oct. 1954). Both features have been reprinted many times. Assisted by Dr. Whatsit, Shermlock Shomes battles against Arty-Morty.

Sherrinford Holmes

1) *The Incredible Umbrella*, featuring Sherrinford Holmes as well as Sherlock Holmes. Marvin Kaye (Doubleday, 1979). Sherrinford Holmes, assisted by Ormand Sacker, exists because of a "dimensional transfer" in a fantasy involving literary characters from an "unpublished manuscript."
2) The name Sherrinford Holmes is an alias used by a supposedly dead Sherlock Holmes in *Lestrade and the Hallowed House* by M.J. Trow (Regnery Publishing, 1999).

Sherringham Holmes

Sherringham Holmes is a one-time corruption of Sherlock Holmes' name in "The Case of the Wrong-Wise Boots," a story in *Sherlock Holmes's School for Detection* by Simon Clark (Constable Robinson, 2017). Holmes' client has supposedly been dead for two years.

Sherslav Glomsky

"The Adventure of the Sinister American," featuring Sherslav Glomsky. John Boardman. *Double Action Detective and Mystery Stories*, No. 19 (Aug. 1959). Glomsky investigates the case of a vanished football player. Assisted by Dr. Ivan Vatsov, with Inspectors Gregsov and Lestradsky.

Sherwood Hoakes

The very first parody of Sherlock Holmes was "Adventures of Sherwood Hoakes: An Interrupted Honeymoon" by C.C. Rothwell (writing as "A Cone and Oil") in *Ludgate Weekly* (April 9, 1892). This story was quickly followed in the same magazine by "Adventures of Sherwood Hoakes: The Yellow Cockroach" (May 28, 1892). Both are reprinted in *My Evening with Sherlock Holmes*

(John Michael Gibson and Richard Lancelyn Green, eds.; Ferret, 1981).

Sherwood Holmes

The Very Great Grandson of Sherlock Holmes, featuring Sherwood Holmes. Bill Majeski (Dramatic Publishing Co., 1976) and *Sherlock Holmes' Grandson Goes Hollywood* (Dramatic Publishing Co, 1988). Although not quite up to his grandfather's abilities, Sherwood Holmes nevertheless manages to solve some murder mysteries.

Sherwood Homes

1) *The Case of the Disappearing Business Traveller*. British Overseas Airways Corp. (Nov. 1967). Assisted by Dr. Whartson. An advertising booklet.
2) "The Adventure of the Roof-Top Marauder," featuring Sherwood Homes. Bruce R. Beaman. *From the Mantelpiece* (Dec. 1978). Assisted by Waffles.

Sherwood House

Sherwood House and Doctor Waters appear in "He Digs Candy: A You-Solve-It" by Laird Long. *Mystery Weekly Magazine* (Oct. 2016). House investigates the theft of a bag of candy from one of Waters' sons.

Sherwood Lang

Some Cases of Sherwood Lang. C. Warren Delves (Drane's, 1924). Assisted by Dr. Warner in four short stories: "The Curse," "A Discovery in Devon," "The Disappearance of Mr. Reynolds," and "Mr. Kerr, Financier."

Sheryl Lock Holmes

Sheryl Locke Holmes Mysteries are a series of short stories by Cassie L. Exline, published by Wild Child Publishing. They include "Amber's Mysterious Death" (2009), "Ruby's Deadly Secret" (2010), "Opal's Disappearance" (2011), and "Dragon's Pearl" (2013). Assisted by Dot Watson, Sheryl Lock Holmes inherits an antique shop and finds herself investigating cases related to characters named for gemstones.

Shih Lok
"The Adventure of La Soupe Chinoise," featuring Shih Lok. Mac-Lean O'Spelin. *Ellery Queen's Mystery Magazine* (Oct. 1975). Assisted by Wa Tze-na.

Shilah Coombes
"The Adventure of the Rubber Pipe: A Memoir of Shilah Coombes, Chronicled by His Friend Dr. Thatson." Anonymous. In: *Twenty-Five Detective Stories* (George Newnes, Ltd., 1910). A young woman consults Coombes about her father's mysterious death, leading to an anarchist plot.

Shirknot Holmes
An Adventure of Shirknot Holmes (1902), a play featuring E. Howard Shepard as Shirknot Holmes, apparently staged in London at the Royal Academy Schools Show, the annual exhibition for final year students. Shepard later became famous as the original illustrator of *The Wind in the Willows* by Kenneth Grahame and *Winnie-the-Pooh* by A.A. Milne.

Shirley Combs
1) "Latest—Desiccated Detective Stories, Boiled to the Bone," featuring Shirley Combs. Anonymous (as "A Conning Goil"), in "The Fingerprint Failure." *Los Angeles Sunday Tribune* (Apr. 27, 1913). Reprinted in *Sherlock Holmes in America* (Bill Blackbeard, ed.; Harry N. Abrams, 1981). "The great girl detective" Shirley Combs discovers how the fingerprints of a dead criminal were found on a circus safe. A promised second tale, "A Double Voiced Detective Story," never appeared.
2) Shirley Combs makes an appearance in "The Case Book of James Thurber," one of the stories in *Thurber Country: A Collection of Pieces About Males and Females* by James Thurber (Simon & Schuster, 1953). Reprinted in *Thurber on Crime* (Mysterious Press, 1991). How "the Case of the Young Woman Named Sherlock Holmes" led to the discovery of a bride-to-be named Shirley Combs.

Shirley Holmes
1) Shirley Holmes, "famed style sleuth" was "on the trail for smart new dress accessories" in an advertising campaign for Charles A.

Stevens & Co., a Chicago department store (*Chicago Daily Tribune*, Oct. 19, 1932). In a series of shopping adventures, Shirley Holmes makes discoveries about handkerchiefs, handbags, gloves, and perfume.

2) *The Holmeses of Baker Street: A Play in Three Acts*, featuring Shirley Holmes, by Basil Mitchell, opened at the Lyric Theatre of London (Feb. 14, 1933) and was produced in various other theatres in Britain and America. *The Adventure of the Queen Bee*, an adaption of the play in novel form by Frederic Arnold Kummer, appeared in a four-part serial in *Mystery Magazine* (July-Oct. 1933). Kummer and Mitchell are together credited with "The Canterbury Cathedral Murder" (*Mystery Magazine*, Dec. 1933), which was reprinted in *The Misadventures of Sherlock Holmes* (Ellery Queen, ed.; Little, Brown & Co., 1944). All three are reproduced in *The Adventures of Shirley Holmes* (The Battered Silicon Dispatch Box, 2003). The daughter of Sherlock Holmes is assisted by Joan Watson.

3) "Shirley Holmes, Policewoman." Bill Finger (writer) and Jerry Robinson (artist). *Batman*, No. 28 (DC Comics, Apr./May, 1945). Alfred meets policewoman Shirley Holmes while walking in the park. When he tells Batman about her, he decides to send her undercover to expose a racketeering operation.

4) "A Case of Facsimile," featuring Shirley Holmes. Viola Brothers Shore (*Ellery Queen's Mystery Magazine*, Oct. 1948). Shirley Holmes solves a crime at the Edgar Allan Poe School with the aid of Samantha Spade, Regina Fortune, Nerissa Wolfe, and Elsie Queen. Assisted by Jean Watson.

5) *If Sherlock Holmes Were a Woman: A Comedy in One Act for Seven Girls*, featuring Shirley Holmes and Dotty Watson. Tim Kelly (Baker's Plays, 1969). A college student with a fixation on Sherlock Holmes investigates the suspicious death of her dormitory housemother.

6) *The Case of the Fallen Dickey: A Mystery Melodrama*, featuring Shirley Holmes. Written by Dan Stone and presented in Washington, D.C., in Feb. 1975. Shirley Holmes was portrayed by Allyson Handley.

7) "Shirley Holmes, Supersleuth of Baker Street." A comedy skit on Season 1, Episode 13, of *Cher*, a variety program on CBS. A turn of the century barrister reports a double murder to Shirley

Holmes (Cher, in full Sherlockian costume) and her assistant Dr. Wanda (Carol Burnette).

8) "The Adventures of Sherlock Holmes' Dumber Sister, in The Case of the Mislaid Pussy!" featuring Shirley Holmes in eight pornographic photographs. *Game Magazine* (July 1976).

9) *Clues for Supersleuths*, featuring Shirley Holmes. By the editors of *Read Magazine* (Grosset & Dunlap, 1978). Illustrated by Jody Taylor. A Xerox Education publication in which young people are encouraged to "be a detective" and solve "a mystery a minute."

10) *Shirley Holmes and the Case of the Spanish Indian*, by Peta Masters and Geraldine Griffith, presented for twelve performances by Theatre Venture of London at the Tom Allen Center (Feb. 16-Mar. 3, 1983). Anna Gilbert portrayed Shirley Holmes, the great niece of Sherlock Holmes who is his equal in deductive skills.

11) *The Family Jewels*, featuring Shirley Holmes. Andy Gregg (The Dramatic Publishing Co., 1984). A one act comedy play. The famous Twitchwell family jewels are stolen during the dinner party under the nose of Shirley Holmes.

12) *My Tenderly Beloved Detective* (1986), featuring Shirley Holmes. A Russian comedy feature film. Produced by Ekran; directed by Aleksei Simonov; written by Grigori Gorin and Arkadiy Khayt. Yekaterina Vasileva appeared as Shirley Holmes, with Galina Simonova as Jane Watson.

13) "The Adventures of Shirley Holmes (Headlock Holmes' Ugly Sister)." Don (Duck) Edwing (writer and artist). *Mad's Creature Presentation* (Warner Books, 1993). Also featuring Dr. Watsnew, Mrs. Crudson of 221 Half-Baked Street, and Holmes' brother Micrin.

14) Shirley Holmes appeared in four children's books in the *Shirley Holmes Case Book* series by Robin Kingsland (Collins, 1993): *The Case of the Missing Case*, *The Case of the Hollywood Soap Star*, *The Case of the Shiek's Missing Shake Maker*, and *The Case of the Illegal Sherbert Running Gang*. Shirley Holmes matches wits against the ruthless Molly Harty, the schoolgirl gangster.

15) *The Adventures of Shirley Holmes*, a Canadian television series that aired for 52 episodes in four seasons, 1996-2000. Produced by the Credo Entertainment Group and distributed by Forefront Entertainment and the Disney Channel. Meredith Henderson portrayed Shirley Holmes, the grand-niece of Sherlock Holmes.

16) A series of eleven stories in seven books for young people, all from Collins (HarperCollins), were based on the series *The Adventures of Shirley Holmes*. Various authors produced the books in 1998 and 1999, including Judie Angell, Narinder Dhami, Sue Mongredien, Stella Paskins, and John Whitman. *The Adventures of Shirley Holmes: The Essential Case File* (1998), by Paskins and Mongredien, is a general overview of the series.

17) Shirley Holmes, the niece of Sherlock Holmes, was featured in a comic stage adaptation of *The Hound of the Baskervilles*, written by Kent R. Brown. Assisted by Jennie Watson. Presented by the Young Artists Ensemble in Thousand Oaks, California (Nov. 2014), with Leilani Toone playing Shirley Holmes.

18) Shirley Holmes, a young woman living on Manhattan's upper west side, is assisted by fourth-year medical student Jack Watson in two stories by Keith R.A. DeCandido: "Identity" in *Baker Street Irregulars* (Michael A. Ventrilla and Jonathan Mayberry, eds.; Diversion Books, 2017) and "Six Red Dragons" in *Baker Street Irregulars: The Game Is Afoot* (Michael A. Ventrilla and Jonathan Mayberry, eds.; Diversion Books, 2018).

19) Shirley "Shy" Holmes is an alias for the character Alice Cassell in *Who Killed Sherlock Holmes?* by Paul Cornell (Pan Macmillan, 2017). Book 3 of the "Shadow Police" series, in which the ghost of Sherlock Holmes is murdered.

Shirley Holmquist

Shirley Holmquist & Aunt Wilma: Whodunit? Janet Letnes Martin (Martin House Publications, 1988). A collection of 14 stories in which two ladies of Scandinavian descent in Heartsberg, Minnesota, Shirley Holmquist and Wilma Watson, solve small town mysteries.

Shirley Lock Holmes

Shirley Lock Holmes is an alter-ego of Angelica Pickles, a character in *The Rugrats Movie* (Paramount Pictures, 1998). Directed by Igor Kovalyov and Norton Virgien; written by David N. Weiss and J. David Stem. Voiced by Cheryl Chase. Shirley Lock Holmes was a toy action figure for marketing the movie, and she also appeared in *The Rugrats Movie Sticker Book* (Landoll, 1998).

Shirley-Lock Holmes

Shirley-Lock Holmes was featured in several comics strips by Owen Thomas in *The World of Spelling* (D.C. Heath & Co., 1978). A classroom textbook utilizing the "Heath Spelling Program."

Shirlick Holmes

Shirlick Holmes and the Case of the Wandering Wardrobe. Jane Yolen (Coward, McCann & Geohegan, 1981). A teen detective and her three friends decide to solve a mystery concerning vanishing antiques that has baffled the chief of police in their small town.

Shirt-Lock Holmes

Shirt-Lock Holmes is an online marketer of various items, including custom t-shirts, hoodies, and novelty apparel. The graphic logo depicts Sherlock Holmes in deerstalker.

Shirtlock Holmes

Shirtlock Holmes was a nickname "officially bestowed" on Sascha Tillmans, "a jersey detective of the highest order" in Jan. 2012 by Joe Johnston of Scotland. Johnston owns the website "The Global Obsession," dedicated to his "quest to collect an official football (soccer) shirt from all 211 national teams in FIFA."

Shoelock Holmes

1) *Shoelock Holmes's Last Case* was a play staged by Murder for Hire, a murder mystery production company based in Binghamton, New York, in 2001. Inspector Kemper identifies the characteristics of boots and pumps while solving the mystery.

2) Shoelock Holmes is a one-time designation for a character in "The Adventure of the Main Six-Year-Olds: Let's Play Damsel in Distress," a story by Rainbowjack2000 on fimfiction.com, a fan fiction site based on the animated series *My Little Pony*. "And what are you supposed to be? Shoelock Holmes?" Posted Nov. 21, 2013.

3) Shoelock Holmes is a company in Singapore specializing in the repair of footwear and leather goods, key cutting, and locksmith services. Incorporated June 21, 2015.

4) Shoelock Holmes "can identify people in the bathroom without seeing their face," according to Will Pfaffenberger of *The Smiley Morning Show* on WZPL-FM Radio of Indianapolis (March 16, 2017).

Sholomon Hume
Study in Emerald (Estudio en Esmeralda), featuring Sholomon Hume. Alberto Lopez Aroca. *Fábulas Extrañas*, Nos. 29 and 30 (1997). A science fiction novel, later released in paperback (Ilarion, 2012). Sholomon Hume encounters Dr. Yun H. Walruss to investigate the death of 7 billion inhabitants of the planet Doilette, also known as Esmerelda.

Shore Rock Halmes
Shore Rock Halmes is a corruption of the name Sherlock Holmes in *Wilde About Holmes* by Milo Yelesiyevich (Comic Masque, 2008), one of many names used within a bizarre hallucination that occurs when "a delirious Holmes" suffers from "a cocaine frenzy."

Shoreflock Hums
Shoreflock Hums is a corruption of the name Sherlock Holmes in *Wilde About Holmes* by Milo Yelesiyevich (Comic Masque, 2008), one of many names used within a bizarre hallucination that occurs when "a delirious Holmes" suffers from "a cocaine frenzy."

Shorelock Gommes
Shorelock Gommes is a corruption of the name Sherlock Holmes in *Wilde About Holmes* by Milo Yelesiyevich (Comic Masque, 2008), one of many names used within a bizarre hallucination that occurs when "a delirious Holmes" suffers from "a cocaine frenzy."

Shorelocked Holmes
Shorelocked Holmes, a pirate detective, drawn by Koko Gonzales, appeared in *The K-Zone Bulletin*, the on-line publication of *K-Zone: Where Kids Rule*, produced by Summit Media of the Philippines. He was one of the 18 Holmes parody characters to take part in "Crisis of Infinite Holmes" (Aug. 2008), an adventure involving Sherlockian characters working together to save their concurrent universes.

Shoreluck Hams
Shoreluck Hams is a corruption of the name Sherlock Holmes in *Wilde About Holmes* by Milo Yelesiyevich (Comic Masque, 2008), one of many names used within a bizarre hallucination that occurs when "a delirious Holmes" suffers from "a cocaine frenzy."

Shorl Rock Hums

Shorl Rock Hums is a corruption of the name Sherlock Holmes in *Wilde About Holmes* by Milo Yelesiyevich (Comic Masque, 2008), one of many names used within a bizarre hallucination that occurs when "a delirious Holmes" suffers from "a cocaine frenzy."

Shorlrock Homes

Shorlrock Homes is a corruption of the name Sherlock Holmes in *Wilde About Holmes* by Milo Yelesiyevich (Comic Masque, 2008), one of many names used within a bizarre hallucination that occurs when "a delirious Holmes" suffers from "a cocaine frenzy."

Shortwave Ohms

"The Adventures of Shortwave Ohms (and Watt's Son): The Mysterious Case of the Voice of the Galapak Ghost." Ralph Perry. *FRENDX* (North American Shortwave Research), Apr. 1973. Reprinted in the same publication in Dec. 1978.

Showman Hoyle

"The Great Security Bank Mystery." Isaac Anderson. *The Smart Set* (Dec. 1902). Reprinted in *As It Might Have Been: A Collection of Sherlockian Parodies from Unlikely Sources* (Robert C.S. Adey, ed.; Calabash Press, 1998). The great detective Showman Hoyle is called when a night watchman awakens to find that the bank has been robbed.

Shrock Holmes

"The Adventure of the Psychedelic Sleuth," featuring Shrock Holmes and Dr. Harcourt. Bradley Kjell. *The Loft* (Rock Valley College), No. 13 (Jan. 1968). The story was revised and republished as one of Kjell's "Tide Pooles" stories in *Shades of Sherlock* later that year.

Shroomlock Holmes

Shroomlock, a mushroom version of Sherlock Holmes, is a character in the single-player video game *Mario Party Advance*, developed by Hudson Scott and published by Nintendo. Released in 2005.

Shrr'lok of Kholmes

"The Case of the Purloined L'Isitek," featuring The Shrr'lok, leader of the race of Shrr'loks on the planet Kholmes. Josepha Sherman. In: *Sherlock Holmes in Orbit* (MJF Books, 1995). Assisted by Dr. Alwin Watson, an archaeologist.

Shumlock Holmes

"Around the World in 80 Hours, Part II: Melementary School" featuring Shumlock Holmes. Michael Gallagher (writer), and Dave Manak and Marie Severin (artists). *Alf*, No. 23 (Marvel Comics, Dec. 1989). Alf recalls "Melmac's greatest detective, my ancestor Shumlock Holmes." Assisted by Dr. Watroast, Shumlock Holmes battles Professor Melmoriarity over the production of illegal naugahyde.

Shurl Holmes

"The Case of the Defective Doyles," featuring Shurl [Holmes] and Watts. Martin Gardner. *Isaac Asimov's Science Fiction Magazine* (Jan.-Feb. 1978). Reprinted in *Isaac Asimov's Science Fiction Anthology* (David Publications, 1978). A mathematical puzzle.

Shurl Rock Gommes

Shurl Rock Gommes is a corruption of the name Sherlock Holmes in *Wilde About Holmes* by Milo Yelesiyevich (Comic Masque, 2008), one of many names used within a bizarre hallucination that occurs when "a delirious Holmes" suffers from "a cocaine frenzy."

Shurlacombs

Shurlacombs was a "big friendly creature" created by E.T. Reed for "Mr. Punch's Animal Land: The Coneydoil or Shurlacombs." *Punch* (Feb. 26, 1898). A caricature of Arthur Conan Doyle, described as "very shrood and saggacious."

Shurlikes Tosnoop

Shurlikes Tosnoop, the famous "Scientific Detective Extraordinary," appeared in five stories by Conrad H. Ruppert in 1932: "The Great Scientifilm Mystery" (March), "Bigger and Better Blunders" (Apr.-May), "The Missing Tarzan" (June), and "The Paul Robberies" (July-Aug.), all in *The Time Traveller*, as well as the two-part "Tosnoop's Trying Task" in *Science Fiction Digest and Fantasy Magazine* (Sept. and Oct., 1932). Assisted by Watzis.

Shurlock Guck

Shurlock Guck was the way "Sherlock Guck, the Eskimo Detective" referred to himself in eight appearances in *The Katzenjammer Kids* Sunday comic strips by Rudolph Dirks (Apr. 28-June 30, 1907). Distributed by the Hearst Newspaper Syndicate. Guck has his offices in an igloo and frequently disguises himself as polar animals.

Shylar Holmes

The Adventures of Shylar Holmes. Stephen Daniel Williams (Carlton Press, 1966). Assisted by Dr. John Whatley. A collection of three tales featuring Shylar Holmes, a detective living at 21B Barlow Street in Houston, Texas.

Shylock Bones

1) "The Röntgen-Ray-Der," featuring Shylock Bones. Phil May (as Mr. "M—"). *Phil May's Winter Annual*, 1895. A tale involving photography and art thieves, with the use of X-rays as a means of detection.

2) *Shylock Bones: A Burlesque on Sherlock Holmes*. Harry L. Newton (W. Rossiter, 1906). Among a series of "Will Rossiter's acts, plays, sketches, etc., for amateur and professional."

3) Shylock Bones was a character in *Savageland* by Walter Ben Hare, the annual stage production of The Savage Club of Cornell University (May 3, 1912). A two-act musical comedy concerning the search for a hidden statue and a "bucket of pearls." Shylock Bones was portrayed by T.L. Tewksbury. The play was adapted and performed by numerous community theatres through the 1930s, often with the character name changed to Sherlock Combs.

4) "Shylock Bones." Joe Archibald (writer & artist). *The Funnies*, No. 1 (Dell Publishing, 1929). A comic book appearance. Archibald also drew the *Shylock Bones* comic strip for distribution to American newspapers in the 1920s.

5) "Shylock Bones." *Wild*, No. 4 (Interstate Publishing Co., June 1954). Ernie Bache (artist); Dick Ayers (pencils and lettering). Shylock Bones and Dr. What'sup encounter Lord Fossil, who collects the heads of famous detectives including Dick Tracer, Joe Thursday, Charlie Chance, and the Skin Man.

6) Shylock Bones is a game piece character in *Why*, a board game by the Milton Bradley Company, originally released in 1958 and re-released in 1967. Other pieces are Sergeant Monday, Dick Crazy, and Charlie Clam.

7) "Scientific Bureau of Investigation," featuring Earl Fuller as Shylock Bones, "the investigator of scientific principles." A series of 30 episodes filmed in 1976 by WKNO, the PBS affiliate in Memphis, Tennessee. The 15-minute segments aired in repeats for 17 years.

8) "The Case of the Missing Lunchroom," featuring Shylock Bones. William A. Carpenter. *The OPS-BS Flier* (Oregon Physicians Service-Blue Shield, Nov. 1979-Mar. 1980), in three parts. Assisted by Dr. Whatsit.

9) "Rap… Rap… Rap…" featuring Shylock Bones, "the greatest ghost detective of them all." In: *Favorite Scary Stories of American Children*. Richard and Judy Dockery Young (August House Publishers, 1990).

10) *The Mystery of the Monsters' Big Ball*, featuring Shylock Bones. An interactive cabaret show. Written by Mal and Jenny Tibbetts, for Ruby Productions. Performed at the Emu Sports Club of Leonay, Australia (Oct. 31-Nov. 14, 2015). Shylock Bones was portrayed by Matthew Avery, with David Attrill as Doctor Watsup.

11) *The Fantom of the Music Hall* (2016), featuring Shylock Bones. Written by Ralph Ashby. A dinner theatre production, first presented at the Mousetrap Theatre of Redcliffe, Australia (Nov. 18, 2016).

Shylock Combs

"Shylock Combs, the Great Detective, and Dr. Hopson: The Adventure of the £2 Note." Vincent Mientus. *Prescott's Press*, No. 11 (Sept. 1991). Combs and Hopson, trying to preserve their dwindling resources, must discover the fate of their last banknote, last seen affixed to the mantle with a hypodermic needle.

Shylock Hames

Shylock Hames and Whatson appeared in two stories by Dale Nelson: "Clews in the Mews" in *APA-5*, No. 37 (1973) and "The Adventure of Sebastian Moron" in *APA-5*, No. 38 (1974). Both were reprinted in *Shot Scott's Rap Sheet*, Nos. 2 and 5 (1975).

Shylock Haynes

Shylock Haynes was a repeated corruption of the name Sherlock Holmes in *W.G. Grace's Last Case* by William Rushton (Methuen, 1984). "Watson could be very irritating," so Grace, the famous cricketer, "wondered how Mr. Shylock Haynes had coped with his peevishness."

Shylock Hoax

"The Case of the Missing Fink." Richard J. Needham. *The Globe and Mail* (June 26 and 27, 1975). *The Daily Plummet* sends for Shylock Hoax to find its aged columnist, Rodney J. Noodlebaum.

Shylock Holmes

1) "The Remarkable Pipe Dream of Shylock Holmes" by Clay M. Greene (1899) was a burlesque skit parodying both William Gillette and his famous play. "What is the difference between Gillette and the ice wagon?... Nothing," since "he wrote the play himself and knows that nothing can happen to him." Debuted at Koster & Bial's Music Hall in New York (Nov. 20, 1899) and added to various shows in the area over the next year.

2) "Shylock Holmes: A Sleuth Whose Sensibilities Were Trained Down to a Wonderful Acuteness." Leon Harman (*The Jennings Daily Record*, Nov. 7, 1901). Reprinted from the humor magazine *Judge*. Watson faints from astonishment over the bizarre deductions of Shylock Holmes.

3) Shylock Holmes is mentioned in several chapters of "Hashimura Togo—Detective," a series of stories about the Japanese character written by Wallace Irwin and distributed by the Associated Press (Nov. 20, 1910-Feb. 26, 1911). In such adventures as "Hon. Sarah Berhardt's Secret of Youth" and "The Horrible Mystery of the Rockefeller Institute," Togo dons his "Shylock Holmes cap of deduction" and raises his "Shylock Holmes eyebrows."

4) Shylock Holmes was the detective character in "Skylark Bones," a short stage play produced for the Railroad Y.M.C.A. of Topeka, Kansas, in 1913. Tom McVeigh performed as Shylock Holmes; the play also featured Dr. Swanson and Moore-Airity. Produced under the direction of Linna Bressette.

5) Shylock Holmes appears in an episode of "Letters of a Japanese Schoolboy" by Wallace Irwin (*Los Angeles Times*, Oct. 21, 1923).

Shylock Holmes, "Famous tracker" must use "new whiskers" as a disguise to prevent being recognized, since he looks like "Hon. William Gillette who makes razors."

6) Shylock Holmes is mentioned in the comic strip "Our Boarding House" by Bill Freyse (Nov. 9, 1945). Maj. Hoople is missing $47, "filched by some light-fingered cutpurse." His employee Jason asks, "Whyn't you deduct the crime lak mistah Shylock Holmes?" Syndicated by the Newspaper Enterprise Association.

7) Shylock Holmes is a one-time corruption of Sherlock Holmes' name in *Ten Years Beyond Baker Street* by Cay Van Ash (Harper & Row, 1984). A local policeman, described as "an affable idiot," persists in addressing Shylock Holmes, much to the irritation of Sherlock.

8) Shylock Holmes is a one-time corruption of Sherlock Holmes' name in *Sherlock Holmes and the Boulevard Assassin* by John Hall (Breese Books, 1998). "Am I to impersonate this—this Shylock Holmes?"

9) Shylock Holmes is the brother of Clewlow and Pycrust Holmes in "The Case of the Open and Shut" by Douglas Moreton. *The Unrelated Adventures of Clewlow Holmes* (Cadds Printing, 1998).

10) Shylock Holmes is one of ten "alternative names for Sherlock Holmes" proposed by Mrs. Hudson in *Nursing Holmes*, a two-act play by Cenarth Fox (Fox Plays, 2009). Holmes discovers the list in his landlady's personal scrapbook.

Shylock Homes

1) *Shylock Homes: His Posthumous Memoirs.* John Kendrick Bangs (The Dispatch-Box Press, 1973) consists of a series of ten stories which appeared in *The New York Herald* and various other newspapers in 1903. A shortened version of one of the tales, "Mr. Homes Solves a Question of Authorship," is reprinted in *The Misadventures of Sherlock Holmes* (Ellery Queen, ed.; Little, Brown & Co., 1944).

2) "Shylock and the Disappearing Pennant Race Case," featuring Shylock Homes and What's On. Bob Hertzel (*The Cincinnati Enquirer*, May 8, 1977). Homes searches for the cause of the Cincinnati Reds' collapse in the race for the National League championship.

3) "Shylock Homes and the Case of the Lifted Locket." Joe Cata-lano (writer) and John Severin (artist), credited to "Moe Riarty." *Cracked*, No. 162 (Major Magazines, Sept. 1979). Reprinted in *Cracked Annual*, No. 20: "The King-Sized Cracked Movie Mara-thon" (Globe Communications, Summer 1986). Assisted by Dr. Whatson and Mrs. Sudson, Shylock Homes pursues a talking blob.
4) "The Super Snooper," featuring Shylock Homes. Dick Malmgren (writer and artist). *Mad House Comics*, No. 125 (Archie Comics, Aug. 1981). Assisted by Whatson, Shylock Homes investigates the case of a dog supposedly kidnapped from her wealthy, yet boring, owner.
5) Shylock Homes is featured in two short on-line videos by Cool N. Inc. (YouTube, Feb. 8 and Mar. 8, 2016), supposedly trailers for a fictitious film, *Shylock Holmes: Strings of the Marionette*. As-sisted by Dr. John Wilson, Shylock Holmes (portrayed by James Bean) searches for escaped villain James Marionette.

Shylock Homestead
In Dahomey: A Musical Farce (1902), featuring Slylock Home-stead, was the first full-length musical written by and starring African-Americans to be performed on Broadway. Bert Williams portrayed Shylock Homestead, who is hired along with Rareback Pinkerton to find a lost casket. Book by Jesse A. Shipp; music by Will Marion Cook; lyrics by Paul Laurence Dunbar.

Shylock Hommes
"The Adventure of the Ripper's Scrawl." *The Adventures of the Second Mrs. Watson*. Michael Mallory (Deadly Alibi Press, 2000). Jack the Ripper taunts Sherlock Holmes with a decoded message: "Shylock Hommes be Damned." The story originally appeared in *Murderous Intent Mystery Magazine*.

Shylock Hound
1) Shylock Hound is the brother of Sherlock Hound in *Hound in the Highlands* by Brenda Sivers (Abelard, 1980). The life of a very noble dog is threatened by a mysterious curse involving some ghostly bagpipe-playing.
2) Shylock Hound is the name of a "detective hound dog" plush stuffed animal toy produced by Dakin, Inc., in 1983.

Shylock Hyams

Shylock Hyams was a play presented by Herbert Landeck and Company at the Royal Hippodrome Theatre in Dover, England, in May 1915, and the next month at the Camberwell Palace in London. Landeck portrayed Shylock Hyams, a second-rate detective mistaken for Sherlock Holmes.

Shylock Jones

Shylock Jones, a detective, figured in a mock trial by the Law Students' Debating Society (1894). E.C. Redhead assumed the role of Shylock Jones.

Shylock Oames

"The Adventures of Shylock Oames: The Sign of Gore." F.W. Freeman (*Tit-Bits*, Dec. 3, 1892). Reprinted in *My Evening with Sherlock Holmes* (John Michael Gibson and Richard Lancelyn Green, eds.; Ferret, 1981). A client arrives at Quaker Street to consult Shylock Oames and Wilkins after his nose is cut and his moustache stolen while he was asleep.

Shylock 'Olmes

Shylock 'Olmes is a corruption of Sherlock Holmes' name in *Anno Dracula 1895: Seven Days in Mayhem*, No. 2 (Titan Comics, May 2017). Kim Newman (writer) & Paul McCaffrey (artist). Of a caged and tortured prisoner, a guard at the Tower or London says, "It's *a* detective from Baker Street, ma'am, but not the famous one. Meet the poor man's Shylock 'Olmes, another enemy of the crown."

Shylock Plumes

Shylock Plumes is one of seven parody names in "Prize Detective Story." Anonymous (*The Weekly Magazine*, May 8, 1897). Retitled "Holmes and the Startled Banker" in *As It Might Have Been: A Collection of Sherlockian Parodies from Unlikely Sources* (Robert C.S. Adey, ed.; Calabash Press, 1998). Hemlock Coombs repeatedly changes his name as he makes a series of trivial deductions.

Signor Om-mez

Signor Om-mez, who "as ever perceives everything" is a corruption of Sherlock Holmes' name in "Art, Crime and Enlightenment" by Vithal Rajan, one of the stories in *Holmes of the Raj* (Writer's

Workshop, 2006). An Italian in India, Moresconi, considers himself "a lucky man today, for long have I searched for Mr. Om-mez."

Simon Rolfe

Simon Rolfe, who tries to imitate Sherlock Holmes, appears in two novels by Joseph L. Bonney: *Murder without Clues* (Carrick & Evans, 1940) and *Death by Dynamite* (Carrick & Evans, 1940). Narrated by Henry F. Watson. Rolfe utilizes "psychological logic."

Sir Loch Hoames

Sir Loch Hoames and "his new bride," Dr. Watt-Sun, on their honeymoon in the Ozark Mountains, are called in by Sheriff Les Tradd to help prove the guilt of Professor Maury R. Tee in the "backwood bookworm" murder. "Positive Denial: A You-Solve-It by Laird Long" (*Mystery Weekly Magazine*, Oct. 2017).

Sir Luck Helm

"The Adventure of Sir Luck Helm" by Aan Wulandari Uman, and edited by Rika Moniarti (Synergy Library, 2009). An Indonesian comic novel written for juvenile readers. In his Bakri Street neighborhood, Mengelmalah Sapan assumes the role of Sir Luck Helm. Assisted by his friend Wawan, who assumes the role of Dr. Watsan, they solve a series of six "silly and magical" mysteries.

Skilock Holmes

"The Lift Line," featuring Skilock Holmes. Albert M. Rosenblatt. *The Poughkeepsie Journal* (Feb. 19, 1971). In a column for enthusiasts, Skilock Holmes searches for a mysterious secret location for skiing.

Skylark Bones

1) "Skylark Bones" was a short stage play produced for the Railroad Y.M.C.A. of Topeka, Kansas, in 1913. Tom McVeigh performed as Shylock Holmes; the play also featured Dr. Swanson and Moore-Airity. Produced under the direction of Linna Bressette, at that time an eighth-grade teacher, who shortly thereafter became the first woman factory inspector in Kansas, a long-time women's advocate, and Catholic social reformer.
2) Skylark Bones of Scotland Yard, in full Sherlockian costume, appeared in the *Homer Hoopee* comic strip by Fred Locher (June

9, 1934). Syndicated and distributed by the Associated Press Feature Service.

Skylark Holmes
Ice Age Extinctions: Skylark Holmes and Dr. Janet Watson Investigate the Case of the Arborcidial Megaherbivores. Elin Whitney-Smith. A scientific investigation in mystery form, advancing a new theory of species extinction. A Kindle e-book.

Skylock Peyton
Skylock Peyton was one of seven roles played by Jerry Lewis in the comedy film *The Family Jewels* (1965). Produced by Jerry Lewis Productions for Paramount Pictures; directed and co-written (with Bill Richmond) by Jerry Lewis. Released July 1, 1965. Also featuring Sebastian Cabot as Dr. Matson.

Slipshod Helms
"The Adventure of the Copper Breeches," featuring Slipshod Helms. Cindy Fischer (Last Bow Press, 1978). Assisted by Dr. Thensome.

Slylock Fox
Slylock Fox and Comics for Kids is a daily comic strip first created by Bob Weber, Jr., on March 29, 1987. Distributed to nearly 400 newspapers by King Features Syndicate. Slylock Fox, the fox detective in Sherlockian costume, presents logic puzzles. Assisted by Max Mouse.

Smallpox Soles
Smallpox Soles and Dr. Rotson appear in "The Marischal Manor Mystery." Anonymous. *Alma Mater*, Oct. 31, 1923. A play, reprinted in *As It Might Have Been: A Collection of Sherlockian Parodies from Unlikely Sources* (Robert C.S. Adey, ed.; Calabash Press, 1998). Soles (whose name is often misstated) and Rotson investigate the murder of a small boy and encounter a clever villain who uses poison. Also featuring Mrs. Sudson, Professor O'Myhatty, and Sir Arthur Bone-and-Oil.

Smearlock Holmes
Smearlock Holmes, or Why He's Conan Doyled Himself. Produced by the Barwick Golf Club and performed for its annual dinner at

the Leeds and County Liberal Club in Yorkshire, England (Feb. 1, 1911). Written for the event by club president R.C. Oldham. Smearlock Holmes was portrayed by G.R. Coxon.

Smearlock Homeless

Murder Under the Big Top, featuring Smearlock Homeless and Dr. Witless. A play written by Michael Rusz for the St. Charles Community High School in Michigan. Performed May 6-8, 2011, with Ben Reyhl as Sherlock Homeless and Mark Chad as Dr. Witless.

Snoopy Holmes

1) Snoopy Holmes, assisted by Dr. Woodstock, is featured in the animated film *It's a Mystery Charlie Brown* (1974), written by Charles M. Schulz, the creator of the *Peanuts* comic strip. Directed by Phil Roman. When Woodstock's nest mysteriously disappears, Snoopy plays detective in order to find it.

2) Sherdog Holmes, featuring the comic character Snoopy in full Sherlockian costume, examining the front door of his "Snoopy Holmes" dog house at 221B, is featured on several products, including prints, a pillow case, t-shirts, iPod and iPad cases, and a shower curtain. Produced by 3Second Design and Art. Featured on various on-line marketing sites.

Snowlock Holmes

"S.O.S.! Save Our Santa," featuring Snowlock Holmes. Lio Mangubat (writer) and Koko Gonzales (artist). In the "Puzzle Zone" section of *K-Zone: Where Kids Rule* (2009), a publication and website of Summit Media of the Philippines. The character had appeared previously in Dec. 2006 and Dec. 2007 as well as in *The K-Zone Bulletin* as one of the 18 Holmes parody characters to take part in "Crisis of Infinite Holmes" (Aug. 2008), an adventure involving Sherlockian characters working together to save their concurrent universes.

Solar Pons

1) Solar Pons appeared in what perhaps were the most successful parodies of Sherlock Holmes. The first volume of Solar Pons tales, *In Re: Sherlock Holmes—The Adventures of Solar Pons* by August Derleth (Mycroft & Moran, 1945), was followed by a series of stories, including one novel, that eventually numbered more than

the Sherlockian Canon. Pons attracted his own devotees and an organized society. Solar Pons lived in Praed Street and was assisted by Dr. Lyndon Parker.

2) Solar Pons and Dr. Lyndon Parker were featured in a long series of new stories by Basil Copper, beginning with *The Dossier of Solar Pons* (Pinnacle Books, 1979). Copper began his series after the death of August Derleth in 1971, eventually publishing eight volumes of Solar Pons stories.

3) Solar Pons reappears in twelve new stories contained in *The Papers of Solar Pons: New Adventures of the Sherlock Holmes of Praed Street* by David Marcum (Belanger Books, 2017).

Sonar T. Phoom

"The Parallax Deception," featuring Sonar T. Phoom, the "most famous 21st Century Detective," was an episode in the third season of *Alien Worlds* (1979), a syndicated radio program. Assisted by McGuffin Drone. Sonar T. Phoom was portrayed by Philip Clark.

Sorelock Holmes

"Sorelock Holmes" is a Pokemon-inspired fan art/digital art creation by the artist known as KamiGoat, found on DeviantArt.com. A bug-like creature, Sorel, wears a deerstalker and uses a magnifying glass while riding a "bulbasaur" dressed in a Watson-styled disguise (2016).

Soreluck Hams

Soreluck Hams is a corruption of the name Sherlock Holmes in *Wilde About Holmes* by Milo Yelesiyevich (Comic Masque, 2008), one of many names used within a bizarre hallucination that occurs when "a delirious Holmes" suffers from "a cocaine frenzy."

Sortluck Ohms

Sortluck Ohms and Dr. Wazzat appeared in four stories by Debbie Laubach in *The Medical Bulletin*: "The Case of the Unearthly Visitor" (Mar. 1981); "A Gamey Piece" (July 1981); "The Adventure of the Blind Man's Newfoundland" (over several issues in 1982-83); and "A Little Pastime of Mine" (Winter 1983).

Speedlock Holmes

Speedlock Holmes is an achievement level for day one of "The Election Day Job," one of the "heists" in *Payday 2*, a cooperative first-person shooter video game. Developed by Overkill Software and published by 505 Games. Released Aug. 13, 2013.

Spencer Holmes
Spencer Holmes, the grandson of Sherlock Holmes and Irene Adler, solves crimes in San Francisco in two novels by Denny Martin Flinn: *Killer Finish* (Bantam Books, 1991) and *San Francisco Kills* (Bantam Books, 1991). He resides at 2210 Baker Street.

Spitlock Phones
"The Scarlet Drop: An Adventure of Spitlock Phones, by Sir Kadaver Bonan Oyle." Anonymous (as "Fibulous"). *Fifth Gloucester Gazette*, Aug. 1917. Reprinted in *As It Might Have Been: A Collection of Sherlockian Parodies from Unlikely Sources* (Robert C.S. Adey, ed.; Calabash Press, 1998). Assisted by Wonson, Spitlock Phones undertakes a "most delicate and special mission" in Germany during World War I.

Spurlock Holmes
"Murder in the Blue Room: A Thrilling Complete Mystery in Pictures," featuring Spurlock Holmes. J.A. Patterson. *Detective Picture Stories*, No. 1 (Comic Magazine Co., Dec. 1936). Assisted by Watkins, Spurlock Holmes investigates "Lady Ashley's blue mystery."

Spylot Bones
Spylot Bones is a recurring character in *Leading Comics*, which was published by World's Best Comics, an imprint of DC Comics, in the 1940s and early 1950s. In *Leading Comics* No. 15 (Summer 1945), funny animals such as Spylot Bones began to be featured.

Squirrel-Loch-Holmes
Squirrel-Loch-Holmes is a handmade and hand painted animal character necklace featuring a squirrel in full Sherlockian costume. Produced by Sophisticritters and created by the artist known as Becka.

Squirrel-Lock Holmes
Squirrel-Lock Holmes, a squirrel in Sherlockian costume, is the creation of Jecca All, an artist who placed the image on a wide range of products including a t-shirt, hoody, shower curtain,

iPhone cover, stationery cards, carry-all pouch, and other items for Society6.com, an on-line marketer.

Squirrelock Holmes

"The Adventures of Squirrelock Holmes." Ron Sumner. *The Biblical Evangelist* (1980-1982). Squirrelock Holmes and Dr. Waspon appeared in Sumner's biweekly column for children in 60 issues of the magazine.

Stamford Holmes

1) *The Monte Carlo Telegram*, featuring Stamford Holmes and James Watson. A play by Grant Eustace and Philip Burley. First performed at the Old Whitgiftian Association Clubhouse in Croydon, England, Jan. 26-31, 1976. The sons of Sherlock Holmes and Dr. Watson investigate an unusual death at a luxury hotel in Monaco in 1934.

2) *Second Holmes*, featuring Stamford Holmes. A six-part BBC Radio 4 comedy series, first broadcast Jan. 3-Feb. 6, 1983. Written by Grant Eustace. Stamford Holmes, a reluctant consulting detective and grandson of Sherlock Holmes, was portrayed by Peter Egan.

Stanway Holmes

The Mantle of Methuselah: A Farcical Novel, including Chapter 11, "Stanway Holmes Gets Busy." Langford Reed and Hetty Spiers (Rich & Cowan, 1939). "The famous detective" Stanway Holmes goes undercover: "When I have my net properly spread and all my clues verified, then is the time for me to make use of Scotland Yard."

Stately Holmes

Stately Holmes is one of ten "alternative names for Sherlock Holmes" proposed by Mrs. Hudson in *Nursing Holmes*, a two-act play by Cenarth Fox (Fox Plays, 2009). Holmes discovers the list in his landlady's personal scrapbook.

Stately Homes

Stately Homes is featured in eight parodies by Arthur Porges published in *Ellery Queen's Mystery Magazine* and other specialty publications between 1957 and 2004. All are collected in *The Adventures of Stately Homes and Sherman Horn* (Battered Silicon

Dispatch Box, 2008). Three of them appeared in *Three Porges Parodies and a Pastiche* (Magico Magazine, 1988). Assisted by Sun Wat.

Stevenson Holmes

"The Baker Street Adventure," featuring the comic character Steve Canyon as Stevenson Holmes. Milton Caniff (writer and artist). Originally a story line in the syndicated *Steve Canyon* daily and Sunday comic strip (July 21-Oct. 8, 1985). Reprinted in *Comics Revue*, No. 21 (Manuscript Press, 1987). In an extended dream sequence, Canyon assumes the role of Stevenson Holmes, an "American kinsman of the great detective."

Suburban Holmes

1) "Suburban Holmes, Sleuth of Sleuths: The Great Powder Puff Mystery." Anonymous (as "Slippery Elm"). *San Francisco Chronicle* (October 9, 1921). Reprinted in *Sherlock Holmes in America* (Bill Blackbeard, ed.; Harry N. Abrams, 1981). One of two stories featuring Suburban Holmes, who has a unique "method of deductive detecting."
2) Suburban Holmes is one of ten "alternative names for Sherlock Holmes" proposed by Mrs. Hudson in *Nursing Holmes*, a two-act play by Cenarth Fox (Fox Plays, 2009). Holmes discovers the list in his landlady's personal scrapbook.

Suburban Homes

Lulu's Lost Lotharios (1915), featuring Suburban Homes. A short silent comedy film. Produced by the Thanhouser Film Corporation; written by Lloyd F. Lonergan. A jealous sheriff locks up his rivals, one by one. A detective, Suburban Holmes, assisted by Dr. Wopson, manages to free them. Released Nov. 8, 1915. Suburban Homes is portrayed by Arthur Cunningham.

Sure-Lock Home

Sure-Lock Home and Dr. What's On? Are highly customized home security systems in "The Adventure of the Diode Detective" by Jody Lynn Nye. *Baker Street Irregulars: The Game Is Afoot* (Michael A. Ventrilla and Jonathan Mayberry, eds.; Diversion Books, 2018). They work together to overcome their own programming to defeat an evil hacker.

Sure-Lock Homes
"Dr. Whatnot's Journal," featuring Sure-Lock Homes. John Lock-wood. *The Northwest Current*, a weekly publication in Washington, D.C. (June 18-July 1, 1981, and Sept. 24-Oct. 7, 1981). The villain is Professor Moldy-Arty.

Sure-Locked Homes
Sure-Locked Homes (1928), featuring Felix the Cat. A silent cartoon. Produced by Pat Sullivan Cartoons; directed by Otto Messmer. Released Apr. 15, 1928. Felix is assisted by a web-spinning spider to capture criminals in a haunted house.

Sure-Luck Holes
Sure-Luck Holes is a one-time corruption of the name Sherlock Holmes in *The Master Sleuth on the Trail of Edwin Drood* by Robert F. Fleissner (Xlibris, 2002): Sure-Luck because he was a "lucky man" and Holes because he "holed out" in a golf game.

Sure-They-Lock Homez
"The Gig of the Man (with the Twist)." J.N. (Jerry Neal) Williamson. *The Baker Street Journal*, Vol. 16, No. 1 (Mar. 1966). Assisted by Dr. Whooson. A tale told "in teenage terms" with a glossary "for those who may think young but not *that* young."

Surefoot Jones
"Surefoot Jones." Donald J. Markstein (writer) and Noel Van Horn (artist). *Walt Disney's Mickey Mouse*, No. 261 (Gemstone Publishing, Feb. 2004). Assisted by Watsup, Surefoot Jones seeks the Tuesday Ruby, which he believes has been stolen by Professor Smartie-Artie.

Surelacks Holmes
In response to a negative review of *Sherlock Holmes: A Game of Shadows* on HollwoodChicago.com, David Smith suggested that the film more accurately "should have been named Surelacks Holmes" (June 23, 2012).

Surelick Bones
"Is It Arf?" featuring Surelick Bones. Season 1, Episode 13, of *Dog City*, an animated television series. First aired Jan. 30, 1993. Produced by Jim Henson Productions for FOX Television Network;

directed by John Van Bruggen. Surelick Boncs, a suave English bloodhound detective, turns out to be an art thief.

Surelick Holmes
Surelick Holmes is one of ten "alternative names for Sherlock Holmes" proposed by Mrs. Hudson in *Nursing Holmes*, a two-act play by Cenarth Fox (Fox Plays, 2009). Holmes discovers the list in his landlady's personal scrapbook.

Surelick Holms
The American Adventures of Surelick Holms (1971), "A Hand in Hand Film." A gay pornographic film. Directed by Ralph Ell. Larry Chandler starred as Surelick Holmes, with Frank Massey as Watson.

Surelock Grones
"The Defective Detective," featuring Sherlock Dale imitating the famous detective Surelock Grones. *Walt Disney's Chip 'n' Dale*, No. 17 (Dell Comics, Mar.-May, 1959). "I made myself a hat, found a magnifier glass, and now I gonna make like Surelock Grones" to find an egg stolen from its nest.

Surelock Holmes
1) *Surelock Holmes* (1902), a play by Clay M. Greene. Described as "a travesty" of William Gillette's popular play *Sherlock Holmes*, it was presented by Proctor's Stock Company. First performance was at Proctor's 125th Street Theatre in Jan. 1902, with one-week engagements at various theatres in New York over the following month.
2) Surelock Holmes uncovered the mystery of newly whitened walls in "Short News Notes from Big Four Shops." Anonymous. *The Journal Gazette* of Matoon, Illinois (Apr. 20, 1907).
3) *A Case of Mix-Up*, featuring Surelock Holmes, was a two-scene musical comedy play written by Fred W. Rath, who performed as the title character, for Class Day at the Manual Training High School of Brooklyn, New York (Feb. 2, 1912). "A burlesque on Sherlock Holmes and on wireless telegraphy."
4) "The Invisible Intruder," featuring Sir Surelock [Holmes]. Carl Barks (writer and artist). *Walt Disney's Uncle Scrooge*, No. 44 (Gold Key Comics, Aug. 1963). Uncle Scrooge calls in "the

world's best detective" to unmask the intruder that is causing his giant bed to shake every night.

5) "Surelock Holmes: Home Security Systems" was an episode of *Consumer Survival Kit*, a program "dealing with home security, offering tips on protecting one's home from unwanted guests and fire." Produced by the Maryland Center for Public Broadcasting. First aired Jan. 27, 1976.

6) *The Mystery of the Willing Victims* (1981), featuring Surelock Holmes, an informational film on crime prevention produced by the State Farm Insurance Co. Jeff Smith played Surelock Holmes. Assisted by John Watson III.

Surelock Homes

1) "Surelock Homes' Waterloo." George M. Johnson (*Top-Notch Magazine*, Oct. 15, 1910). A New York reporter interviews the great detective.

2) *The Tongue Mark* (1913), featuring Surelock Homes. A short silent comedy film. Released by the Majestic Motion Picture Company on June 15, 1913. Fred Mace portrays Surelock Homes, who mistakenly arrests a dog for a burglary.

Surelock Jones

Surelock Jones, Detective (1912), a short silent comedy film. Produced by the Thanhouser Film Corp. Surelock Jones, hoping to impress the girl he fancies, fails to solve either "The Mystery of the False Face" or "The Strange Case of the Vanished Heiress." The cast members are unknown. Released Feb. 16, 1912.

Surelock Keys

Some Adventures of Mr. Surelock Keys. Herbert Beeman (The Kerrisdale Kronikle Office, 1913). A collection of six very short stories, written to raise funds for the Organ Fund of St. Mary's Church, of Kerrisdale, British Columbia. Keys lives in Butcher Street and is assisted by Dr. Whenson.

Surelocked Home

"Hounded by Basketballs," featuring Surelocked Home and Dr. Whatsis. A one-act play by "Rollin' Albert" in *Plays: The Drama Magazine for Young People* (Apr. 1976). "A foul crime is blocked by Surelocked Home."

Surelocked Homes

"The Adventures of Surelocked Homes: Making Entry Less Elementary." State Farm Fire & Casualty Co., no date. A 16-page pamphlet spelling out "the advantages of Surelocked Homes and all the other measures you can take to deter a thief."

Surelout Hole

"Surelout Hole, Dr. Worthless in The Case That Finally Ended." A cartoon by Larry Borg. *The Forum* (Inver Hills Community College, May 21, 1976). Final exams are causing students to die of fright.

Sureluck Combs

1) Sureluck Combs, a parody of the Sherlock Holmes in William Gillette's play, appeared in *The Dynamiters*, a burlesque performance by the Hasty Pudding Club of Harvard in Cambridge, Massachusetts (Apr. 26, 1901). F.R. DuBois portrayed Sureluck Combs.

2) Sureluck Combs appeared in the *Doctor Funshine* Sunday comic strip by Bill Weber (Nov. 8, 1964). Dr. Funshine asks Sureluck Combs "to help him find the Pumpkin Patch Phantom."

Sureluck Gommes

Sureluck Gommes is the principal identity of Sherlock Holmes in *Wilde About Holmes* by Milo Yelesiyevich (Comic Masque, 2008) within a bizarre hallucination that occurs when "a delirious Holmes" suffers from "a cocaine frenzy." The Holmes/Gommes name is garbled continuously in the episode, with at least 21 versions mentioned. "Gommes, moonly the shadow knowl themselves."

Sureluck Holmes

1) In *The Adventure of Sherlock Holmes' Smarter Brother* (1975), Sigerson Holmes (portrayed by Gene Wilder, who also directed and wrote the comedy film) refers to his more famous brother (Douglas Wilmer) as "Sureluck Holmes."

2) *Sureluck Holmes, Private Eye*, a play for student actors by Craig Sodaro (Big Dog Publishing, 2007). Sureluck Holmes joins other members of the Nemesis Society to solve the murder of a fellow detective. Assisted by Joni Watson.

3) *Sureluck Holmes and the Band of Assassins*, a musical comedy produced by the Titus Productions Theatre Company of Salt Lake City in 2012. Assisted by Dr. Jane What'son, with Prof. Morry-Arty and Ilene Dover. Brett Anderson portrayed Sureluck Holmes.

Sureluck Homes
Sureluck Homes is a corruption of the name Sherlock Holmes in *Wilde About Holmes* by Milo Yelesiyevich (Comic Masque, 2008), one of many names used within a bizarre hallucination that occurs when "a delirious Holmes" suffers from "a cocaine frenzy."

Sureluck Hoomes
Jack and Jill and Company, featuring Sureluck Hoomes. A stage production of the John Craig Stock Company at the Bijou Theatre in London, Dec. 1906. A revision of Charles Dickens' *A Christmas Carol*. Thomas MacLarnie portrayed Sureluck Hoomes, while John Craig himself portrayed Scrooge.

Sureluck Hums
Sureluck Hums is a corruption of the name Sherlock Holmes in *Wilde About Holmes* by Milo Yelesiyevich (Comic Masque, 2008), one of many names used within a bizarre hallucination that occurs when "a delirious Holmes" suffers from "a cocaine frenzy."

Sureluck Jones
"Pound of the Baskervilles," featuring Sureluck Jones. Season 1, Episode 8, of *Chip 'n' Dale Rescue Rangers*, an animated television series on the Disney Channel. First aired April 16, 1989. Produced by the Walt Disney Co.; written by Eric Lewald; directed by John Kimball and Bob Zamboni. The Rescue Rangers' plane crashes into Baskerville mansion, where Chip assumes the role of Sureluck Jones.

Sureschlock Homely
"Young Sureschlock Homely." Dick DeBartolo (writer) and Mort Drucker (artist). *Mad*, No. 263 (E.C. Publications, June 1986). A satire/parody of the movie *Young Sherlock Holmes*. Assisted by Whatso, with Inspector LaClod.

Surly Homes

"The Martian Who Hated People," featuring Surly Homes. Edward Ludwig. In: *Inside and Science Fiction Advertiser*, No. 7 (Jan. 1955). An alien visitor is detected by Surly Homes and Dr. Watchson.

Syaloch

"The Martian Crown Jewels," featuring Syaloch. Poul Anderson. *Ellery Queen's Mystery Magazine* Feb. 1957). A classic science fiction story, often reprinted, including in *The Science Fictional Sherlock Holmes* (Robert C. Peterson, ed.; The Council of Four, 1960). Syaloch, the Martian detective, is "a seven-foot biped of vaguely storklike appearance."

Thinlock Bones

"The Adventure of the Table Foot." Allan Ramsay (as "Zero"). *The Bohemian*, Jan. 1894. Reprinted in *The Misadventures of Sherlock Holmes* (Ellery Queen, ed.; Little, Brown & Co., 1944). Assisted by Dr. Whatsoname, Thinlock Bones foils a plot targeting a young heiress.

Tide Pooles

1) Tide Pooles and his assistant Dr. Harcourt appeared in twelve stories written by Bradley Kjell in various journals or privately printed. The first was "The Adventure of the Missing Scuttle" in *Shades of Sherlock*, No. 2 (Nov. 1966), and the last was "The Adventure of the Retired Detective" in *The Three Pipe Problem*, No. 2 (Oct. 1971). Pools lived in Beeton Street and battled Professor Mortality.

2) Six additional Tide Pooles adventures, apparently based on the Kjell stories, were written by John Jacobson for various Sherlockian journals, beginning with "The Return of the Redheaded League" in *Shades of Sherlock Annual*, No. 1 (Jan. 1967) and concluding with "The Diogenes Club Murder" in *The Three Pipe Problem*, No. 2 (Oct. 1971).

Timelock Foams

"The Morning Smile," by Wex Jones, was a weekly comedy column written for the Hearst Newspapers between 1914 and 1916. Many of his columns featured a short mystery with solution featuring

"Timelock Foams, the Great Detective" and his assistant Potson. A dozen of these are reprinted in *Sherlock Holmes in America* (Bill Blackbeard, ed.; Harry N. Abrams, 1981).

Townclock Fumes
Townclock Fumes was one of seven parody names in "Prize Detective Story." Anonymous (*The Weekly Magazine*, May 8, 1897). Retitled "Holmes and the Startled Banker" in *As It Might Have Been: A Collection of Sherlockian Parodies from Unlikely Sources* (Robert C.S. Adey, ed.; Calabash Press, 1998). Hemlock Coombs repeatedly changes his name as he makes a series of trivial deductions.

Turlock Loams
Turlock Loams and Dr. Fatso appeared in 42 tales by John Ruyle, all privately printed by the author, mostly under the imprint of the Pequod Press. The first was "The Adventure of the Logophagous Client" in 1971, and the last was "The Adventure of the Beeping Man" in 2000. The tales are collected in *The Canon of Turlock Loams: The Compleat Adventures of Turlock Loams* (The Battered Silicon Dispatch Box, 2013).

Unlock Homes
Unlock Homes and Dr. Wilson appeared in at least two stories by Albert J. Bromley (as "Snowshoe Al"). "The Great Zoo Mystery" in *Clippings* (Chicago, Dec. 1929); and "The Great Flea Mystery" in *The San Francisco Chronicle* (Oct. 2, 1932), in which the owner of "a highly intelligent troupe of trained fleas" has lost one of its stars.

Upchuck Gnomes
Upchuck Gnomes is one of the "great made-up detectives," as conceived by James Parker in his review of Sherlockian volumes in *The New York Times Sunday Book Review* (Oct. 26, 2015).

Urlach Holmes
Urlach Holmes, portrayed by *Fox Football Daily* analyst Brian Urlacher in Sherlockian costume (FOX Sports, Mar. 4, 2014), was the one-time depiction of a "football detective" who "cracks the biggest cases of the NFL offseason."

Warlock Bones

"The Adventure of the Diamond Necklace," featuring Warlock Bones. In: *Misfits: A Book of Parodies*. George F. Forrest (Frank Harvey, 1905). Narrated by Goswell, who is astonished to find that his companion is a jewel thief.

Warlock Holmes

1) Warlock Holmes, a sorcerer detective, drawn by Koko Gonzales, appeared in *The K-Zone Bulletin*, the on-line publication of *K-Zone: Where Kids Rule*, produced by Summit Media of the Philippines. He was one of the 18 Holmes parody characters to take part in "Crisis of Infinite Holmes" (Aug. 2008), an adventure involving Sherlockian characters working together to save their concurrent universes.

2) Warlock Holmes is a bumbling sorcerer in three novels by G.S. Denning, all published by Titan Books: *Warlock Holmes: A Study in Brimstone* (2016), *Warlock Holmes: The Hell-Hound of the Baskervilles* (2017), and *Warlock Holmes: My Grave Ritual* (2018). Assisted by John Watson, with Moriarty appearing "in some form or other."

Warlock Horne

"The Case of the Missing Garter," featuring Warlock Horne and Potson. Peter Pascal. *Heebie Jeebie* (Utopian Press, 1950). An adult themed story.

Warlock-Jones

A Nineteenth Century Miracle, featuring Warlock-Jones, a consulting detective. Louis Zangwill (Chatto, 1897). Warlock-Jones is called in to solve the mystery of a tea merchant whose body was flung through a skylight, but who apparently died from drowning.

Wassup Holmes

"The Crazy Adventures of Wassup Holmes" was a musical sketch on Episode 7 of *Scratch and Burn* (2002), a variety program produced for MTV. Directed by Danny Salles. Erick Weiner starred as Wassup Holmes. The episode was never broadcast, but was made available online.

Wedlock Holmes

Wedlock Holmes, a bridegroom detective, drawn by Koko Gonzales, appeared in *The K-Zone Bulletin*, the on-line publication of *K-Zone: Where Kids Rule*, produced by Summit Media of the Philippines. He was one of the 18 Holmes parody characters to take part in "Crisis of Infinite Holmes" (Aug. 2008), an adventure involving Sherlockian characters working together to save their concurrent universes.

Werelock Holmes

Werelock Holmes, a werewolf detective, drawn by Koko Gonzales, appeared in *The K-Zone Bulletin*, the on-line publication of *K-Zone: Where Kids Rule*, produced by Summit Media of the Philippines. He was one of the 18 Holmes parody characters to take part in "Crisis of Infinite Holmes" (Aug. 2008), an adventure involving Sherlockian characters working together to save their concurrent universes.

Whodunit Stomes

"Mellow Melons," featuring the comic character Wile E. Coyote posing as Whodunit Stomes to cover up his own theft of Elmer Fudd's watermelons. *Beep Beep, The Roadrunner*, No. 84 (Gold Key Comics, Oct. 1979).

Whoreluck Hams

Whoreluck Hams is a corruption of the name Sherlock Holmes in *Wilde About Holmes* by Milo Yelesiyevich (Comic Masque, 2008), one of many names used within a bizarre hallucination that occurs when "a delirious Holmes" suffers from "a cocaine frenzy."

Wormwood Soames

"Wormwood in Bohemia: A Wormwood Soames Adventure." Roger Langridge (writer) and Amy Mebberson (artist). *The Muppet Show Comic Book*, No. 7 (BOOM Kids! Comics, June 2010). Reprinted in *Muppets Family Reunion* (DC Comics, Nov. 2011). The "great detective" Wormwood Soames, assisted by Fozzie, pursues a tapioca thief,

Yale Lock Holmes

"Murder on the Hill," featuring Yale Lock Holmes. *Kenyon Collegian* (Kenyon College of Gambier, Ohio), Dec. 16, 1929. A "novelette mystery story written by members of the class in English 48."

Yalelock Holmes
"The Mystery of the 9,404 Headless Bodies," featuring Yalelock Holmes of Faker Street. Gardner Rea. *Judge*, No. 84, "Mystery Number" (March 10, 1923). Reprinted in *Explorations*, No. 13 (Spring 1991). The detective, "Yalelock of the Hundred Scars," investigates the systematic elimination of bald men.

Zedlock Holmes
Zedlock Holmes is the identify assumed by the character Zed McGlunk in "Elementary, My Dear Coppers." Season 2, Episode 26, of *Police Academy: The Series*, an animated television series. Produced by Ruby-Spears Enterprises for Warner Brothers Television. Voiced by Dan Hennessey. First aired Jan. 7, 1989.

Zerlock Holmes
Zerlock Holmes was a character attending the annual Melbourne Zombie Shuffle. In Sherlockian costume complete with deerstalker and magnifying glass, the zombie was captured on film by the photographic artist and blogger known as Kwirky Kat, who posted the image on his "Photos 'n Phables" site in May 2015.

Zinsheimer Holmes
"J. Zinsheimer Holmes: The Adventure of the Eastside Ball" (Chapter 13) and "J. Zinsheimer Holmes: The Adventure of the Pudgy Leg" (Chapter 15). *Mr. Hobby: A Cheerful Romance*. Harold Kellock (The Century Co., 1913). J. Zinsheimer "had not been reading Sherlock Holmes for nothing," as he solves the disappearance of a jeweler's assets.

Ziplock Holmes
1) Ziplock Holmes, drawn by Koko Gonzales, appeared in *The K-Zone Bulletin*, the on-line publication of *K-Zone: Where Kids Rule*, produced by Summit Media of the Philippines. He was one of the 18 Holmes parody characters to take part in "Crisis of Infinite Holmes" (Aug. 2008), an adventure involving Sherlockian characters working together to save their concurrent universes.
2) "Ziplock Holmes and the Case of the Vanishing Crown Jewel," a murder mystery/comedy show. Christopher Bange. A Feb. 21,

2010, production of The Baggy Pants of Seattle, a clown-based theater company. Also featuring Dr. Watsup.

3) "The Ducks of Rednose: A Ziplock Holmes Mystery." Ian Fraser. National Novel Writing Month (nanowrimo.org, 2016).

Zoolock Holmes

Zoolock Holmes is an artistic portrayal of a rabbit character who assumes the role of Sherlock Holmes in "Zootropolis." Created by the Danish artist Gaia Due Rosendahl for Instagram (@gaiascreations), 2017.

THINK UP A NEW HOLMES!

In *The K-Zone Bulletin* of January 3, 2009, young readers were invited to "think up a new Holmes." The bulletin and accompanying blog are on-line publications of *K-Zone: Where Kids Rule*, produced by Summit Media of the Philippines.

K-Zone had been publishing various parodies of Sherlock Holmes (included in the main list of parody names), so the editors asked their readers to "create your own Holmes... his name and occupation," always using the formula ____lock Holmes, with the possibility of one being used in a story. Numerous suggestions for a parody name and occupation (in addition to being a detective) were submitted, some clever and interesting, and others strained or groan-worthy. (Remember, these are kids.) Here are their ideas.

Armlock Holmes, the astronaut (by Colwin, Jan. 3, 2009)

Artlock Holmes, the artist detective (by NySy, Mar. 13, 2009)

Babylock Holmes, the youngest detective (by NySy, Mar. 13, 2009)

Badlock Holmes, clumsy, but nice and successful detective (by Kenneth Saman, Dec. 20, 2011)

Baglock Holmes, the backpack detective (by Joel, Mar. 29, 2009)

Bigflock Holmes, the animal herder detective (by Jake Advincula, May 7, 2009)

Blindlock Holmes, who can solve cases with his eyes closed (by Tobias Tomas, Oct. 1, 2011)

Bonelock Holmes, a paleontologist detective (by Jake Advincula, May 7, 2009)

Brainlock Holmes, the smartest detective (by NySy, Mar. 13, 2009)

Bravelock Holmes, the bravest detective (by NySy, Mar. 13, 2009)

Brushlock Holmes, the legendary painter (by DSF, Jan. 14, 2009)

Bucklock Holmes, the multi-billionaire detective (by Auser Jann Pagunsan, Jan. 21, 2009)

Candylock Holmes, the candy maker (by NySy, Mar. 13, 2009)

Caninelock Holmes, the dog detective (by Lopez J., May 21, 2009)

Caplock Holmes, the legendary computer typer (by Shawn Kent Aviar, Jan. 4, 2009)

Carlock Holmes, the nurse detective (by NySy, Mar. 13, 2009)

Cashlock Holmes, the cashier detective (by Colwin, Jan. 12, 2009)

Chestlock Holmes, the famous treasure hunter (by Jake Advincula, May 7, 2009)

Cleanlock Holmes, the neat freak detective (by NySy, Mar. 13, 2009)

Coffinlock Holmes, the funeral director (by Mark, Jan. 14, 2009)

Commentlock Holmes, a commentator detective (by Lopez J., May 21, 2009)

Controlock Holmes, video game master detective (by Mark David C. Silencio, Nov. 3, 2014)

Cracklelock Holmes, the robotic detective (by Auser Jann Pagunsan, Jan. 21, 2009)

Crashlock Holmes, the clumsiest detective (by Mark Faune, Jan. 19, 2009)

Curlock Holmes, the policeman (by Colwin, Jan. 9, 2009)

Dancelock Holmes, the dancer detective (by NySy, Mar. 13, 2009)

Dragonlock Holmes, the dragon detective (by Joel, Mar. 29, 2009)

Dramalock Holmes, a movie director and detective (by Jake Advincula, May 7, 2009)

Duhlock Holmes, the stupidest detective (by Lopez J., May 21, 2009)

Dwarflock Holmes, the story keeper (by Mark, Jan. 14, 2009)

Fablock Holmes, the fashion designer and fashion expert (by NySy, Mar. 13, 2009)

Felinelock Holmes, the cat detective (by Lopez J., May 21, 2009)

Femlock Holmes, the one and only female detective (by Joel, Mar. 29, 2009)

Fightlock Holmes, the Kung Fu master (by NySy, Mar. 13, 2009)

Firstlock Holmes, who is first at everything (by Iris, Jan. 11, 2009)

Flexlock Holmes, the elastic-man detective (by Colwin, Jan. 12, 2009)

Flylock Holmes, the pilot detective (by NySy, Mar. 13, 2009)

Foldlock Holmes, foldabot builder and detective (by Mark David C. Silencio, Nov. 3, 2014)

Foodlock Holmes, the diet expert (by NySy, Mar. 13, 2009)

Footlock Holmes, the messenger detective (by NySy, Mar. 13, 2009)

Frankenlock Holmes, a monster detective (by Lopez J., May 21, 2009)

Gadgetlock Holmes, gadget geek and computer shop owner (by Tobias Tomas, Oct. 1, 2011)

Gamelock Holmes, the expert gamer (by Mickey Mouse 16, Mar. 12, 2009)

Gaplock Holmes, the vegetarian detective (by Colwin, Jan. 4, 2009)

Goldlock Holmes, a prospector detective (by Jake Advincula, May 7, 2009)

Hoselock Holmes, the firefighter detective (by Mark, Jan. 14, 2009)

Hungrylock Holmes, who is always hungry (by Tobias Tomas, Oct. 1, 2011)

Icelock Holmes, the Eskimo detective (by Auser Jann Pagunsan, Jan. 21, 2009)

Idolock Holmes, a singing idol detective (by Lopez J., May 21, 2009)

Ionlock Holmes, the chemistry detective (by Colwin, Jan. 11, 2009)

Judolock Holmes, the judo expert detective (by Joel, Mar. 29, 2009)

K-lock Holmes, the official *K-Zone* detective (by Auser Jann Pagunsan, Jan. 21, 2009)

Kicklock (Kickbutt) Holmes, a tough detective, and Ducktor Whatson (by EFC, Mar. 22, 2010, who added short sketch featuring his characters)

Knotlock Holmes, the shoe seller detective (by Janardan Rilloraza, May 15, 2009)

Kunlock Holmes, the anime detective (by Mark Faune, Jan. 19, 2009)

Laptoplock Holmes, a laptop loving detective (by Lopez J., May 23, 2009)

Lockerlock Holmes, the lock master and detective (by Vince Renzo, Jan. 16, 2009)

Mindlock Holmes, who solves the hardest mystery in history (by Strike Ninja, Jan. 21, 2009)

Nolock Holmes, the fattest detective (by Mark David C. Silencio, Nov. 3, 2014)

Numlock Holmes, math teacher detective (by Hizon, Jan. 9, 2009)

Penlock Holmes, the famous comic book artist (by James Cura, Jan. 8, 2009)

Phonelock Holmes, the legendary texter and detective (by CJ, Jan. 4, 2009)

Picklock Holmes, former thief and "The Thieving Expert" (by Denz Jay, Mar. 26, 2011)

Pillowlock Holmes, a sleeping detective (by Lopez J., May 23, 2009)

Plexlock Holmes, an elastic-man detective (by Colwin, Jan 12, 2009)

Pocklock Holmes, Pokemon nerd and detective (by Mark David C. Silencio, Nov. 3, 2014)

Powlock Holmes, the famous super hero (by Mark Faune, Jan. 9, 2009)

Pranklock Holmes, the prankster (by Colwin, Jan. 18, 2009)

Readlock Holmes, the reader and detective (by NySy, Mar. 13, 2009)

Roarlock Holmes, the dinosaur expert detective (by Lopez J., May 21, 2009)

Rocklock Holmes, the legendary rock icon (by Cadmielle, Jan. 9, 2009)

Scarlock Holmes, the legendary monster and detective (by DSF, Jan. 14, 2009)

Scilock Holmes, the scientist detective (by NySy, Mar. 13, 2009)

Shadeslock Holmes, the super cool detective and shades shop owner (by Tobias Tomas, Oct. 1, 2011)

Sharklock Holmes, the shark detective (by Lopez J., May 21, 2009)

Shiverlock Holmes, survival expert in winter detective (by Strike Ninja, Jan. 21, 2009)

Shiverlock Holmes, who solves the scariest mystery (by Strike Ninja, Jan. 21, 2009)

Shrieklock Holmes, who shouts during investigations (by Lopez J., May 21, 2009)

Shrinklock Holmes, the smallest detective (by Lopez J., May 21, 2009)

Sicklock Holmes, the sick detective (by Lopez J., May 21, 2009)

Singlock Holmes, the singer detective (by NySy, Mar. 13, 2009)

Sportlock Holmes, the fit and sports-loving detective (by Lopez J., May 21, 2009)

Spylock Holmes, the spy (by Mark, Jan. 14, 2009, who added a short sketch titled "Who Is Holmes Proof?" on Feb. 5)

Starlock Holmes, the shining movie star and celebrity (by NySy, Mar. 13, 2009)

Sunnylock Holmes, the legendary summer detective (by Strike Ninja, Jan. 21, 2009)

Swordlock Holmes, online nerd and detective (by Mark David C. Silencio, Nov. 3, 2014)

Tinlock Holmes, a robot detective (by Jake Advincula, May 7, 2009)

Toddlerlock Holmes, the detective in training (by Joel, Mar. 29, 2009)

Toylock Holmes, the toymaker detective (by NySy, Mar. 13, 2009)

Transformerlock Holmes, an autobot detective (by Lopez J., May 23, 2009)

Villainlock Holmes, a bad but helpful detective (by Lopez J., May 23, 2009)

Warlock Holmes, the magician detective (by Jake Advincula, May 7, 2009)

Warlock Holmes, the war detective (by Joel, Mar. 29, 2009)

Waterlock Holmes, the marine biologist (by NySy, Mar. 13, 2009)

Wavelock Holmes, the surfer (by Mark, Jan. 14, 2009)

Winlock Holmes, the detective who wins everything (by Bubblecute, Feb. 1, 2009)

Wrestlelock Holmes, a wrestling detective (by Lopez J., May 21, 2009)

Wristlock Holmes, the time expert (by Jay Jules, Jan. 3, 2009)

Zonelock Holmes, survival expert in unknown places (by Strike Ninja, Jan. 21, 2009)

MY DEAR WATSONS

While not quite as numerous as the parody names of Sherlock Holmes, the Watsons by any other name that do appear nevertheless show as much creativity. This list contains only those names utilized in this volume and omits any that are simply "Watson," but nothing more. Also omitted are titles such as "Dr." or "Mr." and the first name "John" or "John H."

Ampson	(Jane Ampson)	Pureluck Holmes (2)
Átsonez		Cerlocio Olmez
Batsin	(Batsin Belfry)	Foreclose Holmes
Batson		Herlock Sholmes (21, 24)
		Sheerluck Holds (1)
Benwat		Shaw La Coombs
Blotzo		Sheerluck Holmes (3)
Bon-Bon		Sherbet Foams
Boobson		Arson Clews
Bopson		Sheerbach Tones
Botson		Sheerluck Coames
Bottson		Sheerflop Soames
Burrows		Shamrock Ferret
Buttsin		Sheerluck Holmes (2)
Catson	(Dr. Jane Catson)	Sherlock Bones (24)
		Sherlock Bones (25)
Chumpson		Padlock Bones (2)
Clodson		Sherlock Combs (4)
Clotson		Morlock Tomes
Cotson		Potluck Bones
Dash		Forelock Combe
Datson		Blaylock Jones
		Hemlock Holmes (11)
Datsun		Sherlock Jones (12)
Dawson		Geoffrey Holm
		Haricot Bones

Doile		Mylock Bloodstalker (1, 2)
Dotson		Forelock Tomes
		Hemlock Jones (11)
		Herlock Sholmes (10)
	(Wactor Dotson)	Herlock Sholmes (25)
		Mereluck Tombs
	(Woctor Dotson)	Shedlock Combs
Dover		Pharaoh Jones
Dragon		Sherlock Combs (2)
Dripple		Sherlock Droopy
Drone	(McGuffin Drone)	Sonar T. Phoom
Fatso		Turlock Loams
Fatson	(Elmer Fatson)	Hemlock Jones (9)
		Herlock Shomes (13)
		Sheerluck Jones (9)
Flopson		Froglock Holmes (1)
		Shamrock Holmes (2)
Flotsam		Brainy Domes
		Bumlock Tomes
		Headlock Holmes (3)
		Herlock Shomes (15)
		Ozone Holmes
		Shamrock Holmes (2)
Flotsom		Hemlock Stones (1)
Goswell		Warlock Bones
Gotsome		Hairlock Combs (4)
Gottsom		Herlock Shomes (17)
Harcourt		Shrock Holmes
		Tide Pooles (1)
Hopson		Shylock Combs
Hotbun		Rex Homes
Hotsam		Herlock Shomes (15)
Hotson		Mycock Bones
		Padlock Bones (1)
		Sheerluck Jones (7)
		Sherlock Bones (21)
Jobson		Purlock Hone
Jotson		Herlock Sholmes (14, 22, 26, 27)
		Lockjaw Bones (3)
		Padlock Domes
		Padlock Jones (2)
Klutzdam		Finlock Combes

Larker		Molar Vons
Matson		Herr Lock Söames
		Skylock Peyton
Motson	(Boniface "Bon" Motson)	Clewlow Holmes
	(Tom Motson)	Hairlock Jones
Muffin		Sherlock Soames (2)
Neeps		Sherlock Haggis
Notsaw		Pollack Hmms
Omston	(Chon Omston)	Saeloc Holmes
Ouatson	(Doc Ouatson)	Charles Kolmes
Parker	(Dr. Lyndon Parker)	Solar Pons (1, 2)
Plotsam		Herlock Shomes (15)
Poston		Herlock Shomes (9)
Potsdam		Porlock Moans
Potsom		Hemlock Shomes
Potson		Chubb-Lock Homes
		Chubblock Homes
		Forelock Domes
		Hawkeye Soammes
		Herlock Sholmes (17)
		Herlock Shomes (6)
	(Dr. Samuel Potson)	Picklock Holes
		Sheerluck Gnomes
		Sheerluck Holmes (4)
		Sherlock Bones (7)
		Sherlock Soames (1)
		Timelock Foams
		Warlock Horne
Proctor		Sherbert Foams
Rotson		Herlock Shomes (8)
		Shamrock Holmes (2)
		Sheerluck Jones (1)
		Sherlock Romes (2)
		Smallpox Soles
Sacker	(Ormand Gesundheit Sacker)	Kreplock Holes
	(Ormand Sacker)	Sherrinford Holmes (1)
Sandwort		Hoskell Chomers
Schultz	(Dr. Henry Schultz)	Lockley Soames
Scotson		Dennis Bones

		Sherlock Romes (1)
		Sherluck Bones
Snotson		Hemlock Stones (3)
Spitzen		Sheerluck Jones (2)
Spotson		Herlock Shomes (10)
		Oilock Combs
		Sheerluck Bones (9)
		Sheerluck Homes (2)
		Sheerluck Jones (8)
Spotzum		Sherlock Roams (1)
Sotwun		Herlock Sholmes (23)
Squatson		Hemlock Foames
		Hurlock Shoams
Stupid	(Dr. S.J. Stupid, M.D.)	Sherlock Höek
Sun Wat		Stately Homes
Swanson		Shylock Holmes (4)
		Skylark Bones (1)
Swatson		Beerlock Foams
		Doorlock Combs
		Fetlock Jones
		Herlock Holmes (2)
		Herlock Sholmes (5)
	(Juan Swatson)	Herlock Shomes (19)
		Lockjaw Bones (1)
Swotson		Heddlock Phones
Thatson		Shilah Coombes
Thensome		Slipshod Helms
Totson		Sherlock Gnomes (1)
Twatson		Sherlocko Homo
Tweany		Mooch Sheckls
Vasser		Shadrach Chomes
Vatson		Sherlock Combs (4)
Vatsov	(Dr. Ivan Vatsov)	Sherslav Glomsky
Voltson		Sherlock Combs (3)
Votson		Herlock Sholmes (6)
Wa To Son		Sherdog Bones
		Sherlock Bones (23)
Wa Tsn		Sherk Oms
Wa Tze-na		Shih Lok
Waddus		Dudley Jones
Wadjsen		Sa Haapu

Waffles		Sheila Holmes
		Sherwood Homes (2)
Walker	(Jim Walker)	Sanford Haus
Walnut		Fetlock Holmes
Walruss	(Dr. Yun H. Walruss)	Sholomon Hume
Wanda		Shirley Holmes (6)
Warner		Sherwood Lang
Wan-seung	(Ha Wan-seung)	Seol-ok
Wantbun		Sheerluck Bones (8)
Warsaw		Kerlock Shomes
		Petlock Holmes
Wasserman		Sherlock Cohen
Waspon		Cockroach Bones
		Squirrelock Holmes
Wat Sun		Sher Lok Holmes
Watchme		Hemlock Soames
Watchpot		Neville Boyles
Watchson		Surly Homes
Watdaughter		Padlock Bones (5)
Waters		Sherwood House
Watkins		Dorlock Homes
		Philo Holmes
		Sherlock Domes
		Spurlock Holmes
Watney		Schlock Homes (1)
Watnot		Holmlock Shears (2)
		Sheerlock Omes
Watroast		Shumlock Holmes
Watsan		Sir Luck Helm
Watsdotter		Sheercrocked Moans
Watsis		Padlock Homes
Watsnew		Headlock Holmes
		Shirley Holmes (13)
Watso		Fellock Holmes
		Hawkshaw (1)
		Sherlocko
Watson	(Billy Joe-Bob "Bubba" Watson)	Hamhock Holmes
	(Dickter Watson)	Shercock Bones (2)
	(DJ Watson)	Poplock Holmes
	(Doktor Watson)	Sherlock Holmz
	(Dot Watson)	Sheryl Lock Holmes
	(Dotty Watson)	Sheer Luck Holmes (3)
	(Dotty Watson)	Shirley Holmes (4)
	(Dr. Alwin Watson)	Shrr'lock of Kholmes
	(Dr. Janet Watson)	Skylark Holmes
	(Dr. Mike Watson)	Shamrock Holmes (1)

	(Henry F. Watson)	Simon Rolfe
	(Jack Watson)	Shirley Holmes (17)
	(Jamie Watson)	Charlotte Holmes (5)
	(James Watson)	Stamford Holmes (1)
	(Jane Watson)	Shirley Holmes (11)
	(Jean Watson)	Shirley Holmes (3)
	(Jennie Watson)	Shirley Holmes (16)
	(Jimmy Watson)	Shelley Holmes
	(Joan Watson)	Sherly Holmes
	(Joan Watson)	Sherman Holmes
	(Joan Watson)	Shirley Holmes (2)
	(Joni Watson)	Sureluck Holmes (2)
	(Nigel Watson)	Sharlock Holmes
	(Proctor Watson)	Sherlock Jones (15)
	(Watson Bee)	Sherlock Hums (1)
	(Watson Mouse, M.D.)	Sherlock Ferret
	(Wendy Watson)	Padlock Holmes (8)
	(Wilma Watson)	Shirley Holmquist
Watsup		Mukluk Gnomes
		Sheerluck Bones (5)
		Sheerluck Cracky
		Sherlock Homie (1)
		Shylock Bones (10)
		Surefoot Jones
		Ziplock Holmes (2)
Watt-Sun		Sir Loch Hoames
Watts		Hemlock Holmes (9)
		Herlock Soames
	(Jonny Watts)	Sheridan Hume
		Shurl
		Sherlock Ohms (1, 3)
Watts-On		Sherlock Ohms (7)
Watt's Son		Shortwave Ohms
Wattson		Sherlock Ohms (8)
Wattsun		Sheerluck Ohms (2)
Wattsey		Padlock Bones (4)
Wawan		Sir Luck Helm
Wazzat		Sortluck Ohms
Weistson	(Ronald Weistson)	Hermlock Holmes
Westcott		Horlock Shem
Westieson		Sherlock Hound (5)
Weston		Brihtric Donne
		Enoch Bone
		Sherbourne Rath
Wetsuit		Shamrock Cohen
Whartson		Sherwood Homes (1)

What's On		Sheerluck Jones (6)
		Sherbet Jones
		Shylock Homes (2)
		Sure-Lock Home
What's-it		Shamrock Holmes (2)
What's-on		Shamrock Holmes (2)
What's-up		Shamrock Holmes (2)
What'son	(Dr. Jane What'son)	Sureluck Holmes (3)
What'sup		Shylock Bones (5)
Whatley		Shylar Holmes
Whatnot		Herlock Shomes (18)
		Sure-Lock Homes
Whats-on		Sheerluck Roams
Whatsis		Hawk-Sure
		Surelocked Home
Whatsit		Nerdslock Combs
		Sherlock Bones (11)
		Shermlock Shomes
		Shylock Bones (8)
Whatso		Shamus Homes
		Sureschlock Homely
Whatsome		Sheerluck Bones (4)
Whatson		Doorlock Homes (1)
		Hamhock Bones
		Hemlock Holmes (13)
		Padlock Holmes (2)
		Sheerluck Combs
		Sheerluck Coombes
		Shercock Bones (1)
		Sherlaw Kombs
		Shylock Hames
		Shylock Homes (3, 4)
Whatsup		Pureluck Holmes (1)
		Shamrock Jones
		Sheerluck Goof
	(Dr. G. Whatsup)	Sheerluck Houses
		Sherlock Snoop
Whatswine		Sherlock Hams (2)
Wheaton		Sherbert Cones
Whenson		Surelock Keys
Whetstone		Sherlock Stones
Whoopson	(Dr. Jon Whoopson)	Shellack Homes
Whooson		Sure-They-Lock Homez
Whopper	(Doctored Whopper)	Shamrock Wolmbs
Wilkins		Shylock Oames

Wilson	(James Wilson)	Cedric Coombes
		Sherman Horn
		Shylock Homes (5)
		Unlock Homes
Wimpy		Barratt Holmes (1, 2)
Winston		Sherlock Hound (1)
Wiston		Sherlark Honed
Witless		Smearlock Homeless
Witsend		Shearlock Combs
		Sheerluck Holds (2)
		Sheerluck Holmes (5)
Witsno		Herblock Stones
Witson	(Jimmy Witson)	Sheer Luck Holmes (1)
Wonson		Spitlock Phones
Woodsen	(Jane Woodsen)	Charlotte House
Woodstock		Snoopy Holmes
Wopsome		Hemlock Bones (2)
Wopson		Suburban Homes
Worthless		Surelout Hole
Wosit		Sherlock Sooty
Wotsing		Burdock Rose
Wrotten-clew		Sherlock Blake (2)

THE WILY PROFESSORS

Artie Morey
Arty-Morty
Furriarty
Goryarty

Inferiority
Kooparity

Maharishi
Mariarty
Marionette
Marty
Mary Arty
Maury R. Tee
Melmoriarty
Mire Arty
Moldy-Arty
Moledigger
Molly Arty   (Plofessor Molly Arty)
Molly Harty
Montiarity
Moore-Arity
Moratorium
Morearteries
Moreorlessity
Moresconi
Moriartsky
Moriratty
Moritorium
Morry-Arty
Mortality
Mortuarity
Mortuary
Morty
Notoriety
O'Myhatty
Proriarty   (Mofessor Proriarty)

Doorlock Homes (1)
Shermlock Shomes
Purrrlock Holmes
Hemlock Foames
Sherbet Jones
Sherlock Goof
Herlock Solmes
Sherlock Mario
Saurian Holmes
Naughton Jones
Shylock Homes (5)
Schlock Homes
Sheer Luck Holmes (3)
Sir Loch Hoames
Shumlock Holmes
Sherlark Honed
Sure-Lock Homes
Harelock Holmes
Sher Lok Holmes
Shirley Holmes (13)
Brainy Domes
Shylock Holmes (4)
Shercock Bones (1)
Sheerluck Bones (9)
Sheerluck Goof
Signor Om-mez
Shedlock Homes
Sherlock Bones (25)
Sherlockz Homz
Sureluck Holmes (3)
Tide Pooles (1)
Shamus Homes
Sheerluck Coombes
Charles Kolmes
Padlock Domes
Smallpox Soles
Shedlock Combs

Smartie-Artie
Yom Tirra
Yuraliarty

Surefoot Jones
Sherlock Sholem
Padlock Holmes (2)

THE PERPETRATORS

Abbott, Russ
Abrams, Fred
Adair, Gilbert
Adler, Charlie
Adrian, Jack
Aiken, J.B.
Aikman, Anthony (as "Sir Arthur Go-on Foil")
Albrecht, Howard
Alcala, Alfredo
Alexander, Barbara
Alexander, Sue
All, Jecca
Ambrose, Marylou
Amelin, Michel
Anderson, Brett
Anderson, Isaac
Anderson, Poul
Ando, Yuma

Angell, Judie
Anonymous (as "A. Coining Doyle")
Anonymous (as "A. Conning Goil")
Anonymous (as "A. Donan Coyle")
Anonymous (as "A. J. P.")
Anonymous (as "C O'M")
Anonymous (as "Castor Oyle")
Anonymous (as "Croton Oyle")
Anonymous (as "D-Double-E")
Anonymous (as "E. Alson Canoy')
Anonymous (as "Exile")
Anonymous (as "Feathered Fox")
Anonymous (as "Fibulous")
Anonymous (as "John Watlock")

Barratt Holmes (1)
Herlock Shomes (5)
Schlock Holmes (2)
Brainy Domes
Hemlock Bones (7)
Sheerluck Holds (1)
Sheerluck Roams
Sherlock Jones (12)
Mylock Bloodstalker (1)
Sherlock Bones (11)
Blaylock Jones
Squirrel-Lock Holmes
Hemlock Holmes (13)
Sherlock Yack (1, 2)
Sureluck Holmes (3)
Showman Hoyle
Syaloch
Sherdog Bones
Sherlock Bones (23)
Shirley Holmes (16)
Padlock Holmes (3)
Shirley Combs (1)
Herlock Sholmes (9, 18)
Sheerluck Bones (5)
Potluck Bones
Hardas Stone
Sherlock Romes (1)
Bumlock Tomes
Hoskell Chomers
Forelock Domes
Girlock Holmes
Spitlock Phones
Sherlock Cones (2)
Sherlock Foams (2)
Sherlock Phones
Sherlock Roams (2)
Sherlock Watson (2)

Anonymous (as "John Watlock") (cont.)	Sherlock Zones
Anonymous (as "Ka")	Herlock Shomes (1)
Anonymous (as "Knight of Time")	Sherlock Combs (5)
	Sherlock Homes (2)
	Sherlock Moans
	Sherlock Roams (2)
Anonymous (as "Miniature Bucky")	Sherlock Clones
	Sherlock Drones (2)
	Sherlock Gnomes (2)
	Sherlock Groans (4)
	Sherlock Roams (2)
Anonymous (as "Ole Doc Watson")	Herlock Sholmes (12)
Anonymous (as "Rainbowjack2000")	Shoelock Holmes (2)
Anonymous (as "Rollin' Albert")	Surelocked Home
Anonymous (as "Selah")	Hemlock Bones (3)
Anonymous (as "Sir Arthur Donan Coyle")	Herlock Sholmes (17)
Anonymous (as "Slaba Eyce)	Foreclose Holmes
Anonymous (as "Slippery Elm")	Suburban Holmes (1)
Anonymous (as "Suatel")	Heddlock Phones
Anonymous (as "T.P.J.")	Herlock Sholmes (22)
Anonymous (as "The Bark")	Herlock Sholmes (15)
Anonymous (as "Yaffle")	Picklock Homes
Anonymous (in "Prize Detective Story")	Badlock Tombs
	Hemlock Booms
	Hemlock Coombs
	Padlock Booms
	Sherlock Rooms
	Shylock Plumes
	Townclock Fumes
Anonymous (in "The Marischal Manor Mystery")	Hamlock Shears
	Hamrock Shoals
	Picklock Soles
	Shamrock Holes
	Smallpox Soles
Anscombe, Nicholas	Sherlock Moans (2)
Archibald, Joe	Shylock Bones (4)
Armstrong, Anthony	Holmlock Shears (2)
Armstrong, Tom	Sherlock Hounds
Arnold, A.F	Sherlock Watson (1)
Aroca, Alberto Lopez	Sholomon Hume
Arons, Rich	Brainy Domes
Arriola, Gus	Sherlock Hums (3)
Artist (as "Adrienne D.")	Dalock Holmes, Sherlock Dalek
Artist (as "Caffrey")	Sherlock Jones (4)
Artist (as "Becka")	Squirrel-Loch-Holmes
Artist (as "KamiGoat")	Sorelock Holmes

Artist (as "Kwirky Kat")	Zerlock Holmes
Artist (as "MM")	Harlot Holmes
Artist (as "Mr. Broom")	Sherlock Drones (1)
Artist (as "Taz")	Artlock Holmes
Artist (as "Wells")	Charles Kolmes
Ashby, Ralph	Shylock Bones (11)
Asher, Max	Padlock Bones (7)
Aston, Hugh	Sherlock Ferret
Atkins, John	Hamhock Holmes
Austin, Philip	Hemlock Stones (1)
Avery, Matthew	Shylock Bones (10)
Avryl, Georges	Sherlhock Holmès
Ayers, Dick	Mylock Bloodstalker (1)
	Shylock Bones (5)
Babcock, James W.	Padlock Bones (5)
Bacchi, Amanda	Sherly Holmes
Bach, Richard	Shamrock Ferret
Bache, Ernie	Shylock Bones (5)
Bachelor, Andrew	Sherlock Homeboy (2)
Bailey, Hilary	Charlotte Holmes (3)
Bailey, Olive	Shadlock Bones
Baker, G. Graham	Sherlock Oomph
Ballard, S.M.	Nerdslock Combs
Ballentine, Carl	Sherlock Domes
Bange, Christopher	Ziplock Holmes (2)
Bangs, John Kendrick	Raffles Holmes
	Shylock Homes (1)
Baratz-Logsted, Lauren	Sherlock Bones (24)
Barks, Carl	Surelock Holmes (4)
Barr, Robert (as "Luke Sharp")	Sherlaw Kombs
Barranco, Victoria	Sherlark Holmes
Barrett, Cheryl	Sheer Luck Holmes (3)
Barry, Josh	Hairlock Combs (2)
Basara, Pat	Sherlock Jones (17)
Bateman, W.G.	Hemlock Jones (6)
Baumann, Károly	Sherlock Hochmes
Beaman, Bruce R.	Sherwood Homes (2)
Bean, James	Shylock Homes (5)
Beattle, W.	Shccrluck Bones (6)
Beckley, Zoe	Herlock Shomes (16)
Beeman, Hebert	Surelock Keys
Beletic, Kitty	Charlotte Holmes (2)
Bellafronte, Priscilla	Egglock Holmes
Benson, Dan (i.e., Donato Alfredo Boccio)	Herlock Sholmes (24)
Benson, Scott	Sherlock Höek

Bhangoo, Sandy	Sherlock Jones (16)
Bigwood, John	Sherlock Bones (25)
Bingham, Ralph	Padlock Bones (5)
Bischoff, Simon	Sherlock Bones (5)
Bishop, John	Barratt Holmes (1)
Blackiston, Clarence	Sheerluck Jones (1)
Blackman, Edwin, Jr.	Sherlock Bones (7)
Blackman, Malorie	Sheer-Luck Holmes (4)
Blair, Edward S.	Sheerluck Jones (2)
Boardman, John	Sherslav Glomsky
Boccio, Donato Alfredo (as "Dan Benson")	Herlock Sholmes (24)
Bode, Doc	Sherlock Roams (1)
Bonney, Joseph L.	Simon Rolfe
Borg, Larry	Surelout Hole
Bosco, Don	Sherlock Hong
Bosman, Herman Charles (as "Ben Eath")	Lockjaw Bones (3)
Bostwick, Mary E.	Padlock Bones (9)
Boucher, Anthony	Sherk Oms
Boyd, Alex	Sherlock Clones (1)
Boyer, Wilbur S.	Shearlock Hollmes
Braczyk, Paul	Petcock Holmes
Bradley, Milton	Shylock Bones (6)
Bressette, Linna	Shylock Holmes (4)
	Skylark Bones (1)
Brierly, Edmund C.	Hairlock Combs (2)
Brogan, Walter	Schlock Holmes (1)
Bromberg, Andrew	Sherlock Jones (13)
Bromley, Albert J. (as "Snowshoe Al")	Rex Homes
	Unlock Homes
Brookins, Gary	Sherlock Homey
Brower, Otto	Sheerluck Jones (7)
Brown, Adam	Sheerluck Bones (6)
Brown, John	Sherlock Cohen
Brown, Kent R.	Shirley Holmes (17)
Buchwald, Art	Hamhock Bones
Budd, Robin	Sherlock Homely
Buggé, Carol	Sherlock Helms (2)
Bulandi, Danny	Mylock Bloodstalker (1)
Buonocore, Bud (i.e., Bob Lynn)	Shamrock Cohen
Burley, Philip	Stamford Holmes (1)
Burton, Tim	Sherlock Homely
Bush, Rick	Mycock Bones
	Sherlock Bones (21)
Butler, Ellis Parker	Philo Gubb
	Shagbark Jones

Cabot, John Paul	Sharlowe Com's
Cami, Pierre Henri	Loufock-Holmès
Caniff, Milton	Stevenson Holmes
Carey, Ed	Shedlock Holmes
Carnegie, Joseph	Sherlock Kush
Carpenter, William A.	Shylock Bones (8)
Carter, Laura	Charlotte Holmes (2)
Cassatt, Chris	Sherlock Homey
Catalano, Joe	Schlock Holmes (1)
	Shylock Homes (3)
Cavallaro, Brittany	Charlotte Holmes (5)
Caverno, Steve	Shamrock Houses
Cecil, Kevin	Sherlock Gnomes (4)
Ceder, Ralph	Sherlock Sleuth
Chandler, Larry	Surelick Holms
Charnock, Ian	Sherlock Bones (18)
	Sherlock Hoomes
Chase, Cheryl	Shirley Lock Holmes
Cher	Cherlock Holmes (2)
	Shirley Holmes (7)
Chester, S. Beach	Herlock Soames
Christelle, Ruth	Sherlock Yack (1)
Clare, Jenny	Hairlock Combs (2)
Clark, Eric D.	Sherlock Hams (1)
Clark, Harold Asa	Sherlaw Combs
Clark, Philip	Sonar T. Phoom
Clark, Simon	Sherringham Holmes
Clarkson, Steve	Shearlock Combs
Clifford, W.H.	Padlock Holmes (5)
Cohen, Sol	Padlock Bones (1)
Colan, Gene	Hemlock Shoals
Coldeway, Anthony	Sherlock Boob (2)
Colman, Clarence	Padlocked Homes
Comber, Bobbie	Pureluck Jones
Conklin, Bill	Fellock Holmes
Cook, Will Marion	Shylock Homestead
Coon, Francis	Hemlock Bones (6)
Cooper, Jack	Sherlock Bones (5)
Coote, Jay	Sheerluck Coames
Copper, Basil	Solar Pons (2)
Coquet, Georges	Charley Colms
Coran, Pierre	Charlock Halms
Corbett, Matthew	Sherlock Sooty
Coren, Alan	Sher Lok Holmes
Cornell, Paul	Shirley Holmes (17)
Corning, Leavitt	Shedlock Combs

Court, George	Sheerluck Bones (4)
Coxon, G.R.	Smearlock Holmes
Craig, John	Sureluck Hoomes
Crawfurd, Oswald	Purluck Hone
Crummel, Susan Stevens	Sherlock Bones (22)
Cuffari, Christina	Herlock Holmes (1)
Cummings, Jim	Sheerluck Bonkers
Cunningham, Arthur	Suburban Homes
Curtis, Allen	Padlock Bones (7)
Cusworth, A.B.	Sherlocks Combs
Daniels, Mickey	Sherlock Hawkshaw
Davis, Jack	Sherlock Hemlock (2)
Davis, Jacquie	Purrrlock Holmes
Davis, Sammy, Jr.	Sherlock Jones (11)
Dawson, Les	Sherlock Murphy
Dawson, Peter (i.e., Ronald Goulart)	Philo Combs
de Forrest, Charles	Sherlock Doyle
de la Casinière, Nicholas	Loufock-Holmès
DeBartolo, Dick	Sureschlock Homely
Debeck, Billy	Shellac Holmsburg
Debussy, Claude	Sherlock Key
DeCandido, Keith R.A.	Shirley Holmes (18)
DeCarlo, Mike	Sherlock Stones
DeLuise, Peter	Momlock Holmes
Delves, C. Warren	Sherwood Lang
Denison, John	Padlock Holmes (8)
Denning, G.S.	Warlock Holmes (2)
Denver, Simon	Sheer Luck Holmes (2)
Depp, Johnny	Sherlock Gnomes (4)
Derleth, August	Solar Pons (1)
Dhami, Narinder	Shirley Holmes (16)
Dias, Earl J.	Shellack Homes
Dickinson, H.T.	Herlock Shomes (11)
Diddy, P.	Sherlock Homeboy (1)
Dighton, John	Pureluck Jones
Dillon, Teddy Lee	Sherlock Dodo
Dirks, Rudolph	Sherlock Guck
	Shurlock Guck
Disney, Walt	Shamrock Bones
	Shedlock Jones
	Sheerluck Bonkers
	Sheerluck Goof
	Sherlock Dale
	Sherlock Goof
	Sherlock Hemlock (3)

Disney, Walt (cont.)	Sherlock Mouse
	Surefoot Jones
	Surelock Holmes (4)
	Surelock Grones
	Sureluck Jones
Dixon, Ben	Hemlock Jones (9)
Donohue, Dorothy	Sherlock Bones (22)
Dorgan, T.A. "Tad"	Curlock Bones
	Curlock Holmes (1)
Dorricott, Ian	Sheer Luck Holmes (2)
Doty, Gene	Sherlook Ohms
Dreschnack, Edward H.	Hemlock Bjones
Drew, Sydney	Sherlock Blake
Drucker, Mort	Sureschlock Homely
DuBois, F.R.	Sureluck Combs (1)
Dunbar, Paul Laurence	Shylock Homestead
Duncan, David E.	Sheridan Hume
Dunlop, Ed	Sherlock Jones (18)
Eath, Ben (i.e., Herman Charles Bosman)	Lockjaw Bones (3)
Eaton, Leo	Sherlock Jones (15)
Eckfeldt, Robert	Mukluk Gnomes
Edwards, Earle	Sherlock Woof
Edwing, Don "Duck"	Headlock Holmes (2)
	Shirley Holmes (13)
Egan, Peter	Stamford Holmes (2)
Elder, Bill	Shermlock Shomes
Elderdice, Raymond	Sheerlock Holmes
Eldridge, Jim	Sheer-Luck Holmes (4)
Ell, Ralph	Surelick Holms
Ennenga, India	Sherlock Pinky
Eulberg, Elizabeth	Shelby Holmes
Eustace, Grant	Stamford Holmes (1, 2)
Evans, Fred	Sherlock Pimple
	Sherlockz Homz
Evans, Will	Sherlockz Homz
Ewart, S.T.	Herlock Sholmes (7)
Exline, Cassie L.	Sheryl Lock Holmes
Faassen, John	Sherlock Bones (14)
Fahrney, Milton J.	Padlock Bones (8)
Farmer, Bill	Sherlock Goof
Fayne, Eric	Herlock Sholmes (27)
Feininger, Lyonel	Sherlock Bones (2)
Feist, Felix E.	Philo Holmes
Fell, David	Sheerluck Holds (3)

Ferguson, Walter (as "Sir Arthur Cannon Ball")	Hurlock Shoams
Feuillerat, Jadeyn	Harelock Holmes
Fields, W.C.	Sherlock Baffles
Finger, Bill	Shirley Holmes (3)
Filchock Fred	Hemlock Shomes
Finnigan, Tim	Herlock Holmes (1)
Fischer, Cindy	Slipshod Helms
Fish, Robert L.	Mooch Sheckls
	Schlock Homes (1)
Fisher, Nealee	Sherlock Foams (2)
	Sherlock Gnomes (3)
	Sherlock Tones (2)
Fitchett, Carlton	Old Cap Jones
Fitzgerald, Eddie	Brainy Domes
Fleissner, Robert F.	Sheer-Luck Holmes (5)
	Sure-Luck Holes
Fletcher, Terry (as "Fletch")	Sheer-Luck Holmes (3)
Flinn, Denny Martin	Spencer Holmes
Florence, Richard W.	Sherlock Jones (14)
Flynn, Greg	Sherlock Bones (10)
Fok, Clarence Yiu-leung	Sherlock False
Forrest, George F.	Warlock Bones
Foster, Bob	Sherlock Moose
Fowler, Gene	Arson Clews
Fox, Cenarth	Mereluck Holmes
	Shamrock Holmes (2)
	Sheerluck Holmes (11)
	Sherlock Bones (20)
	Sherlock Groans (2)
	Sherlock Thrones
	Shylock Holmes (10)
	Stately Holmes
	Suburban Holmes (2)
	Surelick Holmes
Franklin, Stanley A.	Shelook Holmes
Fraser, Ian	Ziplock Holmes (3)
Fraunholz, Fraunie	Burstup Holmes
Fredericks, Walter S.	Sherlock Ambrose
Freeman, Bud	Sedgewick Hawk-Styles
Freeman, F.W.	Shylock Oames
Frees, Paul	Hemlock Soames
	Sherlock Ohms (2)
Freestone, Stuart	Herlock Holmes (2)
Freisner, Esther M.	Brihtric Donne
	Sherbourne Rath
Freyse, Bill	Shylock Holmes (6)

Frost, Mark	Sheer-Luck Holmes (2)
Fugate, Bill	Sheerluck Goof
Fuller, Earl	Shylock Bones (7)
Fung, Paul	Old Cap Jones
Furtiner, Zyonimir	Herlock Sholmes (29)
Gallagher, Michael	Shumlock Holmes
Gamm, Arch	Sherlock Jones (6)
Gask, Arthur	Naughton Jones
Gardner, Martin	Shamrock Jones
	Sheerluck Brown
	Shurl Holmes
Gassner, C. Bryan	Hamhock Holmes
Gifford, Dennis	Sheerlock Omes
Gillespie, Helen	Sheerluck Jones (4)
Gilmer, Reuben	Sherlock Blake (1)
Gittings, John G.	Charlock Coombs
Goldstein, Jack	Sherlock Ohms (5)
Goldstone, Richard	Philo Holmes
Gonzales, Koko	Armlock Holmes
	Capslock Holmes
	Cellblock Holmes
	Flintlock Holmes
	Grimlock Holmes
	Harlock Holmes
	Hemlock Holmes (12)
	Laugh-a-Lock Holmes
	Lovelock Holmes
	Matchlock Holmes
	Morelock Holmes
	Padlock Holmes (7)
	Shorelocked Holmes
	Snowlock Holmes
	Warlock Holmes (1)
	Wedlock Holmes
	Werelock Holmes
	Ziplock Holmes (1)
Gorin, Grigori	Shirley Holmes (12)
Goulart, Ronald (as "Samuel Josep	
and Peter Dawson")	Philo Combs
Gould, Henry W. (as "Patrick	
O'Conan Donegal")	Sherlock Shamrock
Grant, Barry	Cedric Coombes
Grant, J.W.	Hemlock Holmes (4)
Gray, Harold	Hawkshaw (2)
Green, Sam	Shamshock Phones

Greene, Clay M.	Shylock Holmes (1)
	Surelock Holmes (1)
Gregg, Andy	Shirley Holmes (11)
Greicar, Hunter and Carrie	Harelock Holmes
Greig, Edwin A.	Shercock Bones (1)
Grevstad, Eric	Sherbert Cones
Griffith, Geraldine	Shirley Holmes (10)
Gross, Yoram	Sherlock Bones (10)
Gross, Tudor	Kerlock Shomes
Grushkin, Ed	Herlock Domes
Gupta, Mehul	Sherlock Ohms (8)
Guy, Alice	Burstup Holmes
Hagman, Larry	Sherman Holmes
Hague, Clarence	Hurlock Sholmes (1)
Hall, John	Shylock Holmes (8)
Hallewell, Kevin	Sheerluck Bones (10)
Halliday, Gemma	Fablock Holmes
Hamilton, Charles (as "Hector Hutt")	Sheerluck Homes (2)
	Sheerluck Jones (8)
Hamilton, Charles (as "Peter Todd")	Herlock Sholmes (14)
Hamilton, Lloyd V.	Sherlock Bonehead
Hamilton, Shorty	Padlock Holmes (5)
Handley, Allyson	Shirley Holmes (6)
Hansard, Paul	Sherlock Snoop
Hare, Walter Ben	Sherlock Combs (1)
	Shylock Bones (3)
Hargrove, Dean.	Sherman Holmes
Harman, Leon	Shylock Holmes (2)
Harris, Edward M.	Sherlock Watkins
Harris, Jack C.	Mylock Bloodstalker (1)
Harrison, Jack	Herlock Sholmes (20)
Harrison, Terence	Shedlock Jones
Harte, Bret	Hemlock Jones (4)
Hasson, Ron	Shamrock Holmes (4)
Hausner, Jerry	Hemlock Holmes (8)
Haver, S.C.	Hemlock Holmes (3)
Hayward, Linda	Sherlock Hemlock (1)
Heath, Lester	Sherlock Jones (8)
Heather, Bob	Sheer Luck Holmes (3)
Hegenberger, John	Sherlocko Homo
Henderson, Meredith	Shirley Holmes (15)
Hennessey, Dan	Zedlock Holmes
Henry, O.	Shamrock Jolnes
Henson, Jim	Sherlock Hemlock (1)
	Surelick Bones

Herbert, Paul D.	Herblock Stones
Hering, Henry A.	Herlock Shomes (10)
Herman, Al	Sherlock Bones (5)
Herman, Julius (as "Herbert Skimpole")	Horlock Shem
Hertzel, Bob	Shylock Homes (2)
Herzel, Roger W.	Fetlock Holmes
Hewson, Isabel Manning	Shadlock Bones
Hibbert, Jimmy	Hawkeye Soammes
Higgins, John	Hemlock Bones (7)
Hill, Headon	Radford Shone
Hines, Willie	Sheerluck Ohms (2)
Hinkley, Jane E.	Sherlimerick Holmes
Hitchcock, Laura	Kermlock Holmes
Hobart, George V.	Sherlock Baffles
Hockensmith, Steve	Morecock Bones
	Sheerluck Jones (11)
Hoffman, Sanford	Hemlock Holmes (11)
Hoke, Howard M.	Doorlock Combs
Holman, Scott	Sheer-Luck Holmes (6)
Holt, Michael	Sherlock Jones (10)
Holton, Walter	Holmlock Blake
Hoover, Richard	Pureluck Holmes (2)
Hopkins, L.C.	Herlock Shomes (8)
Hoppe, Arthur	Sherlock Helms (1)
Horrigan, Michael Anthony	Herlock Holmes (1)
Horowitz, Floyd	Hairlock Holmes (1)
Horowitz, Rick	Headlock Holmes (3)
Hubbard, Guy H.	Padlock Holmes (2)
Hubbell, Ned	Creighton Holmes
Huddleston, Jeffrey R.	Cherlock Holmes (1)
	Sherlark Honed
Humphrey, Joanna	Sheerluck Houses
Hutt, Hector (i.e., Charles Hamilton)	Sheerluck Homes (2)
	Sheerluck Jones (8)
Hytten, Olaf	Sheerluck Jones (7)
Ipsum, Lorem	Forelock Holmes
Irwin, Wallace	Badlock Holmes
	Sherlock Homes (1)
	Shylock Holmes (3, 5)
Jacobs, Frank	Sherlock Hemlock (2)
Jacobson, John	Shallock Holmes
	Tide Pooles (2)
Janda, Anita	Sherlock Hoelms
Janela, Mike	Psylock Holmes

Jenkins, Roger	Herlock Sholmes (26)
Jerome, William	Sherlock Baffles
Jimenez, Adan (as "A.J. Low")	Cher-Lock Sam
	Sherlock Sam
Jin-woo, Kim	Seol-ok
Jinkins, Jim	Sherlock Pinky
Johnson, George M.	Surelock Homes (1)
Johnston, Joe	Shirtlock Holmes
Jolley, Richard	Sherlock Homeless (2)
Jones, Chuck	Dorlock Homes
Jones, Grenville P.	Sheerluck Jones (5)
Jones, Wex	Timelock Foams
Josep, Samuel (i.e., Ronald Goulart)	Philo Combs
Joyce, James	Shedlock Homes
Judels, Charles	Philo Holmes
Kahn, William B.	Oilock Combs
Kallgren, Kyle	Sherlock Oan
Kane, Bob	Sherlock Klotz
Kane, Joe	Badlock Holmes
Kang-hee, Choi	Seol-ok
Karlson, Katherine	Cerlocio Olmez
Kaye, Marvin	Sherrinford Holmes (1)
Keane, John	Sherlock Bones (9)
Keefauver, Brad	Saeloc Holmes
Kellino, W.B.	Sherlock Blake (1)
Kellock, Harold	Zinsheimer Holmes
Kelly, Tim	Hawkshaw (3)
	Sherman Homes
	Shirley Holmes (5)
Kennedy, Adrienne	Shamrock Wolmbs
Keyes, Michael	Shedlock Jones
Khayt, Arkadiv	Shirley Holmes (12)
Kibbee, Roland	Sherman Holmes
Kiley, Tim	Hemlock Jones (11)
Kim, Artur	Cherlock Holmes (2)
Kimball, John	Sureluck Jones
King, Burton L.	Cocksure Jones
Kingsland, Robin	Shirley Holmes (14)
Kjell, Bradley	Shrock Holmes
	Tide Pooles (1)
Klenhard, Walter	Momlock Holmes
Knox, E.V. (as "Evoe")	Sherlock Soames (1)
Knutsson, Magnus	Hairlock Shomes
Kohut, Penny	Shamrock Holmes (4)
Kovalcik, Terry	Nerdslock Combs

Kovalyov, Igor	Shirley Lock Holmes
Kummer, Frederic Arnold	Shirley Holmes (2)
Kupperberg, Paul	Sherlock Stones
Kurtzman, Harvey	Shermlock Shomes
La Serre, Edward	Sheerluck Jones (1)
Lack, Dion	Sherlock Homeboy (2)
Lamb, Bertram (as "Uncle Dick")	Picklock Bones
Landeck, Herbert	Shylock Hyams
Langridge, Roger	Wormwood Soames
Lasky, Katherine	Shadrach Holmes
Latham, Larry	Sheerluck Bonkers
Laubach, Debbie	Sortluck Ohms
Laughlin, Lori	Momlock Holmes
Laurich, Andrew	Sherlock Homo (3)
Le Hir, J.L.	Hairlock Cholms
Le Minoux, Martial	Sherlock Yack (2)
LeBlanc, Maurice	Hemlock Shears (1)
	Herlock Shoames
	Herlock Sholmes (8)
	Holmlock Shears (2)
Lebowitz, Fran	Sherlock Homes and Gardens
Lederer, Richard	Sherlock Moans (1)
Lee, Robert G.	Sheerluck Holmes (10)
Lehmann, R.C. (as "Cunnin Toil")	Picklock Holes
Leftwich, Charles	Padlock Domes
Lennon, John	Shamrock Wolmbs
Leonard, Robert Z.	Sherlock Boob (1)
Leprince, René	Charley Colms
LeRouge, Gustave	Charley Colms
Leveson, Brian	Barratt Holmes (2)
Levi, Stephen	Sherlock Goof
Lewald, Eric	Sureluck Jones
Lewis, Cass	Shelly Holmes (1)
Lewis, Jerry	Sherlock Fink
	Skylock Peyton
Liebow, Eli M.	Shadrach Chomes
Limoli, Thomas J.	Myron Honize
Lippman, Laura	Sheila-Locke Holmes
Little, Richard Henry	Herlock Sholmes (10)
Locher, Fred	Skylark Bones (2)
Locke, George	Morlock Tomes
Lockwood, John	Sure-Lock Homes
Lofting, Hugh	Sherbert Scones
Long, Laird	Sherwood House
	Sir Loch Hoames

Longergan, Lloyd F.	Suburban Homes
Lorraine, Christine	Puglock Holmes (1)
Lou, Betty	Sherlock Hemlock (1)
Louis, Will	Sherlock Woof
Lovegrove, James	Hemlock Jones (12)
Lovell, Marc	Sheer-Luck Hums
Lovhaug, Lewis	Sherlock Oan
Low, A.J. (i.e., Adan Jimenez	Cher-Lock Sam
and Felicia Low-Jimenez)	Sherlock Sam
Ludwig, Edward	Surly Homes
Lutz, John	Semloh
Lynde, Paul	Sedgewick Hawk-Styles
Lynn, Bob (as "Bud Buonocore")	Shamrock Cohen
Lytell, Bert	Sherlock Brown
Macchio, Ralph	Saurian Holmes
MacDonald, Jeremiah	Hemlock Jones (5)
Macdonald, John Ross (as "Kenneth Millar")	Herlock Sholmes (23)
Mace, Fred	Surelock Homes (2)
MacGill, H.A.	Padlock Bones (3)
Mack, Hughie	Sherlock Oomph
MacLarnie, Thomas	Sureluck Hoomes
Madden, Mary Ann	Sherlock Sholem
Mager, Gus	Hawkshaw (1)
	Sherlocko the Monk
Majeski, Bill	Sherwood Holmes
Mallory, Michael	Shylock Hommes
Malmgren, Dick	Shylock Homes (4)
Maltese, Michael	Dorlock Homes
Manak, Dave	Shumlock Holmes
Mangubat, Lio	Snowlock Holmes
Manifold, Laurie Fraser	Parrot Holmes
	Sherlock Hound (5)
Mantlo, Bill	Hemlock Shoals
Marcoux, Herbert	Herlock Domes
Marcum, David	Solar Pons (3)
Markstein, Donald J.	Surefoot Jones
Marschall, Richard	Hodiah Twist
Marshall, Chester Alan	Sherlock Shamus
Martin, Gail Z.	Shelly Holmes (2)
Martin, Janet Letnes	Shirley Holmquist
Martin, Thomas (as "Tony")	Curlilock Ohms
Marx, Jonny	Sherlock Bones (25)
Masters, Peta	Shirley Holmes (10)
May, Jack	Hawkeye Soammes
May, Phil (as "Mr. M—")	Shylock Bones (1)

Mayer, Larry	Sheerluck Goof
McCaffrey, Paul	Shylock 'Olmes
McCloy, Helen	Hemlock Jones (10)
McCarthy, Cathy	Pollack Hmms
McConkey, Alton	Old Cap Jones
McDonald, Angus	Shamrock Holmes (3)
McGinnis, Mabel	Padlock Bones (2)
McGoldrick John	Hemlock Holmes (9)
McGowan, Robert F.	Sherlock Hawkshaw
McGregor, Don	Hodiah Twist
McGregor, Gordon	Padlock Bones (8)
McKee, Raymond	Sherlock Woof
McLeish, John	Hairlock Combs (4)
McVeigh, Tom	Shylock Holmes (4)
	Skylark Bones (1)
McWilliams, Al	Sherlock Jones (9)
Mears, Charles	Sherbert Foams
Mebberson, Amy	Wormwood Soames
Mellenten, Kate	Sherlock Bones (16)
Mengert, Tom	Sharlock Holmes
Merow, Erva	Sherlock Bones (8)
Merson, Billy	Sherlock Blake (1)
Messina, Roy	Sherlock Cones (1)
Messmer, Otto	Sure-Locked Homes
Michael, Glen	Sherlock Haggis
Michaels, Sean	Sherlock Homie (1)
Mientus, Vincent	Shylock Combs
Mikuriya, Kyosuke	Sherlock Hound (2)
Millar, Kenneth (i.e., John Ross Macdonald)	Herlock Sholmes (23)
Millett, Ben E.	Sheer-Luck Holmes (6)
Milt, Victor	Sherlick Holmes
Milton, Freddy	Hairlock Shomes
	Sheerluck Homes (4)
Minett, Paul	Barratt Holmes (2)
Mitchell, Basil	Shirley Holmes (2)
Mitchell, Bruce M.	Sherlock Boob (1,2)
Mitchell, Edward	Shamrock Holmes (1)
Mitchroney, Ken	Sherlock Höek
Miyazaki, Hayao	Sherlock Hound (2)
Monero, Philip	Puglock Holmes (3)
Mongredien, Sue	Shirley Holmes (16)
Moniarti, Rika	Sir Luck Helm
Monka, Joel	Shellshock Sloan
Monkhouse, Bob	Sherlock Slick
Monkhouse, Michael	Sherlock Moans (2)
Montana, Bob	Sheerluck Homes (3)

Moore, Frank	Sherlock Boob (2)
Moore, John Blair	Sheerluck Goof
Moore, Randy	Sherlock Jones (19)
Mora, Gia	Sheridan Hume
Morecombe, Eric	Sheerluck Holmes (5)
Moreton, Douglas	Clewlow Holmes
	Shylock Holmes (9)
Morgan, Tracy	Sherlock Homie (2)
Morris, Joel	Barratt Holmes (2)
Moss, Larry	Sherlock Hound (2)
Motley, T.	Sherlock Jones (14)
Mouscadet, Jerome	Sherlock Yack (2)
Murphy, Walter	Shaw La Coombs
Myer, Jacob	Sheerluck Holmes (1)
	Sheerluck Homes (1)
Myers, Russ	Sherlock Troll
Nawrocki, Mike	Sheerluck Holmes (10)
Needham, Richard J.	Shylock Hoax
Nelson, Dale	Shylock Hames
Nelson, Jerry	Sherlock Hemlock (1)
Newman, Kim	Shylock 'Olmes
Newton, Harry L.	Doorlock Bones
	Shylock Bones (2)
Nizza, Paul	Doorlock Homes (1)
Noonechester, Kevin	Sherlock Homerun
Nye, Jody Lynn	Sure-Lock Home
O'Neill, Harry	Padlock Holmes (6)
O'Spelin, MacLean	Shih Lok
Ober, Hal	Sheerluck Holmes (7)
Oldham, R.C.	Smearlock Holmes
Ortiz, Juan	Mylock Bloodstalker (2)
Osborne, Maitland Leroy	Hemlock Holmes (1)
Osborne, Margaret	Shedlock Jones
Ostrom, Howard	Sheercheek Holmes
Page, Andrew	Finlock Combes
Park Jae-sang (as "Psy")	Psylock Holmes
Parker, James	Blowback Foams
	Rockhard Scones
	Shadrach Voles
	Upchuck Gnomes
Parkes, Ernest	Herlock Sholmes (16)
Pascal, Peter	Warlock Horne
Paskins, Stella	Shirley Holmes (16)

Patterson, J.A.	Spurlock Holmes
Patterson, June	Sherlock Bones (12)
Pattrick, Robert R.	Sherlock Combs (3)
Perez, Suni P.	Froglock Holmes (1)
Perry, Ralph	Shortwave Ohms
Peters, Elizabeth	Sa Haapu
Peterson, Doug	Sheerluck Holmes (9)
Petkus, Jennifer	Charlotte House
Pfaffenberger, Will	Shoelock Holmes (4)
Pfaeffle, Emma	Charlotte Holmes (5)
Pickerill, Kane	Hairlock Holmes (2)
Pielikis, Aleksas	Pocklock Holmes
Pimple, Dennis J.	Sherlock Jones (14)
Pinkney, John	Sherlock Q. Jones
Place, Frank	Fetlock Jones (2)
Platts, W. Carter	Sherlock Jones (2)
Porges, Arthur	Sherman Horn
	Stately Homes
Powers, T.E.	Sherlocko Smith
Price, Judy	Sherlock Sholem
Proctor, Philip	Hemlock Stones (1)
Prouty, Marsha	Geoffrey Holm
Puhl, Gayle Lange	Sheercrocked Moans
Quackenbush, Robert	Sherlock Chick
Queen, Ellery	Pharaoh Jones
Quermann, Walter	Sherlock Bones (6)
	Sherlock Combs (2)
Radilović, Julio "Jules"	Herlock Sholmes (29)
Rajan, Vithal	Shelley Gomez
	Signor Om'mez
Ramsay, Allan (as "Zero")	Thinlock Bones
Randall, Chris	Hawkeye Soammes
Rath, Fred W.	Sellem Jones
	Surelock Holmes (3)
Razzi, Jim and Mary	Dennis Bones
	Sherluck Bones
Redhead, E.C.	Shylock Jones
Rea, Gardner	Yalelock Holmes
Read, Anthony	Hemlock Bones (8)
Read, Opie	Hemlock Jones (3)
Reed, E.T.	Shurlacombs
Reed, Kevin	Cockroach Bones
Reed, Langford	Stanway Holmes
Reed, Rod	Goldilock Homes

Reems, Harry	Sherlick Holmes
Reese, Kenny	Sherlock Hohms
Reeve, A.S.	Mereluck Tombs
Reeves, Peter Richard	Hawkeye Soammes
Reyhl, Ben	Smearlock Homeless
Reynolds, Harrington	Sheerluck Jones (7)
Reynolds, Harry	Sherlock Combs (4)
Reynolds, Jerry	Sherlock Homerun
Reynolds, Tony	Sherlock Harms
Richmond, Bill	Skylock Peyton
Rickard, Jack	Shamus Homes
Ridenour, Jerrold	Poplock Holmes
Ridout, Ronald	Sherlock Jones (10)
Riley, Andy	Sherlock Gnomes (4)
Riordan, W.L.	Padlock Jones (2)
Ritt, William	Sherlock Hums (2)
Ritts, Mark	Sherlock Jones (15)
Roach, Hal	Sherlock Hawkshaw
	Sherlock Sleuth
Roach, Suz	Puglock Holmes (2)
Roberts, Xavier	Sherlock Otis
Robertson, D.M.	Sheerluck Bones (9)
Robinson, Hugh	Sherbet Jones
Robinson, Jerry	Shirley Holmes (3)
Rogers, Charles Dunbar	Hemlock Jones (7)
Roman, Phil	Snoopy Holmes (1)
Romita, John, Jr.	Saurian Holmes
Rosenblatt, Albert M.	Skilock Holmes
Rosendahl, Gaia Due	Zoolock Holmes
Ross, Scott	Sherlock Hound (3)
Rothwell, C.C. (as "A Cone and Oil")	Sherwood Hoakes
Rozakis, Bob	Mylock Bloodstalker (2)
Rubenstein, Stanley	Sheerluck Combs
Rushton, William	Shylock Haynes
Russell, Fox	Lockjaw Bones (2)
Russell, Harold	Padlock Holmes (4)
Russell, Ray	Hemlock Foames
Rusz, Michael	Smearlock Homeless
Ruyle, John	Turlock Loams
Sacket, Natalie	Sheila Holmes
Salles, Danny	Wassup Holmes
Sato, Yuki	Sherdog Bones
	Sherlock Bones (23)
Sauer, Stephen	Purrrlock Holmes
Scancarelli, Jim	Sherlock Monk

Scharfstein, Sol	Sherlock Sholom
Schier, Norma	Schlock Homes (2)
Schulz, Charles M.	Snoopy Holmes (1)
Schwartz, Jean	Sherlock Baffles
Schwartz, Tony	Hemlock Holmes (12)
Scott, Hudson	Shroomlock Holmes
Scott, Keith	Sherlock Bones (10)
Seaburn, Paul	Sherlock Fumes
Segar, E.C.	Hancock Homes
	Merlock Jones
Seiden, Joseph	Herlock Sholmes (20)
Semon, Larry	Sherlock Oomph
Seong-min, Lee	Seol-ok
Serafinowicz, Peter	Sherlock Kush
Severin, John	Shylock Homes (3)
Severin, Marie	Kermlock Holmes
	Shumlock Holmes
Shackleford, Lee Eric	Sheridan Hume
Sheldon, Theodore Banta	Padlock Holmes (2)
Shen, Dean	Sherlock False
Shepard, E. Howard	Shirknot Holmes
Sherman, Josepha	Shrr'lock of Kholmes
Shipp, Godfrey	Sheer Look Holmes
Shipp, Jesse A.	Shylock Homestead
Shore, Viola Brothers	Shirley Holmes (4)
Silverstone, Lou	Shamus Homes
Simonov, Aleksei	Shirley Holmes (12)
Simons, Dave	Hemlock Shoals
Sipherd, Ray	Sherlock Hemlock (1)
Sivers, Brenda	Sherlock Hound (1)
	Shylock Hound (1)
Siviter, William Henry	Herlock Shomes (3)
Skimpole, Herbert (i.e., Julius Herman)	Horlock Shem
Skurski, Bill	Ozone Holmes
Sloan, Mark	Mycock Bones
	Sherlock Bones (21)
Smalley, Phillips	Homelock Shermes
	Homlock Shermes
	Sherlock Doyle
Smith, David	Surelacks Holmes
Smith, Jason	Barratt Holmes (2)
Smith, Jeff	Surelock Holmes (6)
Smith, Robert A.	Sherlock Duck
Smith, Robert B.	Padlock Holmes (2)
Smith, Ronald L.	Sheerluck Holds (2)
Smith, Webb	Hemlock Shears (2)

Snyder, Eugene Edmund	Lockley Soames
Soans, E.H.	Sheerluck Jones (6)
Sodaro, Craig	Sureluck Holmes (2)
Spiers, Hetty	Stanway Holmes
Spinetti, Victor	Shamrock Wolmbs
St. Clair, Robert	Fetlock Jones (1)
Stafford, T.P.	Sheerluck Gnomes
Steadleman, Pvt.	Hairlock Combs (3)
Stem, J. David	Shirley Lock Holmes
Stephani, Vincent	Sherlock Holmz
Stevens, Charles A.	Shirley Holmes (1)
Stevenson, John	Sherlock Gnomes (4)
Stone, Arthur	Sherlock Sleuth
Stone, Dan	Shirley Holmes (6)
Stone, Neil J.	Shelley Holmes
Stringer, Lew	Sherlock Hams (2)
Sullivan, Pat	Hurlock Sholmes (3)
	Sure-Locked Homes
Sumner, Ron	Squirrelock Holmes
Sutherland, John	Haricot Bones
Swain, Mack	Sherlock Ambrose
Swan, Barbara	Sheerluck Holmes (4)
Swift, Howard	Hairlock Combs (4)
Swoyer, Alfred Edward (A.E.)	Herlock Shomes (13)
Symons, Julian	Sheridan Haynes
Szymanski, Michael	Sherlock Abodes
Taft, H.W.	Hemlock Jones (6)
Takahashi, Yoshimitsu	Sherlock Hound (2)
Taylor, Jody	Shirley Holmes (9)
Tewksbury, T.L.	Shylock Bones (3)
Thierry, James Francis	Hemlock Holmes (7)
Thomas, Danny	Sheer-Luck Holmes (1)
Thomas, Owen	Shirley-Lock Holmes
Thomas, Sherry	Charlotte Holmes (6)
Thompson, D.C.	Sheerluck Bones (8)
Thorpe, M.H.	Hemlock Holmes (3)
Thurber, James	Shirley Combs (2)
Tibbetts, Mal and Jenny	Shylock Bones (10)
Tillmans, Sascha	Shirtlock Holmes
Tiner, Ron	Sherlock Hams (2)
Todd, Dylan	Airlock Holmes
Todd, Peter (i.e., Charles Hamilton)	Herlock Sholmes (14)
Toles, Claude Eldridge	Hemlock Holmes (2)
Tomashefsky, Steven	Sherlock Ohms (3)
Toone, Leilani	Shirley Holmes (17)

Travaglia, Simon Paul	Herlock Shomes (18)
Trow, M.J.	Burdock Holmes
	Sherrinford Homes (2)
Tryon, Leslie	Shamrock Homes (2)
Tubb, Miles	Dreadlock Holmes (1)
Twain, Mark	Fetlock Jones (1)
Uman, Aan Wulandari	Sir Luck Helm
Urlacher, Brian	Urlach Holmes
Utechin, Nicholas	Porlock Moans
Vallarian, R.C.	Sherloc Holmes
Van Ash, Cay	Shylock Holmes (7)
Van Bruggen, John	Surelick Bones
Van Horn, Noel	Surefoot Jones
Vasileva, Yekaterina	Shirley Holmes (12)
Vaughn, Margaret	Sherlock Jones (6)
Versandi, Bob	Hemlock Jones (4)
Veiller, Bayard	Sherlock Brown
Veysey, Arthur	Goldilock Holmes
Virgien, Norton	Shirley Lock Holmes
Virlojeux, Henri	Herlock Sholmes (28)
Volk, Stephen	Sheeur-Loque Holmes
Wakshul, Gary Louis	Kreplock Holes
Walker, Ashlynn	Sheila Holmes
Walker, H.M.	Sherlock Hawkshaw
	Sherlock Sleuth
Wallace, Karen	Sherlock Hound (4)
Ward, Jay	Hemlock Soames
	Sherlock Ohms (2)
Warner, Penny	Hemlock Bones (9)
Watkins, Candace	Froglock Holmes (2)
Watson, Malcolm	Sheerluck Jones (1)
Weber, Bill	Sureluck Combs (2)
Weber, Bob, Jr.	Slylock Fox
Weems, Walter	Sheerluck Jones (7)
Weine, Al	Hemlock Shomes
Weiner, Erick	Wassup Holmes
Weinstein, Sol	Sherlock Jones (12)
Weiss, David N.	Shirley Lock Holmes
Wells, Carolyn	Picklock Holmes
West, D.C.	Sheerflop Soames
West, Wendy	Sherlock Bones (12)
Weston, Charles	Sherlock Pimple
Whelan, Ed	Padlock Homes

White, Pearl	Homelock Shermes
	Homlock Shermes
Whitman, John	Shirley Holmes (16)
Whitman, Vincent	Sherlock Bug
Whitney-Smith, Elin	Skylark Holmes
Wickline, Dennis	Sheer Luck Holmes (1)
Wilcockson, Ray	Sheercheek Holmes
Wilder, Gene	Sureluck Holmes (1)
Wilder, Marshall P.	Sherlie Holmes
Wilder-Wokoun, Constance	Charlotte Holmes (4)
Williams, Bert	Shylock Homestead
Williams, Stephen Daniel	Shylar Holmes
Williamson, J.N.	Sheerbach Tones
	Sure-They-Lock Homez
Wilmunen, Jon V.	Neville Boyles
	Sherlock Hoax
Wilson, Bear	Sherlick Holmes
Wilson, Flip	Hemlock Jones (11)
Wilson, Gahan	Enoch Bone
	Sherlock Soames (2)
Wilson, H. Chilver	Shamrock Homes (1)
Wilson, Kevin	Shamrock Houses
Wilson, Roy	Sheerluck Bones (2)
Wilmer, Douglas	Sureluck Holmes (1)
Winter, Keith	Sheer Look Holmes
Wise, Ernie	Sheerluck Holmes (5)
Wodehouse, P.G.	Burdock Rose
	Dudley Jones
Wood, Tim	Sherlock Bones (16)
Wyman, Jamie	Sanford Haus
Yache, Fernando	Sherlock Stones
Yager, Rock	Padlock Jones (3)
Yarbrough, Ira (as "Yar")	Sherlock Jones (7)
Yeats, Jack Butler	Chubb-Lock Homes
	Chubblock Homes
Yelesiyevich, Milo	Charlake Hams
	Chelovick Homes
	Churlhack Halmes
	Churlhock Halmes
	Curllock Halmes
	Forelock Hums
	Quarrelrock Hums
	Sharl Homes
	Shayluck Hums
	Shore Rock Halmes

Yelesiyevich, Milo (cont.)

Yeong-eun, Yoo
Yolen, Janet
Young, Judy Dockery
Young, Richard
Yust, Larry

Zamboni, Bob
Zangwill, Louis
Zazove, Ben

Shoreflock Hums
Shorelock Gommes
Shoreluck Hams
Shorl Rock Hums
Shorlrock Homes
Shurl Rock Gommes
Soreluck Hams
Sureluck Gommes
Sureluck Homes
Sureluck Hums
Whoreluck Hams
Seol-ok
Shirlick Holmes
Shylock Bones (9)
Shylock Bones (9)
Sheerluck Hums

Sureluck Jones
Warlock-Jones
Sherlock Gnomes (4)